PRAISE FOR *AN IMPOSSIBLE RETURN*

Winner:

Prix Maison de la Presse 2020
Prix Louis-Guilloux 2020
Prix du Salon du Livre du Mans 2020
Prix du Roman Métis des Lecteurs et des Lycéens
Grand Prix des Blogueurs Littéraires 2020
Prix Paul Bourdarie de l'Académie des Sciences d'Outre-Mer 2021
Prix Cardinal Perraud 2021
Prix des Lecteurs du Var
Prix du Deuxième Roman de Grignan
Prix Belles Plumes
Prix Yaka'Lire
Prix Escapages

Finalist:

Prix du Livre France Bleu / PAGE des libraires
Prix des libraires
Prix Françoise Sagan
Prix Orange
Prix des lecteurs Babelio

"A book about exile and impossible love, but nevertheless about hope too. It is an ambitious and sweeping story written with sensitivity that renders a geopolitical and human tragedy through its credible and endearing characters."

—*L'Orient Littéraire*

AN
IMPOSSIBLE
RETURN

AN
IMPOSSIBLE
RETURN

A Novel

CAROLINE
LAURENT

AMAZON **CROSSING**

Text copyright © 2020 by Éditions Les Escales
Translation copyright © 2022 by Jeffrey Zuckerman
All rights reserved.

Previously published as *Rivage de la colère* by Éditions Les Escales in France in 2020. Translated from French by Jeffrey Zuckerman. First published in English by Amazon Crossing in 2022.

Published by Amazon Crossing, Seattle

www.apub.com

Amazon, the Amazon logo, and Amazon Crossing are trademarks of Amazon.com, Inc., or its affiliates.

ISBN-13: 9781542035019 (hardcover)
ISBN-13: 9781542032339 (paperback)
ISBN-13: 9781542032346 (digital)

Cover design by Leah Jacobs-Gordon

Interior images: Courtesy of Chagos Refugees Group

Printed in the United States of America

First edition

To my mother
To all the Chagossians in exile

Islands where time flowed unhurriedly . . .

Shenaz Patel, *Silence of the Chagos*
trans. Jeffrey Zuckerman

The truth remains: through the fight taking root
Devotion is useless; you must be brute.

Racine, *Bérénice*
trans. Manuel Rève

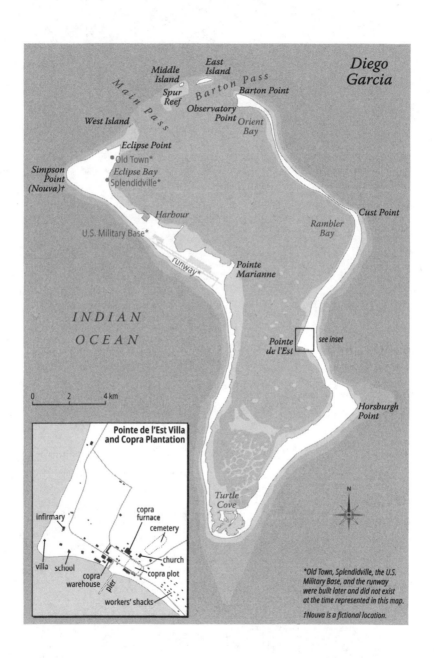

Diego
Garcia

East
Island

Middle
Island

Spur
Reef

Barton Pass

Barton Point

Main Pass

Observatory
Point

Orient
Bay

West Island

Eclipse Point

Old Town*

Simpson
Point
(Nouva)†

Eclipse Bay
Splendidville*

Cust Point

Harbour

Rambler
Bay

U.S. Military Base*

runway*

Pointe
Marianne

INDIAN

OCEAN

Pointe
de l'Est

see inset

0   2   4 km

Horsburgh
Point

Pointe de l'Est Villa
and Copra Plantation

infirmary

copra
furnace

cemetery

villa   school

church

copra
warehouse

pier

copra plot

Turtle
Cove

N

workers' shacks

*Old Town, Splendidville, the U.S.
Military Base, and the runway
were built later and did not exist
at the time represented in this map.

†Nouva is a fictional location.

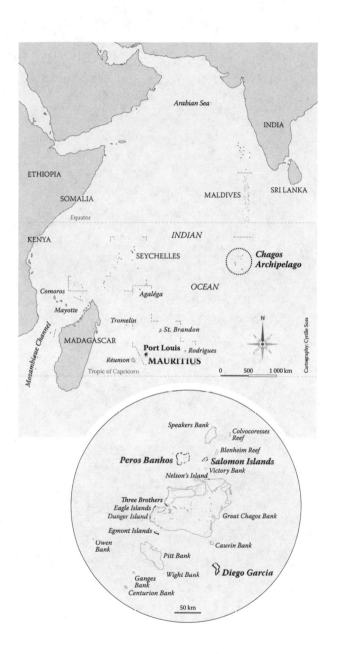

I

It's not much, hope.

A prayer for oneself. A wisp of dream crushed in the hand, thousands of glass shards, the palm bloodied. A refrain conjured up one morning in weak sunlight.

For us, children of the islands up there, it's also a black flag with gold and turquoise shimmering. A pound of flesh claimed so long ago that it actually feels normal to live with a ripped-open belly.

Well, go on. Stare at the horizon. Only the dead have the right to sleep. To give up the fight is to betray yourself. To betray yourself is to abandon your kind.

My mother.

I can see her again, standing beside the path, her face half-drenched in light, half-sunk in darkness. Tall and barefoot. She didn't have the words, but that didn't matter; she had something better: a look. *Get up, my son. Don't go back to sleep. You've got to stand strong. With faith, nothing will be impossible for you . . .* Faith, the second standard. Three letters spell God, and God recovered His wrath, His fire, His rending, His unrelenting pain.

I don't have faith. I'd rather speak in terms of hope. Hope is ordinary life as it always should be: oriented toward an elsewhere. Not a goal, not an objective, an *elsewhere*. A secret place where, at last, everyone will belong. A just place.

Mine exists.

An island lost in the expanse of the Indian Ocean, an overly flat and empty and calm strip of sand, a particular clarity in its waters. The sea like a country. This island that nobody knows is my hope, my land.

See, your absence has changed nothing. Even without you, Mama, I keep going. I'm ready.

Twelve hours by plane to Paris. Then a train to The Hague, a connection at Rotterdam. I won't have time to visit the Eiffel Tower. I'd have liked to, though. To make my way to the top, and that way, for once, I'd be the one looking down on everyone else.

Sorry.

I'm not going as a tourist. I've never been a tourist. What's a tourist, anyway? A white man in Bermuda shorts and flip-flops coming to Mauritius to forget that he's made money?

There won't be any strolling around in The Hague, either. All I'll see of the Netherlands will be the International Court of Justice. The world's eyes will be on us.

A duel.

Justice is the cruel stepsister of hope. It has you believe that it will save you, but what can it save you from when it always comes after the worst? A verdict is no remedy for anything. It's no consolation. All the same, sometimes, it does purge one's heart. The only deliverance I'm striving for is that: purgation. Bringing the guilty crashing down. Upending the established order. You didn't ask for any of that, Mama. This wrath is mine alone.

When the people before me are bowled over—"Your courage, honestly, your strength, after all these years . . ."—I have no idea what to say. Courage is the weapon of those who have no choice. We will all, in our poor lives, have to be courageous at one moment or another. Just you wait.

March 1967

Aim for the eye, and you'll hit the head.

The lagoon was still, as smooth as glass. The trade winds had tossed the night's dark waves; now their breath was calm. Marie looked one last time at her prey, raised her fishgig high, and killed it with a sharp blow aimed between the coral.

Aim for the eye, and you'll hit the head. Forget everything else around it. Nail it!

Her mother's words came through her gestures—islander memory, ancestral memory, passed down to girls over so many centuries. Her body knew. Soon she would be handing this down to Suzanne.

Marie felt some resistance at the end of her harpoon. The octopus released a cloud of ink. Too late: it had been caught. She dragged the creature out of the water while whooping in victory, then stuck a wire in its beak. With a soft sound, the rod cut through the flabby brain.

)(

In the distance, the air was already tinged gold and white. She'd been tracking the creature for too long. It had to be six in the morning, and the work on the copra plantation would be starting now. Marie cursed herself. Once again Josette would have to explain her absence to old Félix. She could imagine her sister's look. *Oh, there you are now, I'm all ears . . .* With an apologetic smile, she'd confess: the call of the sea, so violent, so irrepressible, the prey curled up in the rocks' crevices, made time disappear. She'd take her place on the plot of land, pull out her machete, and, after splitting the first coconut, whisper into Josette's ear, *I'll cook you a nice fricassee.* Her sister would give her shoulder a gentle slap—all good.

The octopus slung over her back, Marie began walking across the sand when a shadow on the horizon stopped her. She squinted, made out a gray speck at the north end of the channel. Sometimes, she knew, desires could be so strong that you could clearly make out the shape of things that didn't exist. And what she wanted above all, in the Diego Garcia dawn, was to be the first to spot the cargo ship. For days the whole island had been on tenterhooks. The *Sir Jules* had left Port-Louis and was traversing the Indian Ocean. Old Félix had relayed the administrator's message: the church needed to be decked out, the warehouses readied, as the ship wouldn't be long now.

Every time the *Sir Jules* or the *Mauritius* stopped at the Chagos archipelago, Marie forgot about her daily grind. A kingdom spilled onto the island's beaches. Commodities that couldn't be found on Diego, like rice, flour, or sugar, overflowed on the pier; wine, cloth, soap, medicine, and beauty products went into the reserves, and men from afar—the cleric, the captain, less frequently a doctor—brought them distractions and news. So many dreams. Marie looked straight ahead. At the other end of the world, people lived in snow. Snow . . . the very word made her shiver. She had to imagine a huge white coat draped over the world's body, or so she'd been told. But the only white coat she'd ever known was the beach of Diego Garcia, as immaculate as a tortoise eggshell.

In her line of sight, the gray speck came into focus. As pinpricks of light began to blink, red and then green, she realized she wasn't mistaken. She waded back into the water, disturbing the cloud of black ink; the purplish water was turning the light a jacaranda-petal mauve. She had to alert Josette, alert the others. There wouldn't be any more work today. The *Sir Jules* was coming! On the path, excitement made her start running, unbothered by the octopus bouncing along her back, her soaked skirt, and the pebbles cutting into the soles of her feet; dust rose up behind her.

"Boat ahoy!"

The men came out of the warehouse, intrigued. Rather than stop, she went to where the women were husking coconuts. Her sister was bent over double, busy turning the white strips of coconut meat to the sun.

"Josette!"

She straightened, stretched out her frame, set her hands on her hips. The machetes stopped; the women turned to look at Marie. Her heart was pounding after running so far. She slumped against the low wall, savoring the moment. This feeling of being the one who knew, the one who'd seen—and, indeed, the one bringing joy—was heady as a mouthful of rum.

"Boat ahoy," she repeated, whispering.

Josette was slack jawed. Really? The *Sir Jules*? Marie nodded, holding up the octopus. The doubtful look on her sister's face gave way to a pure smile. Josette came up, hoisted herself delightedly onto the low wall. *"Alala!"* The women surrounded her, clapping their hands. Josette simpered—the ship would make her the queen of the island, the radiant chosen one.

"Ready?" Marie asked with a nudge. She threw the octopus over her shoulder again, and Josette followed. The strong, salty smell, not unlike that of rotting fish guts, mingled with the sweet aromas of the coconuts heaped like cut-off breasts drained of their milk.

"Put that there! No, over there!" Amid the welter of rowboats, the gunnysacks, containers, and barrels made the activity on the pier feel like a military convoy. Mollinart was giving orders. "Flour to the warehouse." The men shouldered the bags, their skin raw, their foreheads furrowed by the effort. Marie saw Henri and Jean-Joris, both of them bare-chested, sweating. She waved to them; her gaze lingered on one, then the other. Henri was staggering back and forth between the pier and the warehouse, crates balanced uneasily on his head, while Jean-Joris moved slowly, his arms laden with tins. They looked like each other, differences notwithstanding. She knew them both inside and out. Sympathetic, lighthearted. Forgetful.

A new rowboat berthed, bearing bags of sugar. A stocky man with a thick head of hair helped unload it. "Christian!" Josette rushed over. With a smile as pure as a child's, he kissed her cheek. Marie shut her eyes. Bad thoughts were nagging at her, buzzing thoughts she should push away. Her sister's happiness was all too rare on Diego Garcia. Usually men loved and didn't linger—they simply passed through, peaceful retreating soldiers.

"Well? Him, there?" Josette's voice cut through just about all emotion.

"No," Christian responded. "But he's coming, just you wait . . ." He gave her another kiss, heaved the gunnysack onto his shoulders, and waved to Mollinart that he wouldn't stop for long.

Josette shaded her eyes, looking out at the boats. Henri, Jean-Jo, and the other Chagossians, the Îlois, were coming and going, following the administrator's directions in a hubbub of splashing, shouting, and hard work. The noise rose like a wave toward the bright sky before falling back into the sea, which was nearly white with the sun's first rays. A sound suddenly caught Marie's attention. A small boat pulled up with men aboard. Josette trembled. "You think that's him?" It was still hard to see, but she'd have been willing to bet . . . The rowboat bumped up against the pier, setting off a buzz: the priest! It was him, after all! Josette started jumping up and down, impatient, overexcited—a little twenty-five-year-old girl. "Christian!" she shrieked again. "Hurry! Get over here!" He ran over, and the two of them made a beeline for the small boat.

Marie stayed behind, the octopus in her hand, its tentacles brushing the sand. With the growing heat, the smell was becoming more unbearable. She went to splash some seawater on her skin, and from the beach she watched the spectacle. All the pleasure of that morning—her alone facing the *Sir Jules* in the distance—was gone. She'd had a secret to keep. With only a few steps, she could have joined the others, clapped as the boats came, waited for the priest with her sister and Christian, but nothing would change: she'd feel isolated from a group she'd pulled away from, just like her mother, who'd complained in the past about being lonely, even though she never welcomed anyone. She swirled the octopus in the water to stave off her unfounded annoyance. Next to Mollinart, up ahead, Josette, Christian, Henri, Jean-Joris, Félix, and the others were jostling around the rowboat. She kept her eyes on them, taking in the pier and the profile of the cleric who was slowly emerging.

It wasn't the cleric.

The man who'd just appeared was twenty years at the very most, with a slim frame and an odd appearance. His skin, the color of milk tea, seemed to go with his beige jacket, but also—she squinted—his white shoes. She barely had time to look him over before he was swallowed up by the crowd, even as it spat out Father Larronde.

A missionary's beard, a big smile on his lips, a few sparse hairs over a pinkish scalp: he hadn't changed since his last visit to the Chagos.

"My Father!" Josette and the others surrounded him. A woman kissed his hand; another tugged at his cassock. "My Father!" Christian shouldered through the horde and made his way with Josette up to the cleric. Good, they could make their request right away—the thought was a relief to Marie. The feeling that beset her so often wasn't jealousy; it was more impatience, need, like a hole in her belly that nothing would fill.

"Step aside, please . . . Everyone calm down!" Mollinart tried to make his way to the cleric. Marie tried to meet the eyes of the man in beige, but the Îlois were mobbing the visitors. At her feet in the water, the octopus had opened up like a flower's petals. She scrubbed it with sand to remove most of the gunk, rinsed it, then lumbered back onto the beach. The stranger was there, a cigarette between his fingers. Mauritian, he had to be. A city man.

His perfectly coiffed hair gleamed in the sun. His profile was like a bird's, with thin lips and a hooked nose—features that were an odd marriage of harshness and delicacy. She froze, stunned by the truth: this man was handsome. Henri and Jean-Joris had struck her as desirable often enough, because they were there, because they were young, but neither had stirred up in her this soft yet violent, utterly clear feeling of beauty. She took a step toward him, unsure, with a smile that he didn't return.

The smell of octopus on her hands, on her neck; her sopping skirt; her unruly hair; her dark skin dotted with sweat; her too-large feet—she stopped short, ashamed of herself. Swallowed her smile. It didn't matter, in any case. The stranger was looking up and past her, to the now-green sea. She was as good as invisible.

March 1967

Sea spray heavy with sap seeped into his cabin. At last. During his time on the *Sir Jules*, the ocean had lost its smell, dampened by the aromas of soup, engine grease, and upset stomachs. Five days traversing a cauldron. He'd been sick every second of it. When the briny wind finally filled his nostrils, he'd felt reborn; the waves had regained their smell of algae and salt, the sky its clarity. They'd arrived. Gabriel climbed onto the upper deck, teetering toward the railing.

At the end of the lagoon, an unassuming pier and a strip of sand dotted with coconut trees stood out. By leaving Port-Louis, he'd turned his back on a bustling harbor, docks full of containers, buildings under construction, noisy streets, hawkers of all sorts. It was time to flee Mauritius. Time to leave, to get away from himself. But is it ever possible to really leave?

He who had always dreamed of London and lazy afternoons in libraries set down his suitcases. A desert in the middle of the ocean. *When you come back, you'll be so old that all you'll have left to do is die,* Évelyne had said before his departure. His little sister would remain in Beau-Bassin, alone under their father's yoke; he was abandoning her. With a fourteen-year-old's bluntness, her anguish had turned into venom. But maybe she wasn't entirely wrong; he could come back from the Chagos aged, disaccustomed to urban life, with no memory of his London dreams. He only had to take out his binoculars to see the truth across the water: there was nothing but sand and coconut trees—not a single house, not a single structure, not a single street. Not all prisons have bars.

$$\bowtie$$

"Livestock!" roared the captain. Gabriel headed toward the beach beside Father Larronde and Marcel Mollinart. Bald, in khaki Bermuda shorts, the island's administrator, who also owned the copra plantation, had to be in his forties. He was affable, with the nonchalance men assured of their authority had. "My boy, the experience won't disappoint! It's the long-awaited moment . . ." The provisioning followed an unchanging routine. After foodstuffs, other objects, and men was the livestock. "The Îlois don't often get the chance to eat meat, you know." Donkeys, goats, cows, pigs: so many bodies that would feed people and power the oil mill.

The first beasts appeared on the horizon, their vessel gliding across the mirror-flat sea. A song rose up from the shore. The Chagossians kept the rhythm with their hands, their voices lost amid distant, pagan accents akin to those of the Malagasy people during Famadihana—a sacred ritual honoring the dead.

"There's a big ox on the dinghy!" a bushy-haired Îlois suddenly shouted. Mollinart smiled. In Port-Louis, Gabriel had been stunned by the number of seamen it had taken to hoist the animal aboard. First its horns had been wrapped in rags. It took the men two attempts to tie it down in the hold.

The chant rose.

The Îlois' bodies were incredibly dark-skinned, shaped by manual labor, dressed in simple clothes of canvas skirts for women and loincloths made out of better cloth for the men. Gabriel clenched his jaw. What kinds of conversations could he have with them? What kinds of back-and-forths? It only took a glance to figure that they were illiterate. But their voices had a hypnotic depth to them, something that touched the very essence of vitality. No artifice. Just raw force.

"Now that's a beast!" Mollinart exclaimed, pulling him out of his reverie. Gabriel stepped to the side.

Fearless, standing like an idol amid the waves, the animal defied the humans. Its golden hide gleamed, reflected in the ripples it made as it neared; silence fell. A religious silence.

The small boat was about to berth when, all of a sudden, a rock shifted its course. Wood scraping. A wave. In less than a second, everything teetered. The ox was keen to jump out of the boat, but the rigging hobbled it as everything began sinking in the lagoon.

"Alala!" All the Îlois cried out as if with a single throat. The animal tried to get up but immediately fell in the water.

"Get a move on!" the captain yelled. "It's going to drown."

Five of the sailors tugged at its halter, but to no avail. The man with bushy hair rushed over. "Christian, watch out!" One of the rags was coming loose, baring a threatening horn. He pulled away just in time to avoid a goring. The ox struggled for a few more seconds. Then, once its head finally reached the sand, it stopped struggling and started lowing.

Gabriel took in the colossus tossed by the waves. Its sustained sounds were not unlike prayers; it was calling for help. Father Larronde, surrounded by screeching women and children, crossed himself. A murmur ran across the crowd. Christian wrapped his hand around the bared horn and kneeled in the water.

"Well?" Gabriel yelled for his own sake; the echo reverberated within his skull.

After a few seconds, the Chagossian got back up: "Its front leg—it's broken!" He punctuated his comment with twists of his fist. Applause broke out. Shouts of delight, of rage.

Mollinart and the captain walked around the creature, talking briefly. "Christian, come over here." A bit more conversation. The trembling animal was now crying. Mollinart threw his hands up in resignation—"All yours!"—and the crowd chattered.

Gabriel was unmoving as he fended off dizziness. A group of men dripping with sweat brushed up against him. He noticed the gleam of the tools in their thick hands. His heart started pounding even harder. Surely they wouldn't . . .

The metal's reflections forced him to shut his eyes.

At the first blow of the hammer, the animal bellowed in fury, thrust out its legs to defend itself, shook its head, but a second blow, right between the eyes, drew blood and rooted the ox to the spot. Gabriel's stomach clenched. A third blow to the open wound. A fourth. The men, all of them Chagossian, took turns aiming at the same point, where the bone was thinnest and the most brittle. Gabriel opened his mouth, trying to take in air. With each impact, it was as if they were striking his own nose, his own forehead, his own skull. "Go, go! Hit again!" And the ox pleaded. The sound of its flesh giving way was even more unbearable than the sight. All around, the children were huddled up to their mothers, their grandmothers, not daring to move. The men, egged on by stout-legged women, struck warrior poses. An old man in a colonial uniform pulled back at every blow, only to get closer again. To his left, a disheveled young woman was ostensibly looking away from the carnage, a mushy gray thing in her hands, her face turned toward him. He nearly walked her way, but then a new shout stopped him. The sound was different. He forced himself to look, saw the hammer buried in the skull: it had sunk into the soft brain. There was a moment's silence, then cheers moved through the crowd like a shiver down a monstrous animal's long back.

Gabriel sank down onto the beach, distraught. He realized that the sun was high in the sky and the air stifling; he watched as noisy excitement overcame the horde, the taste of meat already on their lips.

"So that's what they call a welcome committee." Mollinart's tone was avuncular. "Well, come along, you've seen plenty for today. They'll carve up that ox. May as well show you the villa." Gabriel rose mechanically and followed the administrator after one last glance at the sacrificial offering.

On the milky-white sand and through the lagoon's clear water, the blood spread its red.

Savage. Slob. Blackie. Thief. Moron. Bastard.

Good for nothing.

Chagossian meant all that when I was a kid. Our accent? Different from the Mauritians'. Our skin? Darker than the Mauritians'. Our pockets empty. Our houses nonexistent.

Don't give them a second thought, my mother said. *Forget them.*

But how can shame be forgotten?

One day, I must have been fifteen, I see a girl on the beach. A redhead. Grand-Gaube isn't a touristy spot. *Redhead* means High White; it means High Whatever. That's how things are in Mauritius: whites, Creoles, mulattos. There's no end to the labels, to madness and mistrust, too. I look at the speedboat in front of me, the bustling pleasure boaters—they're cooking some of their catch. The girl smiles at me. A beauty that makes me sorry not to be older, not to be more of a man. Her hair's flowing lava.

I walk up. Then a guy bursts out of the rocks and gets in front of me, a silly sight in his Speedo and his sunburned skin. This is a private beach.

I don't know what goes through his head. Or rather, I know all too well. He lets out a grunt all of a sudden and then yells, "Scram, you black pig!"

I instinctively turn my head to see who might be behind me. Nobody, of course. I'm alone. I'm weak enough to believe that the black pig wasn't me.

The white guy bursts out laughing.

Not the girl. No, not the girl.

She pays the man no mind as she climbs onto the speedboat without a word.

I flee.

I know one thing now. If the redhead had laughed that day, if she'd been that cruel, I'd never have been able to hold a woman in my arms. I'd have paid dearly for a white man's hate.

March 1967

At Christian's first hammer blow, Marie heard her sister thank God. This meat was unhoped for, a true wedding gift. Father Larronde had set the wedding Mass for the next day at five in the evening. Ever since, it had been pandemonium.

Josette pushed away the mess tin of fricassee. "If I don't finish my dress now, I'll have to wear a sack tomorrow." It was the tenth time she'd said that.

Marie sighed. "Josette. Let's take a break. We have to. After we eat, we'll sew. Promise."

Christian filled his son's plate, a dishful of octopus drowning in rice, beans, pepper, food that would fuel them up. Nicolin hadn't complained one bit while helping to unload the *Sir Jules*, hauling crates and containers. He was only ten. "Makine? Suzanne?"

The two little girls ignored Christian, more interested in the conversation they were having than in what was in their bowls. "When you spin around, Auntie, will your dress make a sun?" The gap in her smile—Suzanne had lost one of her baby teeth—only made her more adorable.

Josette buried her face in her hands: the bust wasn't done yet; there might not even be enough cloth; they really had to get a move on. Marie sighed and slipped her spoon back in the fricassee.

"What about you, Mamita?" Suzanne's two black pupils were raised to hers.

"What about me what?"

"When are you marrying?"

A few years earlier, Marie had been attracted to Henri: that energy, that knobbly body, that roguishness that seemingly naïve teenagers full of love and drama had a habit of cultivating. And, at seventeen years old, what defense did she have against that? Around three in the afternoon, when her work on the plot was done, she went to meet him in the warehouse, by the furnace. The shovelfuls of copra were crackling under the flame. She stuck her metal cup in the water and emptied it with one gulp while watching him, her skirt hiked up to her thighs. There was a first kiss, a first caress. She gave herself over to him, and that same day he hurt her. With a single word. "Your feet, they're like two canoes."

Since she was little, Marie had considered herself pretty, even very pretty. She went barefoot everywhere, embracing the waves and the wind. It only took one word to undo all that, one word to make her feel ugly. *Canoes.* Like a man's feet. But it hadn't kept Henri from rubbing up against her belly, gasping, blissful, his muscles in sharp relief. Feeling stung, she'd turned to Jean-Joris, who also worked in the furnace. Jean-Jo was a gentle giant. Round eyes, high forehead. Never said no. She wanted to believe that there was another man hidden inside him, a more striking one; she was sadly wrong. His gentleness verged on apathy; his good-heartedness on boringness.

Henri, Jean-Jo; Jean-Jo, Henri. After several humdrum months going back and forth between the two, Marie had gotten pregnant.

When she gave birth to Suzanne, she had to resign herself: her baby didn't look like either of her lovers. "Too soon. When they're little, babies look all the same," Josette had said. Now her girl was four, and Marie still couldn't see a thing apart from the nose, the long-lashed eyes, the tight mouth that came from her and her alone. It was always the same old story with Diego Garcia's men: they weren't fathers and were almost never husbands. At best they were memories; at worst, regrets. That neither Henri nor Jean-Joris claimed to be Suzanne's father didn't surprise her. They simply went with the flow, and even went so far as to become best friends. Having shared the same woman, why not share friendship, too?

Marie stroked her daughter's cheek. "You want to know why I'm not marrying?" She paused. "Because I'm just fine without men." A gleam shone in those two black pupils. Christian choked on his wine, and Josette elbowed him. Marie ignored them, her eyes still on her daughter's. Reassured by the calm in her voice, Suzanne gave her a big smile and started eating.

I'm just fine without men.

In her heart, though, that birdlike outline on the pier was etched. She could still see his elegant beige suit, the reddening cigarette, the indifferent gaze—like a very thin thorn digging into her skin.

The sea air mixed with the scent of frangipani flowers. Marie rushed into the waves. The water, almost tinged pink by the late-afternoon sun, was warm and welcoming. She stared off in the distance at a fishing buoy and decided not to stop until she reached it.

The sea. The pleasure of swimming until she was out of breath, out of thoughts. On Diego Garcia, few were those who dared to swim. They were wary of the too-peaceful lagoon. Dark blue depths could suck you right down, and nobody would ever find out what happened—your body would be fodder for crabs, ghosts, and eels.

Marie wasn't afraid of drowning. There had been that trip on a boat with her mother and her sister one Sunday—she must have been five, maybe six. In the clear water, she had seen a shadow wriggle. A silverfish. As she bent over to admire it, a wave higher than the rest threw her overboard. The cold water swallowed her up, dragging her down. No more fish, only salt in her throat, burning nostrils, and a terrible pain in her lungs. But her body made its way back up. The sea instilled her with miraculous gestures, arms tracing the shape of a butterfly's wings, legs kicking like a rear engine, and she'd reached the surface again. Surging out of the water, she inhaled all the air in heaven with her stunned mouth. Ever since, she'd felt free among the currents, invincible; she'd made a pact with the waves.

Marie extended one arm, then the other, gave one last slow kick, and her hand touched the buoy sticky with algae. She caught her breath, her head half-underwater, her hair floating around her like long tentacles. The sun was starting its descent, and soon it would be a red dot swallowed up by the horizon. She thought back on the lights of the *Sir Jules* at dawn. On her sister's panic when she'd realized there wouldn't be enough cloth to finish the bodice. Their aunt Angèle had sorted out the problem in just two hours, setting a yellow cotton triangle just above the waist; that would do the trick, and very nicely indeed.

She slipped under the water, held her breath for a minute. When she poked her head up, her hand still gripping the buoy, the stranger's face was dancing before her eyes. What had he come to the Chagos for? So young. Shoes, cigarette, pinched lips; a washed-up prince. She shut her eyes, then immediately opened them again. No point fantasizing. The young man would leave with Father Larronde at the end of his stay. In three or four days at the latest. What would a man like him be doing on Diego Garcia? Mollinart and his wife were the only Mauritians settled on the island, because that was their job, their status, but him? She recalled the sight of him stumbling in front of the bloody ox. Mixing with them! She let go of the buoy and headed back. The trade winds were at her back, and she quickly reached the sand, turned coppery by the last rays of sun.

What a shame it was all around.

Such a handsome man.

March 1967

Some lacquered furniture with mother-of-pearl inlays, four rattan rocking chairs, a side table, vases decked out with fresh flowers, the waxed parquetry smelling like honey and pepper: everything in the administrator's sitting room added up to a familiar décor. The table at the back was already set—china and silverware gleaming on the starched white tablecloth.

"Ah, here's our young friend," Mollinart said. "Come in, young man. Geneviève's having our apéritifs made."

The woman drew near, her hand held out. Gabriel was caught off guard. Had she forgotten they'd met a few hours earlier? Then he realized. She was waiting for him to kiss her hand. He bent down to the light freckled skin. As he made contact, he was suddenly reminded of a scrubbed pig's hide.

"Is my husband's secretary properly settled in?" she asked warmly.

"Absolutely, my thanks to you."

The administrator sank into his armchair.

"Very good, very good. As I was saying to my husband, Father Larronde and the captain will meet us for dinner. With the boat needing to be unloaded and this whole wedding, not to mention the meat to be carved up, they're delayed somewhat." Geneviève Mollinart pursed her lips. "Those men are rather . . ." She waved her hand in a motion that set her golden bracelets clinking.

An old man Gabriel had seen on the beach interrupted them to set refreshments and alcohol on the low table. He was clad in a white uniform with gleaming buttons that offset the darkness of his skin. Wrinkles furrowed his forehead and carved grooves along his eyes. His age notwithstanding, he still had a childlike look.

"Gabriel," Mollinart said, "may I present to you Félix, the oldest man on Diego Garcia?" The small elder puffed his chest before deflating. "He was already in the service of my predecessor. He's one of my most trusted men. I've named him commander."

Geneviève rolled her eyes.

"Commander?"

"A sort of keeper of the peace, if you will, but rest assured, the Îlois are wholly peaceful; there are never any problems. The prison behind the warehouse has five cells at best, and they're all empty. I've never had to police them. To be completely honest, it's the mill that takes up most of my time. Come along now. Have a scotch with me, will you?"

Gabriel wanted to retch. Here, too, they drowned their thoughts in whiskey. "Just a finger, please. The trip was exhausting, so I'd rather . . . Thank you, thank you." His glass was already half-full.

Mollinart poured himself a good three fingers with a sigh of satisfaction. "Now, tell me. What is the latest news in Mauritius?"

The latest news? Gabriel held back a grimace. It was all bad. Worrisome. He didn't delude himself. When he'd set off, the first protests were already beginning. The island would be torn apart. In six months there would be nothing left but warring camps, communities facing off against one another, winners and losers.

"As you know," he said, "independence has a good portion of the population dreaming of the future, all the Indians are behind

Ramgoolam. The Creoles are against independence, but . . . the referendum will be a rocky one."

Mollinart reached over to the plate of *gâteaux piments* and gulped down two at once, his gaze blank.

"Goodness gracious," Geneviève cut in. "I find politics to be horrifying!" She glanced at her husband, who was noisily chewing and swallowing. "Tell us about yourself instead. The Neymorins are well known in Port-Louis, very good people, of course. But your mother, what family does she come from?"

Gabriel swirled the whiskey in his glass. "My mother?" The administrator waved indulgently at him, as if to say, *Don't feel obligated* or *What's the point?* "My mother's name was Viviaine Petitjean."

"Was?" The woman blinked slowly, savoring the tragedy.

"Yes. She died when I was ten."

※

Gabriel lit a cigarette and let his eyes linger on the shadows of the shore, searching for the outlines of the Indian almond tree his room overlooked. It was the first thing he'd noticed as he entered the bedroom upstairs. A massive tree with glittering leaves. His room was furnished with a wooden desk, a chair, a single bed protected by a mosquito net, an empty shelf, and an armoire. It hadn't taken him twenty minutes to put away his belongings. Clothes, toiletries and medicines, some books, some notebooks, some pencils, and a few photos, including a portrait of his mother, radiant at twenty. He'd immediately set it on the shelf; when he looked at it from his bed, she was smiling at him. It wouldn't be long before he'd lived as many years without her as he had with her. He stubbed out his cigarette in the coconut-shell ashtray and shut the window.

He undressed, pulled on clean underwear, and lay down at last. This first day had left him feeling out of sorts, both relieved and disgusted, exhausted and uneasy. He could still see the hammer sinking into the ox's skull. A sacrifice. A trance.

A sound made him start. It was from outside. He sat up on the bed, turned to the window. With the new moon, no light came through. The sound began again. He cupped his ear, then understood. It was coconuts falling, loosened by the breeze. He let out a nervous laugh and lay back down.

At La Jalousie, when he was a child, similar noises had pulled him out of his sleep. A mango tree planted by his great-grandfather shaded his window and screeched on windy days. Gabriel had been enchanted by the tree, watching its metamorphoses over the seasons: the flower's fuzz stiffened as the fruit bloomed, hardly bigger than an almond; then this almond grew and became a stout heart, orange and green, heavy with a sugar that split its skin. But if they didn't remember to pick the mangos, the flesh wrinkled, turned mushy and brown. In a matter of days it plopped to the ground. Birth and collapse. The rot spread even to the prettiest fruits. Gabriel shut his eyes. Didn't the same, after all, happen to every family?

When the plane takes off, bidding adieu to the greenish sphinx of Lion Mountain and the snaking roads, I think about everything you've never seen, Mother. About everything you'll never see.

The power of engines; the sky above the clouds and the angels who aren't waiting for us there; the impending elections; the Ramgoolam dynasty; power being handed down from father to son; apples imported from Europe or South Africa when we're drowning in lychees, papayas, and pineapples; the latest Bollywood films; our struggles with lawyers, the outcome of trials, maybe justice. Pierrine.

What do people call the memory of what's to come? There needs to be a word—*oracle* and *divination* aren't right—a new word for this compact memory that includes the future. To remember what will happen and what one won't experience.

You, grown so thin over the past weeks, your halting breath already a death rattle. I'd have liked to open up your belly so air could get in and soothe you. Hold on a bit longer. Bettina is pregnant; you'll have a grandchild. The sparkle in your eyes, Mother, and that youthful look you gave me all of a sudden. That light that I'd have loved to catch. But sadness has gotten the better of you. Your tears are heavy with truth.

I won't meet her. I'll miss him.

Him? Her? Your uncertainty is gut-wrenching for me. Whether it's a her or a him, I myself don't know.

Love always comes too late. We've both lost a smile. We make plans to meet in two separate places, by mistake. I'm sorry. Next time? There'll be no next time.

But what am I saying? Of course there'll be one. Thousands of next times! But the older we get, the less right we have to mistakes. Every go around the carousel comes at greater cost. We can't commit to the wrong fights or people or feelings.

You were absolutely right, Mother. You never knew Pierrine. Your granddaughter.

March 1967

A welter of hats bustled around the church steps. Marie was stamping her feet. She'd teased her hair into a bun adorned with big flowers, rubbed her skin with coconut oil—the better to charm, to draw attention. Her bright orange dress, sewn by Angèle as well, thrust up her décolleté.

"Come in, my children." Father Larronde opened the doors and welcomed the guests. She pushed Suzanne up to the front row excitedly. Once everyone was seated, a festive song filled the church. Christian, in a flawless white shirt and pants, made his way to the altar with tears in his eyes, Makine ahead of him, a basket in her hand. The smell of incense settled over the choir, and Marie crossed herself. The cleric waved to Christian before gesturing to the musicians, who began a new song. At the church door, Josette finally made her entrance.

Her hair braided into a wreath, she was resplendent in her white dress with a yellow bodice. The applause was deafening, and the melody grew rousing. With a bouquet of anthuriums in her hand, she made her way up the nave at a trembling pace, Nicolin capping off the procession with a huge church candle. With her round eyes, set off by her thin eyebrows, Josette looked exactly like their late mother.

Marie bowed her head. Stared at her bare feet cooled by the church's stone floor.

"Bigfoot Marie!"

It was so long ago. Her first communion had taken place on her seventh birthday. For the occasion, her mother had bartered with an artisan over in Nouva: a fresh red snapper for a pair of sandals. All the children wore sandals of that sort for church. When Thérèse had tried to slide her feet into the loop, Marie kicked away the sandal. "Stop it, you. Behave!" Her mother had slapped her, to no avail. Marie wouldn't put on shoes.

She could still remember everyone's looks when she'd walked into the church barefoot in a white dress and with tangles in her hair; she could remember her mother's shame, young Father Larronde's indignation, her sister's smile, the teasing, the whispering, the tongues wagging. None of that, however, had held a candle to the new feeling that overcame her, the feeling that meant something akin to "I exist."

"Bigfoot Marie," her mother had nicknamed her, with equal parts irritation and tenderness. Marie had loved it, until Henri, until the shame came. Bodies change. So do men's gazes. Now she would have given anything to be able to pull on shoes that went with her dress. Because in the church's side aisle, his features stoic, was the young visitor. Out of reach.

When Mass let out, the sun was already starting to set. "There you are, big Madame Tasdebois." Marie hugged her sister. Christian had that funny last name: Tasdebois. Pile of wood! They'd laughed over it so many times. And now Josette would bear it for the rest of her days. There was no guessing the twists of fate.

"And here are the sisters." Mollinart rushed over to them, followed by his wife and the stranger. Marie's heart started pounding. The administrator kissed Josette's cheek and gave Christian a firm handshake, while his wife whispered the usual niceties. "Gabriel, allow me to introduce you to the newlyweds. Josette, Christian . . . Their children, Nicolin and Makine . . . And here's Marie-Pierre Ladouceur, Josette's sister. Come over here, my dear, we won't bite. Marie-Pierre, please meet Gabriel Neymorin, my new secretary."

There was a momentary silence as their eyes met. He stuck out his hand, unsmiling. Gabriel. Her thoughts were swirling—first and foremost that he mustn't see her feet. She was wearing her best dress. Was her flower still properly in her chignon? Should she have put on lipstick? When her hand touched his, she was sure for a second that she was dreaming. But she wasn't; his palm was clammy. Henri and Jean-Joris, too, had clammy hands. Her pulse quickened.

"Where's Suzanne?" Mollinart asked. She pointed at her daughter hiding in Angèle's skirt. A shadow flitted across the birdlike face.

⋈

On the beach a huge fire was roaring. Pots were spitting their smoke skyward. The haunch of beef was already exuding a meaty aroma. They started grilling fish as they uncorked some rum. Mollinart and the captain offered the newlyweds a barrel of red wine. "Careful, my children, don't overdo it," the cleric said as he had a drink with them. A few tambour notes rose up from the shore, distracting the couples by the fire. The *séga* was getting underway.

Discreetly, Marie glanced at Gabriel Neymorin. He was younger than she was, clearly not by much, but younger all the same; traces of adolescence remained on his narrow chin, and his features still had some indecision to them. She saw him helping the men prepare the buffet, rather awkwardly, too elegant to be turning the fish over on the fire, looking almost afraid of getting his clothes stained.

The musicians were starting to beat their ravannes gently, to loosen their wrists. The bodies got closer to the flames. Josette and Christian got in the middle of the circle and began swaying their hips, their arms raised, their fists like falling flowers. Marie joined them and clapped her hands to accompany the dancers, and Angèle and the others immediately followed suit. Old Félix launched into the newlyweds' séga with his gravelly intonations, and the children, urged on by the adults, added their voices to his. Around them, men and women were digging into piping-hot chicken legs, gnawing on the coconut-grilled fish, swallowing the roasted ox's blood. Angèle was relishing the crab fricassee. Everyone was licking their fingers, chins dripped with sauce; glasses were emptied and filled anew; everybody's heads were spinning—it was wonderful. The ravannes sped up their rhythm. Josette waved over Marie, who, entranced by the music, got up by the fire to dance. She could make out Gabriel standing back. She threw back her head, puffed up her belly, kept the rhythm with her bare feet on the sand. In the distance the kids were playing, Makine and Suzanne mimicking the women's movements, Nicolin running after a ball. Marie decided to forget about her girl, to forget about Henri and Jean-Joris, who had just joined the circle, to forget everything so she could keep up with the rousing ravannes. "Go on! Dance!" a high voice chirped, and the rhythm intensified. Swaying sensually, she danced the way she sometimes wanted to, for herself and herself alone. She could feel her skin trembling, succulent, and her waist twirled, her breasts undulated, the earth shook beneath her feet. Infected by the general frenzy, soaked in wine and rum, Mollinart joined the group. The captain stumbled in cadence. And when Father Larronde dared to take a few awkward steps, everybody burst with happiness.

Only Gabriel did not move.

Absorbed in the trance, Marie was seized by impatience in the face of his inertia. She danced over to him, hiked up her skirt past her knees, and swayed her hips even more vigorously. When she saw that he was contemplating her, she kept on going, her skirt pulled up, a bit higher now, and a little more, her back bent over. Henri and Jean-Joris began to twirl drunkenly around her and Gisèle and Anne-Lise and Becca, barely disguising their desire. The music kept on defying the flames, the voices soaring up to the comets, and the songs, and the ravannes, and the wild dancing overtook their bodies. Gabriel finally stood up and went to her, leaving his hat on the sand. Marie could almost feel his hands on her breasts, his breath on her lips. But at the last minute, he nodded at her and turned around.

Dismayed, she looked at him sinking into the night. Around the fire, Christian and Josette were entwined. Other couples were joining them here and there. Henri kissed a neighbor, glassy-eyed. When Jean-Joris sidled up to her, she didn't push him away.

March 1967

They sat around the plot, as peaceful as seabirds. Their hands plunged into woven baskets, pulled out coconuts that they set on their skirts. Always the same gestures: raise the machete, split the fruit with a sharp thrust, husk each half before putting it on the ground, the meat exposed to the sun. Then the men would take the copra to the mill. Grindstones pulled by donkeys drew out a thick oil as the husks burned in the furnace.

"The clocks set the time for the day," Mollinart explained. "Work starts at dawn, around six fifteen, and stops in the early afternoon. Then the Îlois go and fish or cook or do who knows what. Come along." They walked up to the workers.

She had turned her back too late; Gabriel recognized her immediately. Marie-Pierre Ladouceur.

Seeing her dance amid the flames two days earlier, he'd been overcome by dizziness. The woman was ravishing. Dark skin with gilded hues. A round face. A supple body, her legs freed. It was too much. That skirt hiked up, swishing, those shrieks, those men around her . . . And her name! It was like a spell that a witch in a book casts on you.

"We export tons of copra every year to Mauritius and the rest of the world. One of your tasks, young man, will be overseeing production with me."

The administrator raised a hand to the women to wave to them. Marie turned when she saw him.

Her startle hurt him. Gabriel bent over quickly. The headscarf holding back her hair revealed her protruding, smooth forehead. Her lips were rounded in a small, sullen moue. But one detail alarmed him. Below her cheeks, small dimples formed tiny wells of love. He felt uncomfortable and kept up with Mollinart so as to get away from her.

"Apart from Pointe de l'Est, where we are, and which is the heart of the island, there are two other villages. Well, you know what I mean by villages. Paths with shacks on both sides. Pointe Marianne to the south and Nouva to the north. On the main island and the islets that make up Diego Garcia, there are about a thousand inhabitants."

Gabriel nodded and followed Mollinart. He came upon a room where a dozen or so children of all ages were playing. He recognized Makine Tasdebois in a corner. The administrator stopped.

"See? I don't even have a teacher for them. In any case, as soon as they're old enough to work, the kids help their parents with fishing or at the mill."

Mollinart then showed him the forge, the infirmary—three beds in a row in a small sheet-metal shack, two boxes of medicine right on the ground, and an old stethoscope gathering dust—the cemetery adjoining the church, protected by century-old banyans, and the garage of his villa, which had been turned into a telecommunications office.

"Here is where you can send telegrams to your family."

Gabriel thanked him.

"Well, I think you've seen all there is to see. Shall we turn to serious matters now?"

In the dimly lit room, towering heaps of registers threatened to tip over. Gabriel took them down one by one to organize them in chronological order. They were mainly account books, documenting business transactions between Diego Garcia and Mauritius, all written in English, records of the transfers of slaves deported from Madagascar to the Chagos. He opened one at random.

> *Date: 17 December 1819*
> *Name of the vessel: Ship Constance*
> *Name of the owner: Mr E. Fouquereaux*
> *Domestic servants accompanying their Masters or Masters' family: 5 Males—9 Females*
> *Place of destination: Diego Garcia*
> *Permanently transferred: 5 Males—7 Females*

Such horrifyingly precise volumes would be a dream come true for historians. He set them aside in a locked cabinet, then collected all the active account books, apart from the most recent one. Sitting at his small desk, he checked off the list of provisions for the *Sir Jules*, as Mollinart had asked him to. In the livestock section, his pencil hovered. On the wedding night, the Îlois had pounced on the unfortunate ox's meat; even Father Larronde hadn't denied himself the pleasure, but seeing the blood trickle had been enough to deter Gabriel from even a bite.

Overcome by a wave of sadness, he shut the register. His existence wasn't all that different from that game of skill Évelyne had always begged to play when they were little: after scattering a handful of sticks on the table, they had to pick them up one by one without moving the others. He did better at those games than at real life. What could his sister really do in Beau-Bassin while he wore himself out recording goods in this thick old book? He'd send her a telegram as soon as he could.

"Well, my boy, is it going well?" Mollinart didn't even glance at what Gabriel was writing as he hunched over a small table from which he pulled out a carafe of whiskey and two huge glasses. "Let's have us a talk, man to man." Again. Whether he was on Mauritius or Diego Garcia, conversations didn't really happen except over a bottle. The administrator pulled a chair over.

"My wife, well, you've likely figured that my wife comes from a family that's rather . . . how to put it . . ."

"Prim?"

"Exactly. Very prim. Talking politics at the dinner table simply isn't done. But here, we're not at the dinner table, are we?"

Mollinart had a knack for setting his fellow men at ease, and this casualness didn't displease Gabriel.

"I'd like to know your thoughts on the referendum." Mollinart had a sip of the drink, which he'd swirled. "How do you feel about the matter? You were there just a week ago. It's no secret, I'll have you know, I'm rather close with Gaëtan Duval."

Of course. The leader of the Mauritian Party. Mollinart supported him, as did the rest of the Creole bourgeoisie.

"If Mauritius gains independence, there'll be upheaval everywhere, even here, on the Chagos. I don't know what the British will do, but one thing I know for sure." His eyes narrowed. "The copra trade may well be affected."

Despite the wide-open window, Gabriel could hardly breathe. No breeze refreshed the room tonight. He'd been tossing and turning for at least an hour, his neck ablaze. The foam of his mattress exuded the foul smell of warm sweat. He ran a hand over his torso: dripping. Everything that day had been oppressive. Marie Ladouceur's moue, the books threatening to tip over, the image of Évelyne, all the way down to his conversation with Mollinart. And to cap it off, a fly was buzzing around his ears. He shook the mosquito net, but it made no difference, the bug's hum amplified by the night's quiet. Gabriel suddenly sat up in bed. That memory. A slap.

Slouching at the kitchen table, he watched the fly, noted its iridescent, blue-green tones. Its feet were kneading a crumb of coconut cake he'd bought on the way home from school. Its proboscis was dripping a clear liquid over the sugar before sucking it up. He swatted it away with the back of his hand. With a thud, the insect stuck to the window.

After finishing his cup of tea, Gabriel set his hands on the table and got up. It was time. He went into the sitting room. In his club chair, a glass of Chivas in his hand, his father was reading the paper and grumbling. Gabriel sat in front of him. He was ready. In his head, he'd run through his line of reasoning ten times already: London was a world capital; the most reputable lawyers were trained there; Benoît was already at Cambridge and could help him settle in there; he promised to work hard to honor the family name; his mastery of English was unimpeachable. The father turned the newspaper page, still utterly absorbed. In the beveled tumbler, the ice had already melted, turning the whiskey pale.

"Good god!" Léon suddenly said. "Listen to this, Gabriel: '1967 will be a decisive year for Mauritius's future,' declared Governor Sir John Rennie on January 5, 1967. At the request of Her Royal Highness Queen Elizabeth II, the Mauritian people will be asked to vote on August 7 and decide whether or not Mauritius should become independent after 157 years of British colonial presence in the territory. Her Majesty's government is not unaware that the winds of change are already blowing across the world. India, Nigeria, and Kenya have already . . .'" He threw *Le Cernéen* onto the table. "Independence? That'd turn everything upside down."

Gabriel picked up the paper, glanced over the headlines. So the rumors were true: Mauritius would soon be able to separate from the United Kingdom. A referendum. British control was hanging by a thread. And maybe that was one further argument to leave.

The father downed his whiskey in a gulp. "Ludna!" The maid rushed in. "Another," he ordered, his shaky hands pulling a cigarette out of his jacket pocket. Ludna made her way into the kitchen and came back with a full glass. "And the ice? . . . You have to spell everything out for this Mozambican."

The dark-skinned *nénène* went to get a bucket of ice and some tongs. The father had always talked this way about nursemaids and gardeners. "Fat Creoles," as he called them, were spared nothing. Gabriel offered Ludna an apologetic smile, a small one, almost a grimace, which the poor woman clung to before leaving.

"An independent Mauritius? Honestly, that'd be a catastrophe. Might as well hand the keys to the whole place right over to the Indians."

"But Gaëtan Duval would allow no such thing," Gabriel said.

"Right you are. The Mauritian Party would never put up with such a possibility."

The father took another swig of whiskey, and Gabriel saw his opening. It was now or never.

"Salam!"

Évelyne was standing in the doorway, a book in her hand, proud of making such an entrance. Gabriel clenched his teeth. Their father hated when she spoke like the commoners; at La Jalousie, only the staff were allowed to speak Creole.

"May we ask what has delayed your return?" their father asked.

His sister was still in her Lorette *collège* uniform, a sky-blue and dark-blue plaid dress and a white blouse that made her look like a little girl even though she was nearly fifteen.

"I took the bus to keep a friend company." She was asking for it, Gabriel knew.

"A friend? What sort of friend makes you get on the bus?"

Évelyne swung her schoolbag and dropped it on the sofa, her eyes ablaze. "Savita Balasamy."

Gabriel blanched; she needed to be quiet.

Their father opened and shut his mouth a few times, as if unbelieving. "You're befriending an Indian girl?" He sprang to his feet and slapped her hard. The act was a shock. Évelyne brought her hand to her reddening cheek, doing her best not to cry.

"I knew it!" she said, running out of the room. "I knew that was how you'd react!" Their father's furious yells redoubled as he followed her into the hallway.

"Stop it, Papa, stop it!" Gabriel shouted as he grabbed him by the arm.

Évelyne disappeared into her room.

"I won't have my girl hanging around Indians! Am I clear?" Then he turned and went into the kitchen, where he poured himself more scotch, his hands shaking.

For months now scenes of this sort had been playing out; the atmosphere in the home was becoming unbearable. Gabriel looked down. That was when he noticed, on the sisal rug in the kitchen, a brown stain. Upon closer consideration, it looked like a bloodstain, in a teardrop shape. The sound of a clenched fist hitting the table forced him to look up.

"A Neymorin woman hanging around a Malbar, well, I never . . ."

Gabriel forced himself to follow the man into the sitting room, where they settled back into their chairs.

"Papa . . ."

"I don't want to hear a word of it!"

That was Gabriel's best chance gone. England was firmly out of reach now. A leaden silence settled over the room.

As he mulled over that scene—why did she have to go and bring up Savita, too?—a gentle buzzing reverberated in the room. That damn fly. After circling once or twice, it landed on the paper. Its velvety body touched the photo of Sir John Rennie. And suddenly, as if insane, it started scratching at the governor's baleful eye.

What does independence mean? Who's independent? Are you independent?

I've long believed in this dream. Freedom, autonomy. Just as applicable to politics as to private life. I love you. I don't love you anymore. If I don't love you anymore, then I'll leave. I can go anywhere. I think I've been fooling myself. Independence—I mean pure, true, absolute independence—doesn't exist.

We're always colonized by someone else.

This fact constrains us.

The Chagos were dependent on Mauritius, which was dependent on the United Kingdom, which was dependent on Europe, which was dependent on the United Nations, which was dependent on the democratic world. Who's heard of us? Diego Garcia? Peros Banhos? Nope, never heard of them. Who knows what the democratic world's inflicted upon us?

Believe me. Our fate affects you all, and certainly far beyond anything you've imagined, or could.

March 1967

Wedged between two shacks, a dog had just given birth. Its fur was short and yellowish. Its tongue wetted its muzzle as its teats were tugged by the litter of puppies.

Suzanne's yells put an end to the quiet of Pointe Marianne. "A dog, a little dog. Please, Mamita, I want a little dog!"

"Look, Auntie," Makine piped up, "funny cute things."

The girls tugged at Marie's nightshirt. They'd woken her up on a Sunday for this? A pair of imps, as incorrigible as rats.

"Please, Mamita!"

"I said no, Suzanne," Marie shouted. "No means no." She had just turned around and crossed the street to go back to sleep when she noticed a silhouette in the distance—hat, beige outfit, city shoes. Gabriel was already waving to her.

Like two arrows, Suzanne and Makine pelted her and kept on tugging at her arm. Marie was furious. Her hair was messy, she was in a nightshirt, she was barefoot. She hadn't seen Gabriel again in a week, and now was when she had to cross paths with him? She pulled herself together and went over to say hello in turn, but he froze. She barely had time to see where he was looking before he turned away, embarrassed. Under the thin cloth of her shirt, she was wholly naked.

"That one." Gabriel pointed at a puppy that seemed weaker than the others. It was trying to get at one of the teats, letting out small growls, its pink muzzle reaching for the sky. Each time, the mother nudged it away. Gabriel clicked his tongue. "You know what's going to happen? That dog's going to kill it. It's too weak."

"Mamita, I want that one! Or it'll die!"

Marie glanced reproachfully at Gabriel.

"Your daughter isn't wrong. Really, I'm sorry," he said with a calmness that belied his words.

Worn down, Marie crouched to the puppy and rolled it around in her hands. Suzanne and Makine gathered around immediately, doe-eyed, to stroke its fur. The puppy mewled more than it barked.

"It needs to be given milk," Gabriel said.

"And who's to give it?"

He looked at her sheepishly, and once again she could feel his eyes piercing the cotton of her shirt, wavering, returning to hers, flitting away. He stammered an apology. Rubbed his arms. His skin was electric. Then she realized: he wanted her. She was still sleepy, but she didn't have any doubt. Yes, he wanted her. He was quivering; he'd betrayed himself.

"Come," she suddenly commanded.

In the sty, where the goat was nibbling at the dry earth, she gave him the puppy and pulled out a stool. She sat beside the kid, set the pail between its legs, slipped her hands under the udder. There was the dog, and there was Gabriel. Both were waiting. She took her time, acting naïve, and started the milk dripping, white and smelly against the metallic sides of the pail. The receptacle filled up quickly. She waved Gabriel over. "Don't move!" She stuck a finger in the milk, held it out dripping to the puppy. The animal started suckling the finger like a nipple. The small tongue licked her skin, scratched at it. The sun was reaching its zenith, and Gabriel's temples were soaking with sweat. She seemed not to notice, did the same thing several times. He couldn't keep himself from shaking.

"M'sieur Gabriel . . . are you sick?"

"No, no, I'm okay. It's the heat." His palms were damp. His lips half-open. He looked at her almost painfully. And suddenly his pain seemed to become hers. She got up immediately, almost yanked the dog out of his hand to give it to the girls.

"Go to Angèle's shack. She'll spoil this little thing for sure."

Away with them. They needed to go now; they needed to be off right away. She could feel her pulse between her thighs. "I'll make the coffee, okay?"

※

She tried to forget the work dress she'd thrown on the ground the night before, the dirty dishes on the table, Suzanne's belongings, the basin of dirty water by the portable stove. "You want sugar in the coffee?" she asked as she pulled the pot off the heat.

"Yes, please."

His jaw was clenched; the vein on his neck stuck out. She sat beside him; the vein became more prominent. She'd have liked for him to venture to make a move first, to say a word first, but his young, well-educated self was clearly petrified. Absorbed into the coffee's vapor, a rich, uncommon smell exuded from his skin, a smell she associated with noblemen, with imported and wondrous fruits. He brought the metal cup to his lips, dared a smile. He scalded himself. Marie couldn't resist. She set her hand on his. He didn't pull away. Then she got up, and he followed suit. She moved in. Dizzying. Her lips reaching out; his answering in response. Skin against skin. She moved his hand to the neckline of her nightshirt, filled her nose and throat and lungs with his scent. Pulled him close. Ran her lips over his stubbly beard, stopped at his ear. Just behind the lobe was a birthmark, a tiny cloud. An impulse overcame her; she ran her tongue over that cloud.

He exhaled. "Don't stop."

She kissed it again, gently, passionately. His body started shaking, almost spasming. She knew he'd never touched a woman before her. She guided him, pressed her breasts to his chest, undid his shirt buttons. She wanted him in her. She slipped her own shirt off and, naked, pushed up against him. He finally landed on the caresses she was hoping for and pushed her to the bed. She flipped him over, ran her lips over his torso, his belly button, moved down farther, then positioned herself above him, her breasts heavy, her belly tensed. The world around them turned radiant.

When they fell, sweat-soaked, back onto the bed, she met his eyes. In them she did not see the tenderness or gratitude or sweetness she'd expected. No, in his gaze all she saw was fear.

March 1967

The teardrop of blood grew, forming a toenail, a finger, spreading in rivulets like a monstrous hand across the kitchen, the sitting room, overtaking the whole house. Sitting in his armchair, the man was smoking a cigar placidly, his feet dangling in the red liquid.

"Papa!" Gabriel yelled.

"No, my son. You're not going to London," the stern voice repeated mechanically.

"Papa!"

The armchair flipped over suddenly. It wasn't his father looking at him anymore, but a gigantic eye with a black eyelid.

Gabriel bolted awake. For several minutes he was gasping; he stuck his hand past the mosquito net, stumbled over to his nightstand lamp. His panting left his heart pounding. The nightmare had felt so real. The specters on the wall amounted to a horrific bacchanal and flooded the room with light.

Everything in his head was swirling. His rushed departure from La Jalousie; the father; Évelyne's goodbyes from the window; Marie, naked in his arms, voluptuous, terrifying, his first time.

A Chagossian woman. A Black woman, even blacker than Ludna, Marie was a working woman who'd never left her island, never held a book, who spoke a Chagos-accented Creole. A woman three years older than him, with one child already. A lowly woman, a mother too young.

On his bedroom shelf, his mother watched him with a smile. He opened the door discreetly and headed for the bathroom to splash some water on his face.

The eve of her death, his mother had called him into the entrance hall. Dressed in a long gown, she stood before the birdcage. A magnificent, monumental one topped by a bulb reminiscent of Indian palaces. Parakeets, weavers, bulbuls, and finches were flitting around. With a hand on his shoulder, she pointed out the two gray-and-blue birds huddled in the back. Gabriel immediately recognized them: the famous lovebirds.

"See them?" she whispered. "You do see them, don't you?"

Of course he saw them. He waited for her to say more, but she simply kissed his forehead without another word.

Gabriel stared at himself in the mirror corroded by salt and time. Disheveled, red-eyed: he looked like a madman.

July 1967

Taming him took months. Four long months. She'd gone slowly, with no sudden movements, and heeded his silences, his absences, sometimes nudging him forward. For weeks, ever since the lessons, properly speaking, some sort of naturalness had arisen between them. The fear in Gabriel's eyes had slowly given way to desire. He grew assertive. Stopped being afraid to knock at her door, to have sex, to play with Suzanne and Mérou—her daughter had insisted on this name for the dog, owing to its gray spots. When they were together, Gabriel opened up, but otherwise he remained discreet, especially because of Mollinart.

Marie didn't feel the same reserve around Josette or Angèle and wished she did. Her aunt had made fun of her. Oh, come on. That little man? Can't even lift a basket of copra? Her sister had warned her: Îlois girl and nice-color Creole? Bad luck for sure. Just look at how he was dressed, how he talked; there was no chance he'd ever be like them. Don't get too attached, or you'll get crushed. Josette didn't laugh.

"But he does, he likes me!"

Her sister shot back. "Sure he likes you—you make him happy now. But look who he is. Look who you are." She wouldn't back down: a master and a slave together never added up to anything good.

Marie wavered for a moment, then his body swept away all doubts. Gabriel was the one she'd waited for all her life, the first man who could actually have a place in her world. She didn't have a father; she didn't have an uncle; she didn't have a brother. Henri and Jean-Jo didn't even exist in her mind. Gabriel was the one and only.

〤

The lessons began after dinner, by the oil lamp's light. Suzanne settled on the back bed, Mérou in her lap. The puppy had miraculously survived despite its frail weight. In a matter of days, its eyes had opened and dense fur had grown over the down. It had started wagging its tail and following them. It and Suzanne were inseparable.

Silence settled over the shack, and Marie waved for Gabriel to start. On the table, the notebook was open to the last page. Tracing rows of letters with an increasingly lively and almost free hand brought her a pleasure she couldn't have imagined months ago. The blank page darkened with ink like what the octopuses squirted at dawn under her fishgig. She turned the gray lines black, even though the rules were still beyond her. Why did a capital *A* turn, in lowercase, to a small circle knotted on itself?

"That's the rule; just follow it," Gabriel said. With a generous gesture, he drew a curved letter, both open and hooked.

"*G*," she announced proudly.

Another letter after that.

"*A*."

He nodded. "And what do *g* and *a* make together?"

She hesitated. "*Ja?*"

"No."

"*Ga*?"

Gabriel smiled.

"But *g* and *e* make *je*. Why don't *g* and *a* make *ja*?"

"Because not all letters can go together. Some need a bridge." He drew a *g* and an *e* and connected them with a *u*. "There you are. Now you have the sound *gwe*. Make sense?"

"I'm stupid, Gabriel. I'll never learn to read."

"I won't have you saying that nonsense."

She picked up the pen again, and a cry escaped her. A cry of surprise, not of pain.

"Marie?"

She felt a new kick in her belly, set her hand on her navel. He looked at her excitedly. Her body had been playing hide-and-seek with her. No nausea or vomiting like with Suzanne. No tugging at her skin. Brownish bleeding on time had her believing that she was still getting her period. Suddenly, she was overcome with a fear of disappointment. She had been dreaming so much of a child with Gabriel, and she hadn't allowed herself to believe in it.

She seized his arm, dug her nails into his skin.

"The baby's moving."

You were in my belly, and I didn't know it. All those weeks that you were there without existing. Yes, you kept to yourself, my son. Until that kick, that awakening.

I listened to you, Mama, sensing things you left unsaid. Sadness blurred your face and infected me. This wavering of my heart still returns at moments. Drowns me. I'm not sure at that point that I'm myself.

What makes an identity? A name, a profession, the color of a passport, a particular alignment of the stars?

Can what undergirds us simply be the love that watched over our birth, or perhaps the inverse, the lack of any feeling?

July 1967

"Évelyne? It's me . . . Hello?"

Only a sputter came through. ". . . house, Gaby?" He squinted, as if doing so could improve the radio connection. ". . . Lorette . . . Mother Superior said, but I . . . in Latin! . . ."

He didn't understand a thing. His sister's voice came through choppily amid static.

"Évelyne? Can you hear me? How are things at home? Are you holding steady?"

For a second the conversation was clear. ". . . to himself. He makes me do all the Sunday scout camps so I don't see Savita . . . And then you know . . . the birdcage . . . ly! . . . I told him . . . do."

It can't be! Gabriel shouted, dangerously close to ripping out the cable, "Hello? Hello!"

Old Félix stuck his head in the garage. Gabriel gestured that the line wasn't clear and covered his ear.

". . . general elections, but . . . we should . . . can't! . . . wear blue . . . you, Gaby?"

He tried to talk reassuringly. "Évelyne . . . I'm going to be a father."
At the end of the line, more static. *No!* he thought.

". . . What . . . say it louder . . ."

He shouted, "I'm going to be a father!"

A screech hit his eardrums, and the line cut out. He hung up the
receiver angrily, his spirits dashed.

"Missah Neymorin?"

Clearly Félix had heard everything. Gabriel waved him in. In the
old commander's hands was a carafe of water and a glass. He drank a
cool mouthful. "Félix. Not a word of all that to Monsieur Mollinart,
okay?"

Since yesterday his head had been spinning.

"The baby's moving."

Marie had grabbed his hand to put it on her stomach. He hadn't
felt anything at first. Then suddenly a bump slid past on the left. Deep
down, something gave way, and he was unable to say a word, do a
thing, apart from cry. A baby. He was going to have a baby. Here, in
the Chagos.

Twenty. Was that a good age to become a father? His had been
fifty and was no example to follow. It wasn't a matter of age. Of what,
then? Of courage, of clear-sightedness? Of love? Marie had revealed him
to himself. Life was only a matter of desire. Of movement. Whether
she was splitting coconuts or throwing her fishgig between the rocks,
dancing in the night or welcoming caresses, Marie was always in
motion—she never waited to be given what she could go get herself.
Soon she would be able to read properly. Soon the world would open
up. A child. His first child.

He went to soak up the Diego Garcia breeze.

"I never trust rumors, Neymorin." Mollinart pointed to the other chair in his office. "That's why I'd rather talk to you one-on-one. Please tell me what I'm hearing isn't true."

His mouth suddenly went dry. The room was sweltering despite the lowered blinds. "What rumors, sir?"

The administrator hit the table. "Oh, not you as well! Out with it!"

Gabriel slumped into his chair. Should he lie? Confess? Betray? His hands clenched the armrests. "It's true."

At those words, Mollinart's scalp turned ruddy. Looking more disappointed than angry, he sank back in his seat.

"I . . . I'm sorry," Gabriel stammered. No, he couldn't say that. He wasn't sorry, not even one bit. Having a child filled him with joy; he was proud; he loved Marie. "Was it Félix who told you?"

"Yes," Mollinart said. "But don't count on it staying a secret. Your little girlfriend will be shouting it everywhere."

It was hot in the room, and the humidity seeped into his thoughts. He tried to right himself. "What does it matter? It's my life."

"Gabriel, with your behavior, you're going to ruin the nice setup we've got on this island!" The administrator was livid. "Are you stupid? It's just like Mauritius here. Everyone has to keep to themselves and stay in their proper place."

Gabriel got up. His sister wasn't allowed to have an Indian friend; he wasn't allowed to have a Chagossian lover. As if mixing never happened, as if Creoles were whites—but they weren't white!

"I must warn you, Neymorin. Don't count on me when it comes to marriage or baptism or anything else."

Gabriel blinked slowly. The furniture was starting to dance, the shelves beginning to float, or maybe he was the one moving helter-skelter amid all this blinding light. Before he passed out completely, he heard himself whispering, "Please, sir, don't say a thing to my father."

August 1967

Swelled by the trade winds, the dress fluttered over her round belly. She dug her feet into the damp sand and saw, caught in the arms of the coral, a spotted cowrie. Fortunately, there was no snail inside. She went to show it to her sister, who was gathering periwinkles.

"Beautiful!" Josette declared.

The lucky find was almost the size of her palm. Delightedly, Marie set it on her belly like a treasure, its spiky opening stuck on her navel. "Listen to that, my Ti Baba."

The sea's song was the most beautiful of all, and her baby, she just knew, could sense its echoes. Josette smiled warmly—she was still wary of Gabriel, but there was no ignoring the baby. Even Mollinart knew about it, and for a month Gabriel had been coming to see her every day, sometimes even spending the night.

Marie started walking again, collecting small gray and gold cowries in the sand as well as ocher-tinted spiral shells and mottled olives. When the bucket was full, she called the children, who were playfully throwing twigs at Mérou. "Come on, kids, let's go!"

As a group, they headed to the church, picking up a few anthuriums along the way. They reached the cemetery fence, went past the banyans. Above the brown creepers, the leaves formed a soft, welcoming green crown. Marie was the first to go down the narrow path, followed by Josette, the children, and the dog. She stopped before the basalt rectangle. A small wooden cross that Christian had painted white topped the grave.

Marie gave Suzanne and Makine the anthuriums to lay in a circle on the slab and let Nicolin arrange the small shells around it. She glanced at Josette, as if to ask if she could herself set down the cowrie. At the center of the circle, the lucky shell gleamed like a flower's heart. Josette reached for her hand, and the two of them, eyes shut, recited the Hail Mary, from which they drew their strength for each of their visits.

Of all her grandchildren, Thérèse Ladouceur had only known Nicolin. And only for a few months at that. The thought saddened Marie. The death of their mother had been sudden. She'd left one morning for the copra plot, machete in hand, and had never reached it. On the red-dirt footpath, they'd found the large knife a meter away from her body. She'd simply collapsed. "Maybe an aneurysm," Mollinart had said despairingly. She had no idea what he was saying but hadn't asked further.

It was her mother's dimples and love of movement that Marie had inherited; for Josette, it was her round eyes and her joyfulness. Who would the baby take after? She imagined a little boy, skin the color of cloves, long lashes, full of energy and intelligence.

"Now and at the hour of our death. Amen."

Marie clutched her sister's hand. Under the sunlight, the shell glittered.

The ground's been gone a long while now. No fields or valleys through my window; the ocean's blue is merging with the deepening night now dyeing the clouds. Each time, I feel like it's a sacrilege. My mother never took a plane. If she could have flown above the heavens, she would have realized that there was no heaven, no paradise other than the one that leaves you with regret. Ditto the childhood that keeps us from growing up and becomes something we miss as soon as it slips away. It's loss, it's pain that creates perfection. But before then? Did you ever tell yourself, Mama, that you were happy on Diego Garcia? That your life was beautiful? That you didn't need a thing?

Maybe.

August 1967

"Good evening, ladies and gentlemen . . ."

Gabriel's ear was glued to the transistor in anticipation. The journalist's voice wasn't as clear as he'd hoped. He'd have to make do. Some mindless music crackled over the radio, delaying the announcement. Mollinart and Geneviève were beside him.

The journalist was talking again. The verdict was nigh. Gabriel envisioned his father, Évelyne, and so many other Mauritians thousands of kilometers away also perched beside their radios with the volume turned up all the way. "General elections . . ." His heart was pounding so hard he was sure he'd heard wrong. Mollinart's eyes were bulging. "Victory . . ." What? "The Mauritian people have said *yes* to independence!" A shriek from Geneviève. "The Mauritian people have said *yes*! . . . Nearly fifty-five percent of the population voted for . . ." Gabriel stood up, sat back down, unsure how to react. The country was barreling into a new era. Mauritius, independent.

The journalist bellowed over and over the name *Ramgoolam*. An Indian man would become the first leader of the Mauritian Republic.

He imagined his sister's smirk, the father's ashen face, the Mauritian Party's blue banners hanging uselessly behind him. Independence meant the downfall of Creoles, whites, Catholics. Geneviève clung to her husband. Mollinart's eyes were moist. Colonialism had been beheaded. The business was in danger. The journalist's commentary continued, but nobody in the room was listening. August 7, 1967. The people had put their finger on the map of the world—and the world had stopped spinning for a moment. Gabriel asked Mollinart for permission to send a telegram to his sister. Every line was busy. He needed some air. He walked out and headed down to Pointe Marianne.

"*Rifrindem*? What's that?" Unable to pronounce the word, Marie burst out laughing. He wanted to explain that it was Latin, but did she even know what Latin was? He immediately scolded himself for the thought; such questions crossed his mind every so often, like weeds that stubbornly resisted uprooting.

"A referendum is a big vote where you say yes or no." Lying beside her, he stroked her bare legs up to her bulging belly. The island's independence was of no concern to her. "You know the Chagos depend on Mauritius. So there will be consequences for us, too."

He recalled Mollinart's fears a few months earlier: Would demand for copra be the same after the British left?

Marie got up on her elbow and glanced at him unhappily. "You don't have to shout at me." She stood up and grabbed her dress to put on.

"Where are you going?"

"To get Suzanne from Angèle's place."

"Sorry, sorry . . . it's just, this news is really important for me, that's all."

She shrugged. "I don't get it. Down with the masters. Always a good thing, no?"

His packet of cigarettes was gone in a matter of hours. He'd lit one after another, first with Mollinart, then by himself, at his bedroom window. Gabriel had been too wound up to stay at Marie's that night. The news had shaken him to his core—more than he'd imagined. What future awaited Mauritius? Nobody knew. On paper, independence was seductive—autonomy, freedom—but did the country know how to steer its course, how to give its children new prospects? Eventually, they'd lose their British passports. Those dreams of England were dashed. Once and for all. He relit a butt. He was in love with a Chagossian woman who was carrying a child by him, and he was still thinking about a career in London? It was like a confession to himself. Two sides warred within his head. The well-born, unhappy, twenty-year-old adolescent jeering at the lost, rebellious young man on the margins. That small bump shifting under Marie's skin obsessed him. That stuck-out navel as round as the sun. "Down with the masters." Who was to say she wasn't wrong?

The father's glasses were back on his nose. "Out of the question. I won't be paying for your studies in London. If you need to travel so much, you can go to the Chagos. I know the administrator is searching for a secretary at the moment."

End of discussion. Gabriel had begged him one last time. Benoît was good and well at Cambridge. Why couldn't he try his luck as well?

"Benoît is brilliant. Believe me, you'd do best to stop comparing yourself to your brother. You're setting yourself up for disappointment."

The disappointment was already there. Gabriel hid in his room. Fury had taken all the wind out of his sails. Évelyne tried to console him with a plate of sweet tamarinds, which he'd barely touched. He wasn't at dinner, either; he took forever to fall asleep.

The next day, he pulled on his uniform, slung his bag over his back, and went out like nothing had happened. But instead of going to school, he veered off toward Rose-Hill. He slipped into the dark alleyways of the bazaar, had a cold glass of alouda at Rachid's, inhaled the incense of the Hindus by the jewelry stalls.

Only Benoît could, only tall, handsome, smart Benoît. His mother had been no idiot. If she'd had a stronger heart, if she'd had enough strength to stave off death ten years earlier, everything in his life would be different. An urge to tear everything down rose up in him, and suddenly he knew what he needed to do.

He left the bazaar hurriedly, ran back to La Jalousie. In Beau-Bassin, everyone knew the house. A huge white wrought-iron doorway, a path lined with flame trees and Judas trees as well as mahogany fences, gray basalt steps, a verandah with pilasters. A model of the colonial style. Seething with fury, Gabriel got there in twenty minutes. His brother's armoires and bookshelves and nightstand—he'd wreck them all.

He rushed up the front steps and twisted the door handle. Locked. He rummaged in his pockets, didn't feel any keys. Forgotten in his bedroom, of course. He tried to turn the handle again, but the door was locked from inside. *I don't care,* he thought. *I'll go around the back.* All the same, it was odd. Foreboding. He slowed down, walked quietly. Through the kitchen windows, he could make out shadows moving. He froze. Vague, disagreeable sounds came through. Something was wrong. He tiptoed, brought his eye to the windowpane, his hands trembling. He could barely breathe.

The father's face was pinched, his pants around his ankles. His left hand clenched the table's edge, his right hand gripped a bare shoulder. The body trapped between his legs was shaking the tabletop rhythmically.

He held back a cry.

Breasts pressed on the table, a resigned face—the woman had tears in her eyes. Ludna.

II

I'll tell the judges where I'm from.

I'll tell them about a land that lets its children live, that doesn't starve them, that respects their memory. My stolen land.

I'll make them hear the crack in my mother's voice.

I'll tell them why my life isn't for living but only for fighting. Not a wasted life, no. A single-minded life. A dedicated one.

I've been fighting from the very beginning. It's inscribed within me.

In forty-eight hours, on Monday, September 3, 2018, at nine o'clock on the dot, the trial will begin. We'll meet on the promenade of the Peace Palace. There are eight of us in the Chagossian delegation. Men, women, children, elders, from three islands: Peros Banhos, Salomon, Diego Garcia. The luggage is heavy. It holds our clothes—dark suits, white shirts—our shoes, our folders. Provisions as well. Food, cakes, green bananas, rice. Two rice cookers. To tide us over for a few days without wasting euros we don't have.

Around me, on the plane, people are sleeping. So many French travelers. How many have heard of the Chagos?

I push up the window shade to watch the night over the ocean, imagine invisible lives, the dark spume of waves. The flight attendant gestures for me to lower it. She's depriving me of Africa's glimmers. The first city we'll fly over, if I'm to believe the on-screen flight map, is Mogadishu, Somalia. Another land of suffering, full of stout hearts. The president of the International Court of Justice, Abdulqawi Yusuf, is Somalian. I want to see some sign in that.

When the future is unclear, we're reduced to this: summoning spirits, turning a trip into an incantation.

December 1967

Peros Banhos and Salomon: the wings of angel Diego. Gabriel set down his suitcase. A one-week mission. Enough time to tour the copra plantations. Mollinart wanted to make sure all was in order on the northern islands. "Are you sure it'll be okay?" Of course everything would be okay. She still had a month left of pregnancy; she'd hold tight. Marie accompanied him to the beach, walking slowly. Suzanne walked ahead of them, bare-chested, Mérou clutched to her bosom.

His perennial Bermuda shorts cinched, Mollinart was already aboard the small boat. As the months passed, his scalp had rounded under the sun's sting. Now he looked like the scarecrow old Félix had stuck in the kitchen garden. Gabriel's hand brushed Marie's, and he kissed her cheek.

"Take care of yourself," he ordered her one last time as he heaved his suitcase. He joined Mollinart. The boat pulled away quickly, driven by Suzanne's farewells. A twinge in his heart. *Let's go. A week is nothing.*

X

The next day, then the one after, the work on the plot seemed even harder. For all her bravado, the exhaustion was bone-deep. Marie couldn't split the coconuts with a single blow or stay focused. At the end of the day, she asked Josette to take care of Suzanne and Mérou for the night. Some calm and some time to herself—that was all she wanted. Josette asked if she was sure, offered to stay with her. Marie was sure. Especially since her daughter loved spending time in Nouva with Makine. Christian had made the shack bigger and set aside a corner for the children—a refuge for games and stories.

As soon as she was home, Marie pulled on her nightshirt. She was hungry but had no energy to cook, so she settled for a few manioc biscuits before passing out in exhaustion on her straw-and-cloth-filled mattress. Night was already falling. She slept until a horrible pain cut through her belly. Unable to breathe, she lay petrified, her hand clutching the mattress. Once the contraction subsided, she groped forward to light the oil lamp she always kept at the bedside. The trade winds were rustling the palm-leaf roof. She set her hand on her stomach, tried to shore up her growing panic. A few minutes later, a new contraction wrenched her insides. She opened her mouth, trying to breathe, floored. She couldn't. Once she caught her breath again, she got up carefully to boil some water. As fast as she could. The contractions would start again, and then . . . The water had started to simmer when a new pain had her reeling. She set down the pot and collapsed into a chair, on the verge of fainting. Her stomach was being stabbed; she rested her head on the table. Suzanne . . . Josette . . . She made a Herculean effort to lift her head, then crossed her fingers. *Oh, Lord, help me!*

When the fourth contraction ripped through her torso, she could no longer hold off the panic. It was too soon—far too soon! The baby wasn't ready, it couldn't be coming now, and Gabriel was out to sea. She forced herself to pour the boiling water into a basin, pulled out some clean rags, and spread a sheet on the ground. The village of Nouva was too far off. Even Angèle was at the other end of Pointe Marianne. She didn't have anyone to count on. She summoned her courage. *No more waiting. Push the table to the side. Make some space.* Another contraction, even more violent, tore through her belly, and warm liquid ran down her thighs, soaking the bottom of her shirt. She reached for the ground, got on all fours, let the groans flow from her mouth. She listened to what nature was telling her and shifted, seeking relief. The contractions were growing regular, her body was working, the baby was making its way out of her, however it could. This was too violent, too painful, it was far too soon, and on her own she wouldn't make it. She grabbed a cloth, put it between her teeth. Bit down with all the strength she had.

How many hours it took until deliverance, she couldn't guess. The night was heavy around her, and then suddenly her skin split, the huge rip came, and she could feel her child crowning. She immediately stuck her hands between her thighs to grab it and pull the child up to her belly.

A hoarse sound rent the air. In her palms, the baby was flailing, unexpectedly big and strong. Marie started to sob, shocked, relieved. She covered its sticky skin with kisses, set it on her breast, her tears mixing with her sweat. The hoarse sound continued. That wasn't normal. The oil lamp shone a wan light through the room. She brought the child closer to the flame, and her blood froze. Around its neck was the twisted cord. The baby would suffocate. *No!* Panicked, she reached for a knife, scissors, her machete, but there was nothing. She couldn't find a thing. With a rage drawn from the depths of her core, she tore the cord uniting them with her teeth.

A sharp cry of freedom filled the room. Her son—it was a boy— cried with all his strength. Tears wrested out like a life song.

December 1967

"Have I mentioned that my wife has always hated the sea?" Mollinart pushed his white piece across the board. "The poor thing has rotten luck. Living on Diego when you don't like the sea . . . Diagonal! I've got you again." It was their third round of checkers on the boat, and Mollinart was racking up losses. Luckily the ocean waves had been kind, and they would be reaching Peros Banhos the next morning. "Geneviève is a landlubber," Mollinart continued, ready to tell all. "She grew up in Beau-Séjour. You know, the sugar estate? That was her father's land, blessed be he. A colossal fortune. Geneviève traveled so much with him. Her dream was Europe, Switzerland, the Alps. She chose a house in Moka to be right by the mountain. A nice view, of course. When I was appointed to the Chagos, she came with me, of course, but . . ." Mollinart moved a piece unthinkingly. "All that's by way of explanation for her being . . . prim. No, no, don't say a word. I know what you think of her."

Gabriel didn't know how to respond. He focused on the game, saw that he only had to move one piece to reach the final row, wavered for a second. Should he pretend to lose? He decided not to: fair's fair.

"Check," he declared.

The administrator glowered. "Again. Well, that's enough for me, if you don't mind." He pushed away the game and made his way over to the cabinet in his room. Came back to sit down at the small table with his leather briefcase. "We need to talk."

※

His finger on the accounts book, his breath heavy with booze, he groaned. "There. See? Production's down. Two percent this month. It's catastrophic. If we don't bring the curve back up, things will turn out poorly. I'm getting warnings every month. Believe me, they won't leave us alone."

"They?"

Mollinart almost shouted, "The British, of course!" He gulped down another mouthful of scotch, and Gabriel apologized, worried. Mollinart was distraught, almost embarrassed. It wasn't just because of the alcohol. "Neymorin. We absolutely need to right the ship. For everyone's well-being." Silence. "Do you understand what I'm saying?"

No, he didn't understand, not one bit. He'd studied the registers closely for months, but he hadn't seen much difference between past harvests and the current one. A small decline, maybe, but not a drastic drop. His calculations weren't anywhere near 2 percent. Not at any point. "What do you want to do?" There wasn't anything to do, in fact. The workers worked hard, and nature followed its course. The island was already covered with coconut trees. If they gave a little less fruit one year, what was there to do but accept that?

Mollinart mopped his forehead. Gabriel noticed the red blotches on his scalp—an oil slick that was spreading. "Independence. It's because of independence." He pulled another paper out of his bag, his hands trembling. "I still don't know how things will turn out for the Chagos."

Gabriel furrowed his brow. "The archipelago will become nothing more than a dependency of Mauritius, won't it? Just like Rodrigues?"

The administrator cleared his throat. "I'm not so sure about that. It's all unclear at the moment. And so long as independence hasn't been officially declared, I'm under orders from the British." The ceremony was set for March 12, 1968, in exactly three months. "They've asked me to sign this." He held out a document. "And when I say 'they,' I mean the English."

"Yes, sir, I understand."

Mollinart stood up again, worried. "They've asked for your signature as well."

Gabriel immediately recognized the royal coat of arms: the lion and the unicorn surrounding the motto *Dieu et mon droit*, the same design as on his passport—but for how much longer?

I, the undersigned, _____, will endeavor for the time being to keep strictly confidential all sensitive facts and information regarding the relationships between the United Kingdom, Mauritius, and the Chagos archipelago conveyed by my superiors, from today and for an unlimited length of time. I understand that any contravention may result in legal action and, if necessary, may be punishable by sanctions under British law.

Signed at Diego Garcia, Chagos, on December __ 1967.

"What's the meaning of this?" Gabriel asked as he set down the letter.

Mollinart's lower lip was trembling. "I don't know, my boy. Security measures, I think."

Gabriel was silent. On the cream paper's letterhead, the small typed letters seemed vaguely threatening. What "sensitive facts" could the

British be talking about? He reread "result in legal action" and pushed away the pen Mollinart was offering him. This litigious tone didn't sit well with him.

"I don't think I'll be signing this."

The administrator's tone was disconcerting. "I'm not sure you have a choice in the matter."

$$\text{\Doublecross}$$

Peros Banhos was identical in every way to Diego Garcia: a string of milky-white sandy islands in water so clear that the tortoises deep down were visible. The warm air tempered by the trade winds encouraged relaxation. A shame. Apart from the evenings, which they spent on the main villa's verandah, Mollinart and Gabriel barely relaxed. After visiting the different areas of the atoll to evaluate the coconut harvest levels, they'd spoken with the Îlois, checked the local account books, calculated a few statistics. On the last day, they made their way anew down the dirt path at the end of which was the copra mill. Huge red-and-black crabs, the same ones as on Diego Garcia, made the coconut tree trunks squeak under their pincers. Barely dressed men were husking the coconuts with stakes driven into the ground. The women removed the pulp while singing, like Marie and the others on the plantation. Gabriel was eager to head back. The feeling he had of time slipping away on these islands where all had been well was growing increasingly unbearable.

"Look how those poor creatures are struggling." Mollinart pointed out two sickly asses meant to power the mill's grinding that stopped every so often to nibble at the dust. A man cracked his whip over the stubborner one. From the stone, an aromatic liquid trickled down into the receptacle.

The commander of Peros Banhos, a fellow named Rosemond, whose callused hands and white hair betrayed a laborer's life on the plantation, shook his head wearily. "We don't have enough livestock, I'll tell you that." It was true that a few extra beasts of burden wouldn't go amiss.

"Why not send a message to the Port-Louis harbormaster's office?" Gabriel asked. "For the next delivery."

Mollinart let out a mirthless chuckle. "I'm afraid the government isn't as generous as it once was."

"But why the government? Can't you talk directly to the farmers? The *Sir Jules* will be back again early next year, won't it?"

The administrator paid him no heed and continued talking to Rosemond, as if he were snubbing a bothersome child.

There was nothing left to attend to on the northern islands. The morning of their departure, Gabriel scooped some Peros Banhos sand into a vial. A memento like any other. Impatience had kept him from sleeping: he'd be beside Marie that very night. Being separated from her for the first time, he felt like his whole body was imprisoned by that absence; he understood how it could drive a man mad. The last few hours felt interminable. Above all, he wanted to share in the emotions of childbirth, to find out whether it was a boy or a girl, to imprint his odor on the baby's skin. The pregnancy terrified him; the very idea of flabby, torn skin made him nauseous, but holding the newborn in his arms, being the first to see it, to name it, that was a wonderful thing.

"Gabriel?" Mollinart's voice brought him back to reality. "Can you come here for a second, please?"

At the back of the villa was the office—a room not unlike the one at Pointe de l'Est, although slightly more cramped. On the table, he immediately recognized the document with the royal header.

Mollinart held out a pen. "Kindly sign, my boy. Don't give me any trouble, please."

Gabriel struggled with his irritation. "I don't want to sign a document I don't understand. What's going on here, for goodness' sake?"

On the administrator's scalp, the red blotches reappeared. "A security measure, as I've said. You're in a strategic role, like it or not, and the British government wants to be assured that you'll hold your tongue. That's all."

Flattered by the phrase "strategic role" despite himself, Gabriel had to remember to hold firm. "What sensitive facts are they talking about? What am I supposed to learn and keep to myself?"

Mollinart sputtered, "I don't know . . . Not much . . . The only thing I've been led to understand is that the Chagos, like I was saying . . . will remain in British hands."

"But how is that possible?"

The administrator held his hands out. Something wasn't adding up, but Gabriel couldn't understand what. How could the archipelago, which was entirely dependent on Mauritius, benefit from being treated differently from the mother island? How could the British disregard the referendum's results? All sorts of questions came to mind, but none of the answers seemed to cohere. He needed more details, more pieces for the puzzle to come together.

"Well, go ahead and sign now." Mollinart was practically pleading.

"I can't, sir. The situation is unclear, and I don't like that."

The administrator leaned back in his chair and said, in a very weak voice, "In that case, I'll have to return to Diego Garcia alone."

The words sank in. Return to Diego Garcia alone?

Mollinart looked down. "In accepting this job as secretary, you signed a contract to work in the Chagos. Not specifically on Diego Garcia. I have the right to appoint you for six months to Peros Banhos or Salomon."

A crushing blow. Gabriel was reeling. Six months on Peros Banhos or Salomon? Good god! What was the point of that?

Mollinart fanned himself, his jaw clenched. "Sign, Neymorin. Don't force me to do something both of us will regret."

A bitter taste filled Gabriel's mouth. Some enormity was underway and already hanging over him. An ultimatum.

As if he owed him this confession, Mollinart added hurriedly, "If I don't give them all these guarantees, they'll close my plantation."

There was no question who "they" was here. A wave of fury overcame Gabriel. The plantation, the business, the crates. His little empire!

"I've invested my life in copra," Mollinart added. "I don't want to lose everything at my age. It's just a piece of paper, Gabriel. Take it. Read it again if you have to."

The urge to rip it up was so strong that he had to tell himself not to touch it. *I, the undersigned, . . . , will endeavor . . .* He let out a long breath, tried to collect himself. Examine the words one by one. Was this agreement such a high price to pay? So he couldn't reveal "sensitive facts." So what? As if any such facts would be shared with him. The administrations tended to protect themselves from everything; paranoia was a sickness that spread through the halls of power. But something held him back.

"Think about Marie-Pierre. About your child."

His child.

With disgust, he picked up the pen and signed.

December 1967

A few warm drops ran down her brother's scalp; Suzanne fearfully jerked her hand back when her fingers touched the fragile skull. Marie picked up the soaked dish towel, dabbed the newborn's back and front, and, after swaddling him in a clean cloth, held him against her breast. The morning sun bathed his dark skin. The baby immediately started suckling.

Joséphin. The name had immediately come to her when he'd opened his round eyes. Joséphin. She liked the clear syllables, the first one accented, the last one trailing off. There was no waiting for Gabriel. The baby was there; not giving him a name would have been bad luck. Warm in her arms, he'd dozed off, his face peaceful. On his neck, a blue streak still marked the cord's imprint.

Marie also slept deeply. Hours later, it was Josette who'd found her amid the blood-soaked sheets. "Mamita!" Josette had pulled Suzanne away, and, at that moment, the baby had woken up. In the middle of all the hugging and kissing, Mérou had started chasing after his own tail.

"And you!" Josette exclaimed, delighted to see Joséphin suckling greedily. "It's like he's eating a big papaya!" She tossed the beans one last time in the pan, turned off the fire, added some salt and pepper to the mixture, and drained the rice before setting a plate before Marie. "Just eat a bit." Josette stroked Joséphin's tender head. "Alala . . . A nice *zilois*, this one . . . Good and dark, good and strong!" And again Marie contemplated her baby: his big forehead, his flattened nostrils, his round eyes—all Chagossian features. She had to concede that the dreams she'd had as a pregnant woman had given him lighter skin, a thin face, almond-shaped eyes. Joséphin let go of her breast, sated.

"Gabriel's coming back soon?" Josette asked.

"Yes. Tonight, I hope."

Josette hefted the baby with a smile. "It's M'sieur Gabriel who makes you big and fat. He'll be proud of this boy, yes."

Marie didn't respond.

In the afternoon, there would be a procession again. For a week now, Félix, Tico, their neighbor Gisèle, Becca, and a few others had come to give her presents and well-wishes. Fresh vegetables, sugar, wine, woven baskets, fish, baby clothes, and even medicine. Like usual, Henri and Jean-Joris held back. Angèle sobbed happily when Marie asked her to be the boy's godmother. She held him close to her paunch and smothered him in kisses. Promised him clothes in nice patterns. Once she'd handed him back, they'd danced the séga. They were celebrating. "Do you need anything else?" No, she didn't need anything else, thank you.

When it was calm again, Marie tucked the baby into the cradle Christian had built. His mouth was wide open as he squinted, forehead creased. Suzanne wanted to hug him. "Later," Marie said. Her daughter looked disappointed. "Go to sleep, Suzanne. I'm tired." It was something bigger than her; she felt torn. Something she couldn't shake. With his thick skin and his rotund eyes, his dark skin gleaming under the oil lamp's light, she had to concede that her son wasn't the one she'd dreamed of.

Three knocks. She started, pulled out of a deep sleep, and stood right up. It was him, at last. Night had long since cloaked the village, and she had to light the lamp, setting it as low as she could so she didn't wake the children. She glanced at the cradle: his arms bent around his head, Joséphin was breathing heavily. Marie opened the door and leaped into Gabriel's arms.

"Ti Baba is here!"

"What? Already?" He kissed her quickly and raced to the cradle. Not a sound. On the wall, the shadows silhouetted his birdlike face shaken by tears. She had never believed that a man could take to a child. That was the domain of women, generally: a baby's smell, a breast's sweetness, a matter of skin and guts. But looking at Gabriel, so moved, one could have thought that he was the mother. He slipped his hands under Joséphin's body and brought him to his lips like a treasure. Their baby woke up and cried a little, pulling Suzanne out of her sleep as well.

All three of them gathered around the cradle. Their breath mingled in the night festooned with insects.

"Little Joséphin." Gabriel was trembling. Marie brought a finger to her lips. *Quiet, the children are asleep again.* He smiled. Fatherhood had changed the man, the lover, the traveler. His eyes shone with a new gleam. It was too much. Yes, it was almost too much. The happiness she'd anticipated at the prospect of seeing her lover again, their joy, their kisses, wasn't as pure as it ought to be. Didn't Gabriel see that huge forehead, those eyes like marbles, that immense head? The thought nagged at her again: Joséphin wasn't handsome. She knew that at one week old the physiognomy was indefinite, but the features, the deepest facial features, were there, carved by nature. In her mouth was a leathery taste. Sticky. The umbilical cord. She pushed aside the sheets, suddenly nauseous.

"Marie?" Gabriel's arm reached around her waist. "Do you want some water? Aspirin?"

She stood up, wiped her mouth. Pushed him away. Her stomach hurt, the skin of her thighs, her crotch, her rear, her breasts—it all hurt. Disgust rose up again, searing her windpipe.

She rushed out of the shack, leaned against its outer wall. The stars brightening the night like a stream of milk. "A nice zilois . . . Good and dark, good and strong . . ." Josette's words echoed in her ear. A need to cry wrenched her gut.

Gabriel sat down beside her, happy, on cloud nine, and hugged her tight. "That's for you," he said, giving her a small vial.

Of sand. That was her present.

"It's from Peros Banhos."

She thanked him grudgingly. Then, abruptly, she uncorked the vial and turned it over. The sand poured forth in an almost human breath, an exhalation, forming a small dune on her feet.

Everything that has a name exists. Men, plants, countries, legends. A name is always the seed of a fate.

I remember that woman in Réunion. An anthropologist. I was delivering a lecture at the university there, in Saint-Denis, recounting our tragedy and raising awareness. She'd been working on our past, our Malagasy ancestors, our culture. She approached me afterward. "Do you know where the word Chagos comes from?" I looked at her ashamedly. No, I didn't know. She told me.

Pedro de Mascarenhas, the navigator, was sailing to the Indies. The discovery of new lands eventually called the Mascarene Islands. I knew the Portuguese had left their traces in the Indian Ocean, yes. Just singing the names of our islands—Diego Garcia, Peros Banhos—made that clear. But I didn't know about the rest. One of the main Portuguese ships was called the *Cinco Chagas*. "*Cinco Chagas* means the Five Wounds, a reference to the Five Holy Wounds of Christ." Hands and feet nailed, the right side pierced by the lance. The Chagos, therefore, bear the name of a ship and of suffering.

After the Passion, Christ was risen. He rose up to heaven in glory and peace. A land being reborn—is that not like God?

January 1968

Slowly, Gabriel set Joséphin on the flour scale. "Five kilos!"

Old Félix let out a long whistle. "That's a big one, that."

In a month, Joséphin had grown considerably. He slept deeply in between each feeding, was almost smiling already, seemed affable and peaceable. Apart from his son, nothing mattered for Gabriel. Even Marie came in second place. "Don't you parade around," Mollinart had ordered him. He'd paraded around. He paraded around with Joséphin at church, at the mill, at the beach, at Nouva, at Pointe Marianne, in the villa, on the pier—everywhere. Mollinart's rebuke was swift: he wouldn't attest to Gabriel's paternity: no declaration, no paper, no nothing. Just another bastard child.

"Doesn't matter," Marie had reassured him. "Here, nobody has papers for their children, you know."

Here wasn't Mauritius. Later, maybe. Later, they'd see. Gabriel wasn't afraid anymore. Happiness had crowded out all thought. Never had he imagined that he could experience this sort of love. Fatherhood had brought him a new sense of completeness; he finally felt useful, responsible. For years he'd chased ghosts. His dead mother. The dream of being loved. Making his family proud. Now, a five-kilo baby made him invincible. Maybe that was a father: a man who had found his place. If only his own had understood that. The harshness he had shown Gabriel and then Évelyne, when she was a teenager, left a permanent void in them. No tenderness, not a single kind word. Only Benoît had evaded his severity. Joséphin would be luckier: he'd be loved, doted upon, raised properly, supported.

"Five kilos already." Marie barely smiled. Her coldness was striking. "A bit big, yes?"

"Better that than too small. Remember, he was born early."

She looked away. Gabriel, irritated, held Joséphin close. Eleven o'clock. He had some time before the next feeding. "I'll meet you at the shack," he said, acting annoyed. In fact, the prospect of having his son to himself for a minute enchanted him. He headed for the garage.

Upon returning from Peros Banhos, he'd tried to send his sister a telegram to announce the baby's birth. To no avail. The connection didn't work. He was dying to hear her voice, to share his happiness with her. Her nephew, her first nephew!

After two rings, a woman's voice reverberated in the handset.

"Évelyne?" He knew the second he asked that it wasn't her. "Hello? I'd like to speak to Évelyne Neymorin, please." The line crackled, and he waited, Joséphin in his lap.

"Gaby?" A clear voice came through.

"Lizard! Hello, Lizard, happy new year!" There was no laugh or well-wishing on the other end of the line. "Évelyne? Can you hear me?" He was sure the connection had cut out, but then her words reached him.

"It's Father. We've just brought him back from the hospital. He had a stroke two days ago." A pause. "He's completely paralyzed on the left side."

Gabriel stood up, making Joséphin start. He would have been less stunned to hear that the man was dead.

"It's hell here," she continued. "Ludna quit on us a few months ago, and her replacement didn't last two weeks. I found a live-in nurse who seems serious, but honestly, I'm not sure about that. Gaby, you need to come back."

He absorbed the news. Joséphin was fidgeting and starting to cry. He patted his back mechanically. "What about Benoît? Can't he come back?" The line was hissing unpleasantly.

". . . already asked. But he's not at Cambridge anymore, apparently. He's finished his studies. I called the secretary yesterday. They don't know what's become of him. They have too many students. Apart from Savita, I'm alone."

"What does Savita say?"

"That you need to come back."

Gabriel felt the air go out of his lungs. His fifteen-year-old sister was being ground down. He offered up another idea. "What if you put him in hospice?" Ludna's breasts pressed against the kitchen table darkened his thoughts again. Hospice would be too good for the man.

"What would I do, then? Live alone at home and be placed with another family because I'm a minor? Not if I can help it. I'm going to get my Higher School Certificate this year, Gaby. You need to come back!"

The thousands of kilometers separating them collapsed amid tears and shrill sobs. He held out the receiver, which set Joséphin, who couldn't stand the sharp sounds, either, crying.

"Lizard . . . ," he stammered. "Do you hear that?" He brought the receiver to the baby's mouth. "That's my son. Joséphin." Silence. "Évelyne?" He waited, on tenterhooks. "I said I was going to become a father . . . Do you remember?" The hissing grew louder over the phone.

"So that actually was what you said." Her voice sounded astonished. "Bring him home with you. You can all come to Mauritius; just don't leave me here by myself. I'm counting on you, Gaby."

There was a small click, and then the line was dead.

※

His fist was hovering at Mollinart's door, his baby perched on his hip. Gabriel took a big breath. Évelyne's idea hadn't been absurd. As he'd mulled it over, he'd come to find it a valid one. In Mauritius they'd have every modern convenience. Joséphin could go to a good school; Marie wouldn't have to work; she could keep house, finally relax. Marriage would be possible. Now that his father was paralyzed, he wouldn't be able to bother them. Of course they'd have to deal with neighbors' disapproving glances, and some aunts and uncles would shut their doors on them, but what did it matter? They'd make do. Leaving Évelyne alone in that situation was simply untenable.

He rapped at the door and was called in. Facing him, the administrator was smoking as he scribbled notes. He looked up, not disguising his surprise at seeing Gabriel with the baby. Ever since returning from Peros Banhos, they'd avoided any sort of personal conversation.

"I'd like to know when the next boat for Mauritius is arriving," Gabriel said.

"For Mauritius?"

"So I can go back. I'm seriously thinking about leaving Diego Garcia."

Mollinart blanched. "What about him?"

"He's coming with me. What do you think?"

"And Marie-Pierre Ladouceur?"

"Likewise."

The man mopped his face, looking genuinely regretful. "That's impossible."

"What do you mean, 'impossible'?"

"They can't leave. Well, they can leave, but they can't come back."

Gabriel felt like he was banging his head on a wall. None of this made any sense. "I'm only asking you when the next boat for Mauritius is arriving," he repeated, gritting his teeth. Évelyne was right. He needed to go back, stop thinking about copra and the administrator's threats.

"You want to know, Neymorin? You really want to know?"

"I want to know what you're hiding from me, yes! Your plan, whatever scheme you're concocting."

Mollinart was wild-eyed. The red blotches reappeared on his scalp. Then, with a fury Gabriel had never seen before, he unlocked a drawer and pulled out a file that he set on the desk. "Read, and you can see for yourself."

At the top of the envelope was a stamp that read *Classified Documents. TS.* Gabriel recalled all the novels he'd read as a teenager.

TS for *Top Secret.*

He set Joséphin on the rug and read in silence.

March 1968

"See. The change of the flags."

Gabriel's hands were trembling. Marie pretended to be interested in the photo but couldn't understand why the image had him in such a state. A man dressed in white, with light hair that showed under his helmet, was lowering a flag. Facing him, a Creole man in a dark uniform was raising a new one with horizontal stripes.

"You can't see it on the fax, but there are four colors: red, blue, yellow, green. Know why?"

She didn't know why.

"Hindus, Catholics, Chinese, and Muslims—the four communities of Mauritius."

"What about us? Where are the Chagos?"

He didn't respond but picked up the other page and pointed to the text. Her reading was still slow and shaky. She kept mixing up letters, tripping over certain sounds. Gabriel helped her, deciphering the syllables with her. With enough patience, the text finally took shape.

Glory to thee, Motherland!
Sweet is thy beauty,
Sweet is thy fragrance,
Around thee we gather
As one people,
As one nation,
In peace, justice, and liberty . . .

She looked up, proud of her progress. "Nice, that." She especially liked the beginning: "Sweet is thy beauty, / Sweet is thy fragrance." It was like a lover talking to his fiancée.

Gabriel kept quiet as he looked straight ahead, even though there was nothing there. For some time now, Marie had noticed that he'd changed. He was colder and more distant with her. He spent long hours cooped up with Mollinart in the office and only came out to sleep. He didn't stay with her very often anymore, even though he did visit the baby every day.

At three months old, Joséphin was the size of a six-month-old. He was a good baby, calm and sweet, and as she rocked him, her eyes shut. As she brought her nose to his skin, a violent love surged within her, but as soon as she opened her eyes, the spell was broken. His huge eyes, his massive forehead, his chubby legs were a source of grief. One day as Gabriel was rocking him, she'd heard him whisper, "Sleep well, little Jo'," and she'd snapped. "Who's this Jo'? His name is Joséphin! Not Jo'. Never Jo'!"

He'd glanced at her as if she were insane. "What's wrong?"

Unable to explain, she feigned a headache and went to bed.

One Sunday morning, she summoned the courage to go talk to Josette. Swaddled in a big cloth, Joséphin was dozing on her back, unaware of his mother's hurried pace. The women settled on the Nouva beach. The sea glittered before them. The sky seemed infinite.

Marie placed her son on a large sheet, then turned to her sister. "I can't take it anymore. With Joséphin . . . I can't take it."

Josette took him into her arms. "You don't love him, is it that?"

Marie stiffened, stung. No. It wasn't that. Things were less clear than that. She loved him, but she didn't recognize him. He didn't look like the child she'd wanted and dreamed of.

"Marie, are you sure Gabriel is the father?"

Her heart could have shattered into a thousand pieces. That was it. That was what had been weighing on her for months. No, she wasn't sure. As she wasn't sure who Suzanne's father was. It was the same curse. "At your wedding . . . ," she stammered. "Gabriel didn't dance with me . . ."

Jean-Jo hadn't been nearly as difficult. With booze on his breath, with the séga pumping through his veins. Gabriel had turned away. She'd felt ugly. Useless. But still pretty enough for Jean-Joris. The dates matched up. March 1967. December 1967. And a little Îlois who was *good and dark, good and strong.*

"You think Gabriel knows?" Josette asked.

Who knew? Maybe. He had to sense something, because he didn't love the boy the way he had before. At that thought, she began to sob. Her sister stroked her hair.

"I thought he was the father, Josette." It was all she'd dreamed of.

The light turned the lagoon into a mirror. Perched beside a basket, Joséphin looked at it listlessly.

"What do I do?"

Her sister bit her lips, staring off into the horizon. "You don't say a thing. To anybody. Not to him. A cat gets burned, it's always scared of ashes."

Men only see what they want to see, she thought. So Gabriel wanted Joséphin to be his son? Well, Joséphin was his son. And would remain so as long as she didn't betray herself.

"What about Jean-Jo?"

Josette's hand came up and immediately fell back down. "Sew that mouth shut, Marie."

She wiped away her bitter tears. "I have to lie to him?"

Josette thought for a second, as if to find the right words, a proverb, that would soften her response.

"Exactly," she finally said resignedly.

March 1968

Classified documents. TS.

Gabriel pulled several documents out of the pouch. The first one was a secret governmental note. Prepared for the British prime minister, Harold Wilson, dated September 22, 1965. It announced that Sir Seewoosagur Ramgoolam would be coming to see him at ten the next morning. The goal was to frighten him with the hope that he might gain independence and frighten him that he might not unless he was reasonable about the detachment of the Chagos archipelago.

The future leader of Mauritius was to come away from his meeting with Harold Wilson with one thing clear in his mind: that Mauritius's independence was conditional upon the "detachment" of the Chagos archipelago.

Then came a document dated November 8, 1965, formally establishing the BIOT—the British Indian Ocean Territory—which united the Chagos and several other island dependencies of the Seychelles: Aldabra, Farquhar, and Desroches. The Chagos, it was underscored, would benefit from special treatment. The archipelago would remain in British hands whatever the outcome of the independence referendum.

Another document, signed December 30, 1966, revealed a secret agreement between the United Kingdom and the United States. Diego Garcia would be made available to the Americans for an initial period of fifty years, with a potential extension of twenty years. A naval base installation was under consideration.

The final document established a provisional schedule for evacuating the island. The Americans were supposed to present at the United Nations a file assembled by the British promising that it was territory free of indigenous inhabitants in order to obtain approval to erect the military base. There were three stages to the British plan. First, people who wished to leave voluntarily would be encouraged, without any mention that return to the island would be forbidden. Then people would be pushed to leave when the deliveries of goods and provisions stopped. And finally, for any who still resisted leaving, force would be used.

Mollinart's voice was low. "I'm sorry, Neymorin." He sank into his chair. "Don't forget: you signed."

As he walked out of the office, Gabriel was reeling. Despite his repeated requests, Mollinart had refused to tell him who had sent him the folder, but there was no denying that an impending, horrific, unfair catastrophe loomed. He held Joséphin close. The whole way to Pointe Marianne, he went back over the details, letting them explode in his head like bubbles of poison. The Chagos didn't belong to Mauritius anymore. The British and the Americans had orchestrated everything in secret, and Ramgoolam had acquiesced—his position as prime minister of the new Mauritian Republic had come at that cost. They would evacuate the archipelago. Gabriel kissed Joséphin's head. If Marie went with him to Mauritius, they would be barred from returning to Diego Garcia. She wouldn't understand, would insist on going back, on raising

Joséphin on the land of her ancestors. She would never forgive him for this betrayal. She'd leave him. If he confessed the truth to her, the repercussions would be immediate: Josette, Christian, Angèle, Gisèle . . . In an hour, the whole island would know. Which would result in that "legal action" in British courts, and nothing would be gained as a result. The truth wouldn't save them; the Anglo-American countdown had already begun, the plan already underway. How could a handful of Chagossians resist? They'd be crushed in a matter of minutes. Should he return to Mauritius alone, then? And be separated from the woman he loved and his son, his dear son? Impossible. So, he had to stay quiet, stay here, and leave Évelyne to her sordid fate, even as disaster loomed.

"What's wrong?" Marie asked when he entered the shack.

He held out Joséphin, who was bellowing with hunger, and collapsed onto the bed.

"What is it?"

Only then did he realize that he was crying. She held the baby to her breast, her eyes still riveted on him in worry.

He exhaled, uttered the first explanation that came to mind. "It's my father. He's had a stroke."

I'd rather not have ever been born. Not have had to endure that. Fifty years of fighting, appeals, solicitations, meetings with lawyers, trials, waiting. "Have some pity for the Chagos!" all the papers say these days. What pity? You can keep it all; I don't want any. Justice, dignity, liberty for these people—what we're asking of our adversaries, the inventors of those values, is to uphold those principles themselves.

I accuse the British government of profiting at our expense and sacrificing us at the altar of the Cold War.

I accuse Prime Minister Harold Wilson of striking us from the map of our own land.

I accuse the Mauritian leaders of that time of betraying independence.

I accuse the colonial elites of leaving us in ignorance—no schools, no books, no revolt.

I accuse the American army of turning our island into a fortress of steel.

I accuse the silence that's cloaked our tragedy for too long.

It's time to drop all pretense.

In the name of my people, living, dead, exiled, uprooted, amputated, old, and young, I call for the end of British colonialism in Africa.

My mouth shall be the mouth of those calamities that have no mouth . . .

March 1970

Once the rice was cold, sugar had to be added, the paste had to be mixed, and then it would rest a few minutes. With Suzanne and Joséphin nearby, Marie took a bit of the mixture in her palm and formed it into a ball. When the sphere was nice and round, she pressed her thumb into it and slipped in the bit of coconut-fried banana, then sealed it and rolled it some more. Suzanne had already gotten to help make rice cakes, but it was Joséphin's first time.

Suzanne protested. "Mamita, he'll be trouble. He doesn't get it!"

Marie stared at her. Her brother was still little; he had to learn, that was all. She swatted the flies from the pot of fish and covered it. For Josette and Christian's going-away gathering, she'd cooked the fruits of her fishing. As if she could have done otherwise. For a year now no ships had stopped at Diego Garcia, and no further provisions had come. No wine. No fresh vegetables, just kidney beans and a few herbs. No meat. She didn't dare to slaughter the chickens in her courtyard: the eggs were so nutritious, and their shells helped plants to grow. Food was scarce. Marie tore a rice cake in two, gave half to Suzanne. The girl made a face.

"What? It's bad?" Marie tasted it. Not enough sugar.

Why didn't the *Sir Jules* come anymore? Or the *Mauritius*, or any other ship? There was no news of Father Larronde, either. She'd never seen the likes of it. Nobody had. They'd stretched their reserves for several months, but now there was precious little left. At this rate there wouldn't be any more rice soon. Or flour.

And Josette was leaving in two days.

Around five in the afternoon, Marie gathered some trochetia flowers and put them in a bucket full of water. A bouquet for her sister, a farewell gift. She placed the pot of fish in a huge basket, set the rice cakes on top, made sure that all the mats were there.

"Salam, salam!" The Tasdebois family came in, accompanied by Angèle. Marie kissed them. Gabriel had said that he'd meet them on the beach a bit later, because he had a report to finish for the administrator. For months now, Mollinart had stolen her man away; night after night was spent working, and Gabriel always came back to the shack looking even more glum, complaining about how tired he was, always so tired. He fell asleep quickly, only to experience nightmares that left him worn out when he woke up. They barely had sex anymore. Only Joséphin still seemed to bring him joy. At two and a half years old, he was clumsy and still chubby. When she saw Gabriel throw his head back laughing, holding the little one close, she shuddered. Her secret was still secret.

"Any news?" she asked Josette, acting happy.

Her sister kissed her cheeks and set a small bowl of black beans on the table. She hadn't found anything better.

"Makine, I made you a surprise!"

Suzanne rushed over to her cousin in excitement and showed her a nice, twisted shell through which she'd run a bit of kitchen twine. Makine immediately put the makeshift necklace around her neck, delighted.

"*Ayo,* my little girlie. My stomach's yelling, it's so hungry!" Angèle declared. She, too, was trying to act delighted.

Christian grabbed the basket. On the beach, maybe the sorrow wouldn't weigh so heavily on them. Mérou darted ahead, making sure every so often that the whole group was following.

"Sugar, flour, rice, vegetable seeds, fruit seeds, chickens, meat, tea, coffee, medicines, cloth, barrettes"—Marie gave her daughter a stern look: *Barrettes? Really?*—"wine, rum, cotton, dishes, sheets, wood, tools."

Josette and Christian nodded.

"Nothing else?"

It was already plenty, but this "plenty" barely covered the essentials. Everything depended on how much things cost, on how accommodating the captain would be. Marie rolled the lead of her pencil on the paper. *A sentence starts with a capital letter and ends with a period.* She remembered Gabriel's rule and was doing her best to follow it. She gave the paper to her sister. "There. If you can't remember everything, give them that."

Down there. In Mauritius.

When they'd realized that Diego Garcia would be cut off from all food supplies, panic had run through the island.

"What's happening, Gabriel?"

"They don't want to buy our copra anymore." He looked down disappointedly.

Marie wasn't sure she understood completely. What did that have to do with the boats not coming?

"Your goods," he said. "How do you pay for them?"

Pay. Of course they had to pay. She was so accustomed to living without money here that she had no idea that the rest of the world followed other laws. On Diego, she could trade a fish for two bunches of bananas. A hand-sewn dress for a bucketful of wine. A fish fillet for a table. But the boats' owners expected something different. The money from copra allowed the Îlois to buy provisions.

"That's what they call *transactions*," Gabriel concluded.

In the meantime, the island was idle. Marie wanted to believe, all the same. A boat would come at last. They couldn't be left in such a state; it was impossible. And indeed, two days earlier, at the north end of the pass, Christian had made out the shadow of a ship. At last! He'd taken his dugout canoe to see it up close: the *Trochétia*—that was its name—had dropped anchor. At last!

Mollinart threw cold water on their hopes. "The *Trochétia* is empty. It's got nothing. I'm sorry. It's coming back from the Seychelles, that's all."

The blow had been painful. Too painful.

"Now that I think of it, my dears . . . The boat is going to Mauritius, after all. If you want, maybe it'll take you." He said that with a smile, as if to encourage them.

That was an idea. They could go to Mauritius to buy what they needed to restock Diego. Christian and Josette had looked at each other in agreement.

"How many moons before we see each other again?" Marie asked while finishing her fish *seraz*.

Josette stretched out her legs on the mat. "The market, the travel, the other boat back . . . A month?"

Christian nodded. Maybe even two months.

"It's good you're not going alone," Angèle said as she took another helping.

Indeed, twenty of them would go; Mollinart's suggestion had won over several families.

Makine fiddled with her necklace, looked imploringly at her cousin. "You should come, Suzanne."

Marie sighed. The trip tempted her as well, but when she'd suggested it to Gabriel, he'd yelled and shouted at her. *Are you crazy? With Joséphin? He's not even three years old. What if the sea is rough? What if he gets sick on the ship? What would you do? No, Marie, absolutely not.*

"Look!"

In the looming night, a small red dot appeared, then a green dot, and the two blinked in turn. Boat lights always seemed unreal. Even the children went quiet. In two days, loneliness would replace races in the sand. Marie herself had never been separated from her sister. Josette had seen her come out of their mother's belly, and not a day had gone by without their talking. Gabriel was right, all the same. What if there was a storm? What if the ocean got choppy? What if they became separated on Mauritius?

Marie suddenly felt unhappy. All the more so because, despite his promises, Gabriel wouldn't be joining their gathering. Angèle's jaws working over the rice cakes was the only sound that broke the silence.

November 1970

A huge airplane runway. Military planes with gray-green jaws, flying sharks, their sides emblazoned **US AIR FORCE**, as orderly as cigars in a box. Barbed wire strung all along the runway to mark the boundary between two realms. A mere glance up reveals an aircraft taking flight in the morning light, scattering the birds. Some will go and drop bombs, maybe, over Iraq, Afghanistan, Vietnam—who knows. That's all the modern world is: a group of splintered territories dominated by a ruthless cold war of nerves fought one millimeter at a time by missiles launched from secret bases; a web of alliances and intimidation, all of it exponentially insane. The powerful don't simply maintain their power but seek to wholly neutralize opposing forces; it's a world where mass media has elevated power above everything else—democracy, freedom, community, peace, justice, and much more. The twentieth century has taken the side of deceit, terror, and hatred.

Smoking from his bedroom window, Gabriel could easily imagine what would become of Diego Garcia. All military bases look the same. Some are simply more strategic than others. The construction plans had been finalized, Mollinart had told him. The island's topography, ecosystem, terrain, limitations, everything had been gone over with a fine-tooth comb. A source close to the London people had confirmed everything. The moment there were no more Îlois, no more animals, no more of anything but a few cooperative Mauritian people, the work would begin.

Gabriel took in the blindingly white strip of sand, imagining the striking blackness of asphalt.

X

"What a shame."

Sitting at the table in his small shack behind the villa, his head tilted back, Félix was unmoving. Dead. There was still a warm plate of rice in front of him. Mollinart clapped his hand to his chest twice to steel himself and then closed the eyes of the old commander.

Mérou barked for a while when Gabriel arrived. Despite Suzanne's endless pleas, Marie had decided to keep the dog in the yard. Ever since Josette had left, she couldn't bear having the creature inside.

"Félix is dead."

She dropped the bowl of coconut bananas she'd been making. The mixture slopped onto the ground, a lumpy mass. "Félix? Our old Félix . . . ," she whispered.

He kissed her forehead. "There'll be a vigil tonight."

She nodded, misty-eyed. He sat her down on the bed. Her wrists were so thin now that she could easily wear children's bracelets. As she'd lost weight, the dimples in her cheeks had deepened into two holes, like thumbprints in a lump of clay.

"Josette never got to say goodbye to Félix," she sobbed.

He kissed her, heartbroken.

"Nine months. Nine months now they've been gone! Where is she? Where?"

When Marie knocked at Mollinart's door that day, as they were checking the latest registers from Peros Banhos and Salomon, his blood had run cold.

"My sister still isn't back. Something's wrong! They ought to have been back in the shack weeks ago."

The administrator tried to reassure her: the Tasdebois family was well and happy in Mauritius; they didn't have enough money to return; maybe the weather was too dangerous for sailing. But it didn't make a difference. She pressed him.

Gabriel's eyes met the administrator's, and he stood up. "She's right. Something serious must have happened." His voice was lifeless, his breath halting. "I'm just as worried as you are, Marie-Pierre, but I have no idea."

"What about the others? Twenty of them went. Nobody's back!"

The world was starting to fall apart. Soon there would be only regret, shattered and guilty memories. The blotches once again appeared on Mollinart's scalp; they weren't so red this time, more pale pink, as if his body had finally decided to stop it with the lying.

"Let me have a chat with the Mauritian harbormaster's office," he finally said. "I'll let you know."

Marie left, buoyed with hope. Once she was gone, Mollinart turned to Gabriel.

"Help me."

"Help you what?"

"To think up a believable story."

Out of the question. Gabriel hadn't slept well in two years. He was chewing his nails until they bled; he wouldn't do this.

"Neymorin, do you want me to tell her that she'll never see her sister again?"

The next day, that was exactly what the administrator did. He went to find her on the plot and pulled her aside.

"My contacts at the Port-Louis office gave me terrible news," he said in a hushed voice. "A small boat wrecked on the coast near Souillac in the south of Mauritius. The sea is always dangerous right around there. A fisherman said he saw a group of men and women, all of them Black, being swallowed up by waves. The description matches up . . . I'm sorry, I'm so sorry."

Gabriel heard a shriek. He ran at full speed over from the villa. Marie was on her knees, sobbing.

The shack, with its solid walls akin to the one at Pointe de l'Est, was dimly lit. A table pushed to the back, two chairs, a small desk, and, set in the middle for tonight, the bed on which Félix's remains rested. The women lit candles, and the shadows danced across the old man's emaciated, already waxy face. Gabriel noticed the wrinkles of his skin, his thin fingers interlocked over his stomach. Peaceful. His skull, without the helmet's protection, betrayed incredible fragility. The old commander was wearing his white uniform, just as he'd wished. Gabriel set a hand on the body and immediately yanked it away, as if burned. The puckish, energetic man was no more. *Where does joyfulness go when the heart stops?*

The men drank in silence; the women fanned the body to shoo away flies. Suddenly, Angèle got up and launched into a melody he'd never heard before, a deep, melancholy one. Gisèle, Becca, Tico, Henri, and Jean-Joris each rose in turn, taking up the song with her. Their voices echoed like in a cathedral's nave. The prayer was underway. "Our Father, who art in heaven . . ." The voices merged and rose in the room. A consoling murmur.

Mollinart and Geneviève piped up as well, the two of them dressed in black. The man's eyes were red as he approached the body and bowed. The woman stayed back and crossed herself several times.

"My friends," he began, "we must honor the memory of a remarkable man, devoted to his island and to his fellow men. When I met Félix Grangé, he was still a worker on the plantation. His liveliness revealed so much about his character immediately. He was the sort of man who . . ."

Gabriel wasn't listening anymore. Across from him, Jean-Joris's round eyes were staring at the corpse. Something nagged at him. In the shadows' flicker, his large forehead seemed like a giant's. His features were hard to pin down. Gabriel had never looked at the man so closely before.

". . . in our heart and in our memory. Amen."

"Amen!" the attendees replied in unison.

"Amen," Gabriel whispered belatedly.

Mollinart started shaking hands, and Gabriel realized he should follow suit. "My condolences." As he waved to Jean-Joris, an inexplicable sadness overcame him.

What about your father?

I've been seeing Bettina for some time now. That tall woman from Curepipe intimidated me. I was awkward. She was self-assured. I met her at a New Year's party some friends were having. She recognized me. At that point, the papers were starting to talk about the Chagos, and I'd given several interviews. My picture was going around.

She was the one who came over, a glass of gin in her hand. Smiling. Natural. She was the one who chose me.

You always talk about your mother, Joséphin.

She said that one morning, as she poured herself a second coffee.

Her courage, her determination . . . I understand it. But she didn't conjure you out of thin air, did she? Well? What about your father?

November 1970

The flower fell on Félix's shroud and among so many others. Marie turned around to cross the path. The spotted cowrie was still there on her mother's grave. The colors had faded, but with a bit of shine, the gleam would be just like new. It didn't matter anymore. She'd gathered shells with her sister and her nephews, and now they were all gone—nine months, the length of a dream, of yet another lost illusion. The son of a Chagossian woman and a respectable Mauritian man? What was she thinking? Nature hadn't granted her such a silly thing, and she'd had to lie, out of love, yes—more than two years of lies already, and she hadn't betrayed herself. *See, Josette, I was strong. Even Félix, rest his soul, never guessed a thing.* She started on the Hail Marys alone.

In the distance, Mollinart was waving his arms. "Meeting at the Pointe de l'Est!"

"My friends," the administrator began after clearing his voice. "I have to share some sad news."

Everyone's ears pricked up. In the distance, she noticed Suzanne in Angèle's skirts, Joséphin in her arms. She'd almost forgotten that she'd entrusted them to her aunt that morning; for some months now she'd been forgetting many things. Her despair was too immense.

"The general situation is bad. Very bad. Our copra isn't selling. Twenty of our comrades went to Mauritius to get provisions and materials to replace the supply ships. Unfortunately, none of them have come back . . . And I've just learned that the British." He paused to gather his thoughts. "The British are going to shut down the copra plantations. Forever. There will be no more work." He held up a hand to hold off the shouts and forced out his last words. "I'm the saddest of us all."

A whisper ran through the audience, like a convulsion, before settling into an icy silence. Marie clutched Gabriel's arms. Her legs were going to give out, or maybe she was shaking. No more work? How would they live?

✕

She slept for twelve hours straight, a long run of frenetic dreams in which Joséphin, now tall despite his child's head, was running a rope around her neck. When she woke up, Mollinart's speech hit her again. No more plantations. No more work. Her sister gone. She stood up, put some water on to boil. Only a bit of Mauritian tea left. On the box it read *Bois chéri, île Maurice*. She'd gotten it from the last supply ship. Such a long time ago that it almost seemed like it had never existed. The smell of vanilla filled the room and gave her courage.

Josette's disappearance couldn't be in vain. If her sister was dead, Marie at least owed it to her to fight for life on the island to resume. Shutter the mill? Out of the question. She sipped the tea, surprised to find an energy in herself that she had thought was gone. Because everything was lost, she had to act.

After preparing a huge basin of water, into which she plopped herself, she scrubbed her skin with a sliver of soap and dug into the roots of her hair, which she'd left unwashed for months. She untangled them with a comb and cut off the ends with a technique her mother had taught her, then reached into the armoire for a container of coconut oil. As she rubbed it in, she realized with shock how thin she'd gotten, rediscovering her body as if she'd been in exile from it. Was she still seductive? She put on the bright orange dress she'd worn to Josette and Christian's wedding years earlier and knotted her hair in a somewhat limp plait.

When Gabriel opened the door, she saw that he, too, was emaciated, his eyes sunken; she hadn't been able to make love to him for months. She smiled at him. Went through the old motions. Gave him a light kiss on the lips. Slipped behind his ear, ran her tongue over the small cloud on his skin.

Then, as if that was all he'd been waiting for, he leaped onto her, devouring her neck, her breasts, his hands blindly groping her. His hunger had returned. His sweaty skin, his member, his back, his hair falling over his face. He slipped under her dress, delved with his tongue, pulled her whole body close against his, came back up, and suddenly he was pushing her against the kitchen table, her dress hiked up. There was no tenderness left in his gestures; it was all brute action. He pushed forcefully into her. She held back a cry of pain. It wasn't working; he was hurting her. What he was demonstrating wasn't so much desire as rage. He was angry with her; he was settling scores, as if he knew—oh! That was it. He'd figured it out about Joséphin. She shut her eyes and gave in.

Geneviève seemed to be fixated on Jean-Joris, who had come to ask for permission to fire up the furnace again.

Mollinart erupted. "What's the matter with you, Geneviève?"

Gabriel himself felt uncomfortable.

"Nothing, nothing. I just think our friend is formidable, that's all. What a force of nature."

Jean-Joris smiled shyly.

"It's good for the furnace," Mollinart said, shooing him out. "Go for it."

She waited until the man was gone to spit her venom. "Don't you think that Joséphin looks an awful lot like him?" There it was.

"Geneviève!" The administrator was livid.

But it was too late. Hurt shot through Gabriel's veins; his muscles, his blood felt almost electric. A hurt borne by how true those words felt. Joséphin. Someone else's son. His round eyes, his dark skin, his stocky frame. Gabriel wanted to believe all that was from Marie, from her Chagossian ancestors. From a long line of strangers. How could he have overlooked such obvious things? The child didn't resemble him at all. This fact undid him; he was glass, crushed under a heel.

✕

"Fill the bucket up to the top, my little coconut." Suzanne nodded and went to milk the neighbors' mule, her small feet stamping the dry earth. For two days now their goat hadn't been producing any milk. It was a catastrophe. Marie thought she was stopped up, but the teats remained empty; the well had run dry. When the neighbors offered their mule for milking, she didn't ask twice. Preserving normalcy had become a battle. But she held her head high, walked up and down the island's paths like always. With Angèle and a few other friends, she had even gone back to splitting coconuts on the plot. Not for Mollinart, not for foreign buyers—no, for them, just for them. In the morning, she got up at five to fish for some shrimp, catch an octopus or two, gather periwinkles or tec-tec mollusks. Christmas was coming, and she'd decided that they'd have themselves a magnificent feast.

Her grit was infectious. Henri and Jean-Joris had come out with a mountain of coconuts for the plot. Tico had come to help them with husking. Life, oddly, was settling into a routine again, and Mollinart didn't protest. Only Gabriel was still distant: *What's the point, Marie? Don't wear yourself out. It's not going to change a thing, you know.* He alternated between stretches of kindness and bouts of darkness; in the space of a day he might give her both a caress and a slap. She dreaded those latter bouts, not because they were aimed at her, but because he also took it out on himself. One night, he'd banged his head on the kitchen table so hard she was scared he'd draw blood. Her imagination was running riot. She still had no idea whether he'd figured it out about Joséphin. He didn't bring it up. He didn't bring up anything, actually. Deep down, she knew what was driving him crazy: his guilt. Gabriel's father was sick in Mauritius, paralyzed, while he was here, thousands of kilometers away. Every time she tried to broach the topic, he let out a nervous chuckle that left her even more perplexed.

She was about to husk some coconuts in her yard when she saw him coming up from the beach, his face wan. A new bout.

"Where's Joséphin?" His voice was threatening, and she was suddenly wary.

"The baby's sleeping. Why?"

He barged into the shack, came right back out. She set down her machete. He made his way to the coconut plantation, and she realized that he meant for her to follow. In her gut, it was like a ticking bomb.

When they were far enough away from the village, Gabriel stopped. "I'm only going to ask you this once. Once." He paused. "Joséphin . . ."

There it is, she realized. *The world's falling apart, and it's falling apart now. You don't say a thing. To anybody,* Josette had insisted.

But Josette wasn't there anymore, and Marie's tears were already betraying her. The jig was up.

Gabriel reeled. The blood drained from his face. "Who?" he hissed.

She bit her lip.

"It was Jean-Joris, wasn't it?"

She hated the sound of that name on his lips, those lips she loved so much, the ones she had loved even before tasting them, those lips she'd waited so long for.

"Gabriel, I swear, I thought . . ."

"You've sworn enough, I'll say." He took two shaky steps backward, then turned his back on her.

To die of pain. Doubt. That's what's killed men in the past, what kills them even today. Is the child mine or not?

I look in your eyes to find mine, Pierrine, and in them I find Bettina's. So much the better. Believe me, you're getting the better end of the deal. Your skin is golden brown. Your hair, perfectly smooth. You're my daughter, I know it, but that's all. *I know it* doesn't mean anything.

It's not a matter of trust—she tricked me, she was faithful, truth or dare—it's a matter of nothing.

The definition of doubt: nothingness sheathed in words.

It's your child. The phrase could be false. So how to know? How to move forward? Women always have us dancing over the abyss.

But we need them to fight the madness rising up around us.

December 1970

He wouldn't see anyone else. From his room, he'd simply stare at the almond tree like a gallows, not think about anything anymore. He'd apologize to Évelyne, whom he'd abandoned for a woman who'd betrayed him from the very beginning. His poor sister! She hadn't responded to a single telegram. Of course she was furious. The father was probably dead, and she was probably rich. No. Damned souls were the toughest ones. Léon Neymorin would hang on until the bitter end. Gabriel thought he could hear a baby's cries. But it was his shame playing tricks on him. *I loved you so much, Joséphin. My baby. My poor little baby.* But now someone else's face was superimposed onto the child's.

"Gabriel! Open up! Please . . ."

Through the locked door, he recognized Angèle's voice.

"It's bad, Gabriel! Suzanne's not well . . ."

Now they were pulling tricks. Suzanne, sick? And they were sending Angèle to him.

"There's blood, Gabriel!"

He got up and yanked open the door. Angèle started back. Unshaven, unwashed—he must have cut a pitiful figure.

"Hurry," she pleaded. "Suzanne's not in good shape."

He took a breath. Realized she wasn't lying.

He'd told himself he'd go into the shack without looking at her, but it was impossible: Marie was sobbing beside her daughter. His fury evaporated immediately, and he rushed to Suzanne. Blood was dripping from her hand. Nearby, Joséphin was crying; his son was crying. He picked him up, kissed his forehead, said something soothing, and gave him to Angèle. "He doesn't need to see this. Take him to Gisèle. Come right back."

Suzanne was shrieking.

"How did she do it?"

Marie rubbed her eyes, smearing red across her forehead. "The pail . . ."

"What do you mean, 'the pail'?" He wet a rag hanging on a chair and wiped the wound.

Marie couldn't get a word out in her shock. Suzanne kept on yelling, yelling. Between her thumb and her index finger, where the skin was tenderest, he found a gash several centimeters long. A deep one. He pressed the cloth to it to stanch the bleeding. By the door, the tinplate pail lay, tipped over.

Angèle returned, out of breath. "Well?"

"Well what?" Gabriel shot back. "Well, nothing!" Panic was rising up in him.

"Show me."

He lifted the cloth: the blood was still flowing.

"You think it needs to be sewn?" Marie whispered.

"I don't know."

"If you want, I can sew," Angèle declared.

He could feel his pulse quicken. It was madness. Without anesthesia, antiseptics, any doctor.

Marie was losing her head. "We need to sew! Angèle! Angèle!"

Her aunt dashed out again. Needle, thread, scissors. What other option did they have?

Gabriel heated up a bit of rum to disinfect the needle and the thread. It was sheer luck that there was still some in the armoire.

Angèle scrubbed her hands with the last of the soap and gave Suzanne a mouthful of unwarmed rum; the taste disgusted her. "No, no spitting!" She made the girl swallow the alcohol; she needed to be numb. When all was ready, Gabriel carefully lifted the bloodied cloth and replaced it with the rum-soaked cloth. Suzanne bent over, crying bloody murder. Marie groaned sympathetically. He pushed her away, gently, but she refused.

"Give her space," Angèle insisted.

She acceded.

"Now!"

Gabriel tensed when the needle pierced the thin skin, immediately seeking out the other stretch of skin. Suzanne started sobbing, her eyes bulging. Her heart was pounding furiously. His was, too. This was unthinkable. He clenched Marie's shoulder, urged Angèle on. She pricked the girl again, drew the thread: a first stitch. Suzanne clenched her eyes shut.

"Don't stop!" Gabriel yelled.

Marie kept on sobbing, and he instinctively held her tight. Angèle kept at her work, making larger stitches to save time. The ordeal seemed interminable. Even the dog, huddled in a corner, seemed terrified. Gabriel dared to glance back at the butchery. From the sewn-up skin, small rivulets of crimson seeped. Flies had gathered, excited by the smell. Suzanne's mouth gaped, frozen in a long, silent scream. Angèle was sweating, and Gabriel was in awe of her strength. He never would have been able to do such a thing; he was suffering as if the needle were piercing him, too.

"It's almost over," he reassured Suzanne.

The little girl didn't react. She was beyond pain. Angèle pulled the last stitch tight, made a knot, and cut the thread. Then, without a word, she fainted.

✕

Exhausted by the operation, Suzanne was deep asleep. Her bandaged hand lay on the bed like an accusation. Angèle had left to go sleep, and Gisèle had agreed to look after Joséphin for the night. Marie hadn't been able to drink the least bit of the broth Gabriel had prepared.

"What now? We stay here? We do nothing?" She'd broken the silence harshly. "How do we take care of her? We need real doctors. Are there any on Mauritius? Do you know one?"

"No, not really."

She thought carefully. "Then we need to find some there."

He reeled at the thought. If she had any idea. Fleeing to Mauritius and then never coming back. Sentencing herself to exile. Better to wait. Who knew? The British might change their mind. Politics wasn't an exact science. Best to keep quiet, like she had. To lie, like she had. Gabriel sighed. The truth was that he wanted to keep Marie close, here, on Diego Garcia. To buy some time.

"You shouldn't go, Marie."

"What?"

He turned to Suzanne, groaning in her sleep, her hand resting atop the sheet. He said, "It's important that you don't leave Diego Garcia. Don't make that mistake. Believe me, you'll regret it."

January 1971

Suzanne's fever was spiking. The herbal infusions weren't helping anymore, and Angèle's stitches had split, revealing a festering wound. Gabriel's sharp words notwithstanding, Marie had begged for her daughter to be taken immediately to Mauritius. Mollinart had promised that a boat would come, but she still hadn't seen a single one. Her anguish had her hair falling out; in the mornings, she'd find small clumps of wiry coils on her pillow.

One Sunday, at the end of the day, as she was preparing some banana purée for Joséphin, she heard a commotion. Voices were rising up to the warm blue sky. "Everybody to the beach! Everybody to Pointe de l'Est!"

She stepped out and stared wordlessly as Gabriel hurried past, his eyes furtive, his face ashen.

"What?"

The man didn't stop.

"Gabriel, tell me!" She thought she was seeing a ghost.

"Everybody to the beach," he continued, moving almost mechanically.

Joséphin rushed to his mother. "What happened, Mamita?"

In bed, Suzanne was groaning. Marie kissed her burning forehead. "I'm coming right back," she promised her daughter. Then, taking Joséphin's hand, she went outside. Curiosity was a better way to draw people than fear. On the path, she saw the whole village making their way down. They were walking slowly and obediently, eyes darting worriedly. She shoved the door shut and joined the procession.

All the Îlois were there, gathered in front of Mollinart's office. The administrator stood over the crowd on a sort of platform, but not alone. Behind him were soldiers. Armed ones. Her guts clenched. Soldiers? Here? What was going on? She heard them giving orders and realized they were British. Gisèle and Becca made room for her beside them. Gabriel was standing by the platform, his eyes downcast. Of the magnificent bird she'd once wanted to domesticate, all that remained was a carcass.

"Something serious is happening," Mollinart said in an unsteady voice. "I've already mentioned that the copra plantation will be closing." A murmur rose up from the crowd. "I'm as sad as you are, believe me. But now there's something else."

He was clearly struggling. Marie tried to meet Gabriel's eyes, but all she could see was his scalp.

"I'll let my boss, Mister John Rawling Todd, speak."

A tall white man raised his arms to ask for silence.

"Who is that?" Angèle asked; she'd just arrived.

"Mister Mollinart has said that the plantations are going to close. That's quite right." He pronounced *Mollinart* and *plantations* with a strong accent. "That is not everything. For reasons of security, the island also will have to close." The man said, "Oh, I'm sorry," in English before catching himself and continuing in French. "You will have to leave the island."

"What? What is that man talking about?" her aunt asked.

Marie could feel her heart bursting. She looked around, saw eyes as dismayed as her own. Leave the island—but why?

"You are in danger. Everyone has to leave. Nobody can live on Diego Garcia anymore," the British man added.

Not live on Diego Garcia? In danger? None of this made any sense.

"Hey! You can say whatever you want!" someone in the crowd shouted. "But I'm staying right here. I'm not going nowhere!" Everybody clapped. They'd been born on Diego, they would die on Diego! What right did these men have to kick them out of their home? And where would they go? How would they get there? Gabriel stepped down from the platform. Marie was shaking. She wanted to take Suzanne to Mauritius, yes, but to have her cared for, that's all. Her head was abuzz. Was this the boat she'd been wishing so long for?

The man continued. "Orders are orders. You have one hour to gather a few belongings. No furniture, nothing bulky. The bare minimum. One hour! The soldiers will go with you."

Shouts filled the air: Go? Leave the island? For where? To do what?

A British soldier gestured for them to be quiet, and Mollinart started talking again, his forehead dripping. "We'll take you to Mauritius! Don't panic; all will be well. We'll explain on board. Hurry along. You heard him: just a few belongings, only the essentials."

Marie wanted to find Gabriel, but amid the crowd, the cries, the questions, she couldn't see him. Mauritius . . . Evacuating the island . . . Leaving . . . Panic washed over her.

Angèle, Becca, Gisèle, everybody was crying. She even saw Henri and Jean-Jo burying their faces in their hands.

"Hurry up!" the soldiers in uniforms were yelling. They cradled their rifles in their arms like babies.

Marie ran to Jean-Jo. She would need help with Suzanne and Joséphin.

"You'll come help me? You'll come?"

He promised, horrified. She looked around, unable to find Gabriel's profile. The horde of people dispersed amid shrieks and sudden silence. Everybody was bewildered. Nobody could live on Diego Garcia anymore. But what about the animals? The chickens, the donkeys, the dogs? One hour.

"Mamita." Joséphin was sobbing.

She covered him with kisses and tried to calm him down. No time. Practicality filled her thoughts, marshaling what little strength she had left.

She got back to the shack out of breath, Joséphin in her arms, and explained to Suzanne, "I'm taking you to Mauritius, my little coconut; we're taking care of you." But they had to hurry. Get up and hurry. The girl's eyes fluttered. Her fever was so high she couldn't really talk, but everything in her face asked, *Is that true, Mamita? Will I stop hurting?* Marie looked away. On the ground she spread out a big sheet on which she threw all sorts of clothes, a pot, some silverware, three bowls, her machete, her oil lamp, a box of matches, and a woven coconut mat. She could bring only the essentials. After a moment, she also slipped in her writing notebook, with the pencil. But what if they didn't have anything to eat? She managed to catch two chickens in the courtyard and stuffed them into a basket with a lid. The birds squawked in terror. Joséphin seemed distraught. Outside, Mérou was barking. Marie focused on what mattered most; she grabbed two jars of grated coconut that she'd filled the week before and that might keep, tossing them into the hodgepodge. As for water, she had no idea. There was no gourd, no bottle that would close. Most of the time, she used her metal cup, but for the trip she would need some other container. The trip. What trip? And Gabriel hadn't said a word! Everything was a blur. She'd been crying for some time and not even realized it.

He'd discouraged her from leaving for Mauritius, but he'd never mentioned soldiers, a forced departure, an island being evacuated. Did he know about any of this? Did Mollinari? Her head was spinning. What if they said no? What if they, the Îlois, didn't leave Diego? What if they stood their ground against this brutal, inexplicable departure? They had no idea what was happening. Why had the British come to find them? They hadn't seen or anticipated a thing. Right then a soldier opened the door. He couldn't have been more than thirty, but she saw a terribly harsh look on his face. His blue, almost white eyes cut through her. He barked out several words she didn't understand, and she mechanically responded, "Yes, yes," frightened by the gun in his hand. Mérou barked even louder. Dripping with sweat, she was so overwhelmed she didn't even react when he grabbed the dog.

She'd gathered all the belongings she could. Her bed, her furniture, her home: those were as good as gone. Even Joséphin's cradle would have to stay. She couldn't take anything else. She couldn't carry heavy things. The air went out of her lungs when she thought of her mother. The grave. What would become of the grave if she wasn't there to bring it flowers? She yelled at the children to be careful, and she rushed to the cemetery, her heart pounding.

The banyans' roots reached under the slabs, as if nothing had changed. The soft green of the foliage seemed all the more painful. She stopped in front of the rectangle of stone. Sad, small spotted cowrie. At Christmas the children had placed flowers that had withered since then. She wavered. The stone was rough, unyielding. It was blank. There was no name on the basalt. All the Îlois knew this tomb was Thérèse Ladouceur's, but if Diego was emptied of its inhabitants, who would remember? She noticed some sea urchin spikes on the sandy earth. The little kids must have brought them here to decorate the grave. The spines were made of a white chalklike material—Marie didn't think twice. Awkwardly, shaken by the tears that ran down her face, she traced five letters on the rock. The five little letters she missed so much, that word from her childhood she could no longer say to the woman who was gone.

The British were everywhere in the village, yelling to hurry up, and all in that impossible, guttural language that made her nauseous. Time was slipping away. Marie noticed the goat tied to its post. Too bad. She hurtled into the shack, tried to think over once more what she'd gathered, and what she could add to it, but the bag was already unbelievably heavy. She had to carry Suzanne, too, because, despite his promises, Jean-Jo wouldn't be coming to help them. She realized she had to give up the chickens, opened the basket, freed them. Where was Gabriel?

"Joséphin, you help me, okay? Don't go far." She set the bag on her head like it was the most spectacular heap of copra of her life. Slowly, she lifted Suzanne with one arm, saying, "Come along, my dear, stay strong," taking care not to touch her wounded hand, and with the other she steadied the bag on her head.

"Mérou," Suzanne whispered. "Ayo, my girl."

Marie didn't know where the dog was. She was so laden down that she didn't even think to glance back at her house. If she had, she would have seen an empty room that reeked with their exodus, the round-bottomed *karay* still full of grease on the counter, the tea gone cold, the gas stove turned off, Mérou's water bowl, the bed on which, in an already long-gone life, she'd loved and given birth.

The scene on the beach was heartbreaking. All the families were jostling against one another with baskets, sheets full of belongings just like the one Marie had tied up, everyone's eyes lost and distraught, so much weeping and incomprehension. Why were they being ripped away from their island? Who had decided this? When would they be back? All was chaos. Beside her, a woman was vomiting a clear liquid.

Marie set down her bundle a bit farther off and laid Suzanne down before going to find Gabriel in the crowd, holding Joséphin in her arms. She elbowed her way through, shoved her comrades, made her way around the beach three times, but didn't see him. She wanted to call out, but her voice faltered in her throat. The children were shrieking above the adults' cries. And the British were watching them closely. There was a commotion, and suddenly Jean-Jo and Henri pushed through the horde with horrified looks. They'd seen! With their own eyes! But what? The animals, the poor animals. Mollinart—he helped the soldiers. The two men were shuddering. They'd taken the dogs! Everyone stiffened. What did they do to the dogs? Henri could barely contain himself. They'd put them in the copra warehouse, and then, one by one, they'd thrown them in the furnace. Marie screamed. What about Mérou? Jean-Jo shook his head sadly. On Mollinart's orders, the soldiers had stuck pipes connected to their trucks into the furnace and turned on the engines. Judging by the sound of their barking, they hadn't died right away. Marie looked up. *My god, my god, please tell me it isn't true.* Gassed. They had gassed the dogs.

Angèle shrieked, "What about us? What are they going to do to us?"

Joséphin burst out crying. Marie held him tight, shocked herself. "My little coconut, it's all *sagren*." The Kreol word for *sorrow* lingered in the air.

The children were disconsolate. She turned back to Suzanne, who looked horrified. Nothing was as it should be.

There was even more jostling as the soldiers called the families up. Marie couldn't move. She felt torn, on the brink.

A soldier pointed at her and said in his incomprehensible English, "How many children?"

She didn't understand. What was he saying?

And then, in French, "How many babies?" She held up two fingers. He said other words that seemed to mean she should go ahead. But Angèle wasn't allowed to come along. Joséphin reached his arms out to her, shouting "Godmommy!" but to no avail. A soldier pushed her toward the shore, and Angèle shrieked. There would be other convoys. The man was saying, "You go now." It was their turn. They were told to put their belongings in rowboats. In the distance, the cargo ship loomed.

Marie's heart felt like a coconut husked raw; now a machete blow was cracking it apart. Gabriel. Where was Gabriel? The sun was descending; soon it would be night. How could she resist, how could anyone keep the men with guns from ripping them away from this land? Everything was hazy, everything was unbearable. Suddenly, in the distance, she saw her beloved looking for her in the crowd. He had a bag in his hand and was trying to push his way through.

"Get on the boat!" a British man yelled. The small boats started moving, coming and going like dreadful insects, long, dark, ominous boats. Marie was swept up in the momentum.

Gabriel was there, just a few meters away. "Let me on! I have to get on this boat!"

She tried to head toward him, but a soldier held her back, pointing to one of the small boats. The English words were harsh: "This one, please." His rifle gleamed. She was forced forward. She wanted to see Gabriel, see him one last time, just once, please, to clutch him in her arms, to explain about Joséphin. He was the father. Jean-Jo was nobody. It was him. Who else could it be? Oh, to kiss that cloud-shaped birthmark one last time . . . From the other side of the pier, Mollinart watched them climbing aboard, his body shaking with sobs. It was too hard.

"Gabriel!" Marie tried to resist. She was the barefoot woman, the one that drowning hadn't drowned. She wouldn't go! But with her two children, one being poor Suzanne, she couldn't put up a fight. She shouted Gabriel's name again, shouted so loud her belly felt like it would rip open. Then the boat shook.

There was enough time to see him rush toward the craft, his thin, birdlike profile a shadow among the shadows. A soldier held him back.

"Marie!" His voice cracked. "Marie!"

It was too late. In a matter of minutes, the shore disappeared into the twilight.

I remember colors.

The rest: erased, forgotten.

The sun sinking into the sea and the sea no longer blue but orange.

The red of women.

The black of the hold. Our bodies packed together.

The gray ashes of a dog.

I remember green, beige, khaki.

And, amid all that, my mother's tears.

November 1973

Joséphin was watching for the storms. When a threatening wind pushed the steel-gray clouds across the horizon, he rushed outside to put down buckets. The sac of the sky split open, letting fall water that hammered the sheet metal. Before the buckets got too heavy, he emptied them in the huge container that served as a cistern. "How much?" his mother shouted. He knew that answering "seven" or "eight" would make her happy, even if he was making it up. When the water reached the black line, half of the reservoir, he was flooded with joy; he'd done his work well. At five years old, Joséphin was master of the rains.

They'd been waiting a good hour in the precarious shade of a flame tree. Usually there were plenty of visits on Sundays, but today a heavy silence, broken only by the distant sound of engines, overpowered the Saint-Georges Cemetery. Marie was succumbing to torpor. To the thick, humid heat of November. On Diego Garcia, there had always been a sea breeze to refresh the air. Not here. In the basin of Port-Louis, the all was stifling. She'd barely been able to breathe for two years now; at times, she was astonished not to have died already.

On the foliage of the papaya tree nearby, she noticed brown spots that hadn't been there a week before. The austral summer scorched all vegetation; only a yellow plant managed to poke through the gravel-covered ground. Joséphin was about to fall asleep when a family came into the cemetery, arms full of flowers. They set the bundle at the foot of a vault and crossed themselves. A couple with a child. She vaguely remembered their faces; their eyes met two or three times a year—Christmas, a birthday, and All Saints' Day—like so many other folks these days. She shook her son. *Come on now!* He grabbed a half-full bucket of water, made his way to the visitors.

"For the flowers."

The woman looked at him in shock.

"One sou for the pail. Some water for the flowers."

Her little giant lumbered over, bent under the weight. Honestly, there was nothing giant about Joséphin anymore. He was looking his age now, maybe slightly younger, in fact. Soon he'd be six. With so little to eat, he didn't give the impression of being a well-fed toddler anymore; he'd lost the baby fat on his legs, and his belly was slightly caved in. His angular face made him seem keen; his round eyes were sunken. He'd never resembled Gabriel so much.

Marie approached the visitors as well. Since she'd begun showing up at the cemetery on Sundays, she'd quickly figured out the best way to work. Always send Joséphin first, to touch the visitors' hearts. Target the women rather than the men.

"Some rain from this water. One sou for the pail, ma'am. Just one sou."

Her bare feet rasped against the gravel, and the mother of the family locked eyes with her. Nod, politely, without a word. A hand on Joséphin's shoulder, sometimes a kiss on his forehead, and then a shift of the feet to hint that they'd leave. "Wait!" the woman always cried.

And Marie would hear the sound of a purse being opened and the woman rummaging around inside. And then it was a done deal. "Take this, sweetie." Joséphin would open his hand and immediately close it around the coins that had fallen into his palm. Then Marie would sound out a short, straightforward phrase—"Thank you, ma'am"—take the pail from her son's hands, water the heap of flowers, bow down, and walk away while whispering, "God bless you."

They waited for the Creole family to leave before jumping in glee. Three rupees! It was their lucky day. With one rupee, she could buy a few zinzli bananas. With two, a loaf of sliced bread. With three, she could buy the soap she sorely needed. There wasn't money on Diego Garcia, but since she'd come to Mauritius, she'd learned how to count.

January 1971

The hold of the *Nordvaer* had turned almost immediately into a furnace. There were about a hundred of them, heaped on top of one another, among the whistling machines. Marie fanned her children with her skirt, fully aware that it was no use. But she had to do something so as not to go crazy. The heat was giving her palpitations. Sweat glued her clothes to her skin. The youngest children's cries mingled with the women's sobbing. Some were passing out, and horrendous, unslakable hunger was scratching at their throats. Suzanne was crying quietly. Marie would have given anything never to hear such crying. Joséphin eventually fell asleep, his fear giving way to exhaustion. An acrid smell reached her nostrils. She hunched over her daughter's bandage, dismayed that she might see it soaked with blood again, but it was still beige. In the air heavy with anguish and so many people's breath, she suddenly realized what the sharp, almost familiar smell was. Something was dripping down her own leg. She slipped a hand under her skirt as discreetly as she could. That was it. The blood was her own. She panicked. She didn't have any cloths, any rags; everything was in her huge sack, stuffed somewhere on the boat. She looked around. Nothing.

If only she'd brought her apron. It must still be hanging off a chair in the middle of her empty kitchen. She burst out sobbing, her whole body shaking uncontrollably, causing Joséphin to wake up. He stared at her for a second, and then did likewise. He was contorting in his shorts, suffocating in the furnace heat.

"Give me those!" she said sharply, pointing at his underpants. He was a baby; he could go around naked. Now all she had to do was ball up the cloth between her thighs. "Give it!"

Joséphin sobbed. "No! Mamita, no, no."

She blinked hard, shocked to be asking such a thing of her baby. But the blood was flowing, staining her dress. Her hands smelled just like the octopus's head on her metal rod.

"Take this." Gisèle, her neighbor back on Pointe Marianne, held out a rag.

Marie unfurled it, realized it was a headscarf for working. The huge white square that they folded into a triangle and knotted at their nape. She glanced at her with gratitude, unable to get a word out.

A chain scraping against the hull. After a backbreaking night, the noise woke her up. Were they dropping anchor already? Between her legs she could feel the cloth soaked by her period. "British! Let us out!" someone bellowed. But nobody responded. Everything around them was dark. Suzanne's forehead was damp, burning.

"Mamita," Joséphin whispered. "When can we go back to the shack?"

If only he knew! If only he knew how badly she, too, wanted to go back home. Voices ringing out reached them. The hatch of the hold opened, letting in a blinding ray of light, and the silhouette of a man made its way down the metal steps. Gabriel! But it wasn't him, not even close. This man was as dark as an Îlois and looked plenty old. Other men followed him, and women, and children—some forty people at least joining their group amid yells and pleas for help.

"I won't go! I won't go to Mauritius!" The man who was trying to fight back was white-haired. "What right do you think you've got?"

The soldier grabbed him by the shoulders and pushed him down to his feet. "Do what we say," he said in harsh English. The old man was about to get back up when another soldier hurtled into the hold. The word out of his mouth was incomprehensible, but not its meaning: *Enough!* Another thrust his head threateningly into the opening. All of them were armed. The man cowered in a corner and stopped moving. Then Marie understood. These were their brethren from Peros Banhos. The British were clearing them out as well.

The heat in the hold only worsened, as they all had to huddle together. The sailors eventually gave them water and a few provisions. The rationing was a dicey affair; Marie had to push and shove to make sure she got something. She was terrified of there not being enough. The British yelled at them to calm down, insisting that there'd be a bit for each of them. She elbowed her way forward all the same. The cloth Gisèle had given her fell at her feet like an overripe fruit. Too bad. She couldn't do anything about it anyhow.

"Stay here, Joséphin. I'll go get us some water." She took a gourd and asked for another for her children. "Bahbee, bahbee," she repeated, mimicking the British word for baby. She gulped a mouthful, let the water refresh her mouth and run down her throat before heading back to the two kids. Joséphin drank several gulps in a row, which made his stomach grumble. Suzanne didn't ask for any. Marie held a hand under her head and had her drink slowly. "It'll be okay, Ti Baba." She wet the girl's face. But within minutes, sweat had broken out again across her forehead.

"More water, please!" someone moaned in the darkness. "Give us more, sailor! Thirsty!"

There wasn't nearly enough for everyone; they'd lied. The chain scraped against the metal. In the distance, an odd, inhuman cry resounded.

"So many animals on the deck! Asses, goats, pigs! Treated better than us, my children!" The white-haired man was sniveling despairingly. An angry whisper rose up.

"And us?" Marie whispered. "What are they doing with us?"

The shock was too great; nobody fought back.

November 1973

Gabriel had imagined this scene a dozen times. He'd walk self-assuredly into the entryway, stop in front of the birdcage. Show them the parakeets, the finches, the bulbuls. The lovebirds. Joséphin would plead for them to be let out. He'd pretend to think, and Suzanne would pipe up, too. Gently, Marie would open the door to set them free.

Gabriel picked up a frangipani branch and broke it in half, then threw the two pieces as far as he could into the sea. The wind tossed them into the foam. His dreams of returning had ferried a whole procession of images. Sometimes it was Évelyne who welcomed him on the quay; other times, Marie was dancing a séga; but most often his dream was a simple one: Joséphin would be running toward him, shouting, "Daddy." The pieces of wood settled by his feet, spat out by the backwash.

Another week to go. When Mollinart had told him that the *Mauritius* would pick them up, he hadn't believed it at first. What pleasure was there in a false promise? He was just as fearful of disappointment as others were of serious illnesses. He'd been waiting three years to go back! After the *Nordvaer* had left, Mollinart himself had sent cable after cable to the Port-Louis harbormasters, insisting that their return be carried out. His messages were always answered with a single phrase: *Complete your mission first.* Their mission? What was their mission supposed to be? To finish archiving the island, to ensure a strong relationship between Mauritius and the United Kingdom, to clear out the place. Since the spring of 1971, American ships had started invading the bay, with absolutely no prospect of leaving. All communication with Mauritius had been heavily monitored to avoid any leaks. In one of the few telegrams he'd been able to send Évelyne, he'd written, in French: *Stuck on DG. Stop. Return date unknown. Stop. Thinking of you. Stop. Your loving brother, Gaby.* She hadn't responded. Around him, the lagoon loomed like a fortification.

One night, maybe a month after the worst of it, there had been a knock at Gabriel's door. The administrator—but of what, apart from decaying memories?—was drunk. Tiny veins had burst all over his cheeks and nose. Ever since the soldiers had arrived, the Diego Garcia cellars had been full to brimming anew with rum, whiskey, and beer.

"I'm screwing it all up!" Mollinart bellowed.

Gabriel had guided him to the bed. "Sit down. No! Don't lie down. Listen to me. Sit."

He no longer remembered who had told him that: never let a drunk man lie down. He'd rushed downstairs to warn Geneviève, passing several officers in khaki uniforms in the sitting room. Only the top brass were living in the villa on the Pointe de l'Est; their underlings and the base staff were living in hastily built barracks some ways off. He rapped at the door and went right in. Geneviève was reading a book; he'd disturbed her.

"Marcel isn't well. Please come."

She followed him upstairs. Seeing her husband drunk and unhappy, she hadn't offered him the least bit of kindness—she hadn't reacted at all. An exasperated sigh, and then, "This place will be the end of him, honestly."

This place, as she said, had been destroyed by politics and national interests. Mollinart and Gabriel were complicit in this destruction, but she was hardly innocent herself.

"Getting himself into a state like this over Blacks," she pronounced.

Gabriel couldn't take it anymore. He sank his nails into her skin, which was as dry and scaly as a snake's. "I hope you lose everything someday. Your belongings, your family, your fortune—everything! But not your soul. That's gone already." He didn't let her get a word in edgewise; he pushed her out violently and locked the door.

On the bed, Mollinart had slumped over like a huge bag of flour, giggling like a madman. "Bang!" he shouted while holding an imaginary rifle. "You didn't get that one!" He tried to sit back up, but to no avail; his body was racked by sobbing. At that moment, Gabriel felt some semblance of friendship toward him.

He'd never have thought he might be capable of forgiving Mollinart, and yet his wife's cruelty had rallied Gabriel to the cause. This change of heart astonished him. But what was so surprising, really? Mollinart had acted the same as anyone else would have: by thinking about himself first. His regrets couldn't undo the deeds he'd carried out, but at least they were sincere. Gabriel hadn't forgotten the look on his face after gassing the animals. An empty, terrified stare. Everything in him bespoke guilt. "I didn't want to . . . But. Those poor dogs . . . ," he kept whispering every so often. "Those poor things."

Several days after the evacuation, Gabriel had fled the villa.

"I'd like to have a word with you, Gabriel, please."

He said no.

"I'm begging you. If you think I'm proud of what I did . . . I know I'm not going to heaven for this."

But hell was right there, all around them, far more real than the dogs' bones in the furnace's ashes, far more horrible than the cracking voice of the woman he loved. As weeks went by, while the island's new occupants—American officials and agents, Filipino and Sri Lankan

141

workers—disembarked in successive groups, his solitude plunged him into terrible anguish. He curled up into himself, read books that immediately disappeared from his thoughts, didn't read them at times, gulped them down like tranquilizers. With nobody to talk to, with no friends, he wouldn't last long.

Preliminary work for the military base's construction had begun. In a year's time, the island would be handed over fully to the Americans. With the British's agreement, the shacks had already been razed, the coconut trees felled, the warehouses and mill destroyed. Gabriel had walked past what remained of Pointe Marianne several times already. The ruins of their home lay amid the vegetation. The goat's post was still standing, the animal's skeleton scattered a bit farther off.

The lagoon's beauty put him off; the ransacked villages put him off; the demolished trees put him off. The merest step on Diego, the merest glance, reminded him of Marie and the children. Suzanne's wound haunted him. They'd waited too long; they'd done too little. Amputation was likely. Angèle knew how to sew dresses, not gashes. With rum for disinfectant! He couldn't believe himself. How had he let that happen? And what about Joséphin? His son. Yes. His son, his pride and joy, his boy, the one he'd raised from the outset. Marie had lied to him, but her lie was nothing compared to his. He'd counted; the nine months of pregnancy corresponded to the months that followed his arrival on the island. He couldn't fault her for having relations before him. All that was such a trifling thing now. On Mauritius, life had to be far more difficult for her. He could have told her that Josette wasn't dead, at least given her that much! But he had no idea where Marie was living, what she was doing. Mollinart had received confirmation that the *Nordvaer* had indeed reached Port-Louis. Nothing further.

Gabriel grabbed his bag and headed toward the cemetery. For the time being, only the church was intact, but for how much longer? Brambles were already starting to overrun the graves. He did his best to keep the area tidy, weeding here and there, discouraged by the unrelenting roots. In front of Thérèse Ladouceur's grave, he kneeled. He still remembered how he'd felt upon discovering, a few days after the deportation, the clumsy letters Marie had scrawled using the sea urchin's spine: мαмαn. A childish, inexpert handwriting. Five small letters that were striking in their poverty. Next to it, the spotted cowrie shell hadn't moved an inch. He slipped it into his pocket.

He pulled the chisel out of his bag.

That was his final mission on the island. The very last thing he'd do before going back to Mauritius and finding those he loved. He would engrave their names into the basalt.

Leave a trace.

"My ancestors were slaves, runaway Negroes. When slavery was abolished, in 1835, they decided to stay on the Chagos and never left the archipelago. I myself was born on Diego Garcia, and I lived there until I was forced to leave in 1971. My mother raised us, my sister and me, simply, passing essential values down to us. It was an education well suited to our life on the Chagos, not to life in Mauritius, which was already a developed country with its own rules, its own economy. Mauritius was fine for short stays, medical visits. Not for living there. This is why we suffered so much after. Back there, people worked in copra and fishing. I split coconuts on the plantation. I never had any work contract. No Chagossian did. What use would it be? Everybody worked; unemployment didn't exist.

"We ate well, healthy things; it was straightforward. On top of our ration of rice, sugar, and vegetables, we could also get some wine every so often. Daily life was peaceful; we went at our own pace. It wasn't a life of business.

"On the Chagos, everyone had a home. If you didn't have one, you picked out some stretch of earth and told the administrator that you'd build something there. In my house there were three of us, my daughter, Suzanne, my son, Joséphin, and myself.

"Religion was important. We said our prayers, and often, with my sister and the kids, we went and laid flowers at our ancestors' graves, especially my mother's.

"When we were forced to leave, we lost all that. We lost our material and immaterial belongings. We lost our jobs, our peace of mind, our happiness, our dignity, and we lost our culture and our identity."

How many times did I read and reread and read out loud this account my mother gave with lawyers' help? How many times did I show it to journalists, historians, university professors, writers, filmmakers here or abroad who expressed interest in our tragedy? Alas, justice isn't a matter of human suffering but of legal formalities. Considering that Mauritius freely agreed to the detachment of the Chagos, how could the Court be swayed that our distress should supersede the law? How could it be argued that a political agreement shouldn't outweigh a people's uprooting if not by tears? That's what we have to attempt.

January 1971

First it was a whispered rumor, a distant sound that slowly grew more distinct. A tinny, unpleasant noise like an enormous jaw snapping shut. The hatch door opened suddenly; air and light flooded the hold's depths. The trip was over. Marie was about to pass out; her throat was bone-dry despite the water; her head hurt; her legs were all pins and needles. Joséphin stood up, buoyed by the fresh air. She tried to smile at him. Suzanne barely opened her eyes. She was a horrific sight with her sweat-soaked forehead and her sunken cheeks. Gisèle helped Marie pull her up. They had to help her step by step to the upper deck, doing their best not to trip despite the blinding sun.

Mauritius.

The dreadfulness was overwhelming. Huge steel containers were piled up on the quays. Terrifying vertical homes as high as stormy waves thrust into the sky. Everywhere it was loud. It was a bewildering urban torrent of roaring engines, honking, shrill tones everywhere, men shouting, bells, and music. Gray dust hovered over everything. This was Port-Louis.

"Get a move on!" The captain, with the help of the English soldiers, led the rest of them down to the harbor. Sailors were unloading their belongings on the quay. Nobody talked. *Help me, oh, Lord, please help me,* Marie thought. She kissed her daughter's forehead. Burning. Sat her down in the shade of a container. "Don't move, Joséphin. I'll get our things." He perched beside Suzanne, exhausted.

There were hundreds of sacks, white sheets, with pans, bowls, cloths. Everybody had more or less brought the same things. Marie rummaged through but couldn't find her bag. The thirst in her throat was unbearable. Where were her belongings? Suddenly she saw a woman pull out a parcel that looked like hers.

"Hey, you! That's mine!"

The woman, whom she didn't recognize, evidently an Îlois from Peros Banhos, undid the knot unthinkingly. Inside, Marie could make out her notebook, and she raced over.

"You take what's mine?" she said sharply.

The other woman turned her head mechanically to the heap of sacks.

Marie dragged her sack across the quay, unable to balance it on her head. Her body hurt so much. Near Suzanne and Joséphin, she made out Angèle's stout silhouette. Momentary relief filled her body. Angèle's eyes fluttered dazedly. Her aunt pointed out the crimson-stained dress.

"Ayo . . . Still hurt?"

She had forgotten. After the third day of travel, she'd stopped caring. Her period, she reassured Angèle. Her aunt patted her shoulder.

"I thought Suzanne still . . ."

The two women walked over to the little girl, who was rubbing her tongue over her lips in thirst. The gourd was empty. Marie collapsed to the ground. Joséphin was huddled beside her; she was waiting. She couldn't bring herself to do anything.

"Get your head up," Angèle ordered her.

No. She couldn't.

"Bigfoot Marie!"

The name brought her back to her senses. Nobody had called her that in years. Her eyes met Angèle's. The smile that slightly bared her gums, the crow's-feet around her eyes: for half a second, her mother's face was superimposed on her aunt's. "Never give up." One of Thérèse's guiding principles. Never give up.

And now?

In the distance, the captain was talking to a few Indian-looking people, Mauritians by all appearances. After a few minutes, the British men disappeared. Two or three sailors waved to them. "Good luck, good luck." They didn't say anything else; they, too, departed quickly. They were going. They were leaving! Angèle was livid. How dare they leave, abandon them here, with nothing and nobody, without a single explanation. Marie wanted to curse them all. But what good would shouting herself hoarse do? She looked around for the Îlois with white hair but didn't see him. What about Gabriel? Where was he? She slumped against the container. She'd had enough.

Amid the bundles, the sheets, the baskets, the makeshift luggage, voices were rising.

"Where do we go now?" Henri asked an agent by the harbor.

She hadn't seen him in the hold, either. The boat had been so big, and there had been so many of them. The Mauritian shrugged. He had no idea. He didn't have a clue about any of this. Nearby, Jean-Jo was wailing like a baby. Nothing was right. They'd been plopped down in Mauritius after an ordeal at sea and left like this, with no home, no information, no help—with nothing at all.

"Mamita," Joséphin whimpered. She turned her head. "Look at Suzanne."

At the corners of her daughter's mouth there was foam. She rushed over to the harbormaster agent. "Hey, you! Don't go! My girl is sick!" The words hurtled out of her bone-dry mouth; she wouldn't leave until she had an answer, some sort of explanation.

"I'm truly sorry, ma'am." The man said that he'd seen other boats come, from Peros Banhos and Salomon especially. "Mauritius signed an agreement with England. The government sold the archipelago; you can't go home anymore. That's all I know." But one thing was clear: some fifty Chagossians were already living in Mauritius. Had been for years. Every day, a woman walked up the quay at three in the afternoon. At first, he'd thought she was insane. She kept saying the same thing over and over: she would go back to Diego. She had to go back to Diego. He'd explained the situation to her a hundred times: the island was closed. No boat would be taking her back. She refused to believe him, came back every day. If they waited a bit, they'd see her.

A woman would be coming to the harbor. An Îlois, a friend, torn right out of the Chagos as well. Marie opened her mouth, seized by irrational hope. A woman? Who wanted to go back to Diego? Would God grant her this gift?

"My girl," Angèle declared, sensing her thoughts. "The sea, it takes you one time. It never gives you back."

But Marie was trembling. They had to wait for her. A Chagossian! Ahead, the heat was making the air shimmer; oil fumes were wafting all around. She could hear the Mauritian man shouting behind her. "Your dress, ma'am! It's dripping blood!"

November 1973

"Why bother? There's no need for it here." Geneviève Mollinart was holding the villa's silver service in her arms. "We can actually make some use of this back home. Look at those Americans. They eat right out of the jar!" She snapped shut the cutlery set and slipped it into her suitcase. "What about that?" A finely wrought soup tureen gleamed on the service trolley. "You want me to think they'll actually make soup? All they'll make is beer." The piece went in along with the service. "Whine all you want, Marcel, but just you wait, when we've got everybody over for dinner, you'll be thankful."

Mollinart looked around for Gabriel. His wife had already filled three enormous trunks with their belongings: clothes, sheets, lamps, decorations, books, folders, pillows, not to mention light furniture. But the dishes and valuables didn't belong to them; all of it had been there when they'd come to Diego Garcia. The bourgeoisie could always be counted on to save the silverware when the world was falling apart.

"Geneviève, please . . ."

"What?"

"Would you look at yourself?"

"Oh, you're one to talk!"

"Now, now," Gabriel piped up, unable to resist a sarcastic remark. "Does it count as stealing when you're stealing from the British?"

She turned her back on him and kept going.

An American officer, who'd taken up residence in the guest room, stopped in front of her. His accent was strong as he asked, "Are you okay, miss?"

)(

His final night on Diego Garcia. Gabriel waited until midafternoon to walk around the whole island alone. He walked all the way to the tip of the western end. Red-and-black crabs skittered away, hiding in holes that his feet immediately crushed, filling them with sand. After a few breaststrokes in the warm water, he returned to the land and sat, the waves breaking along his legs. He couldn't see it from here, but the *Mauritius* was already coming over the horizon on the other side of the island.

Mauritius. He would go and find his country, or rather what had once been his country, even as he abandoned another one that was crumbling apart in his heart. He would go and find Évelyne, who still hadn't responded to him, the Port-Louis buses, the hawkers. Not La Jalousie. He wouldn't dare end up alone with the paralyzed father. The invitation Mollinart had extended seemed far wiser. A few days in Moka, until he found a place of his own. The British government had withheld part of their pay against their final work—for their silence. He'd gladly have turned his back on that money; only the thought of Marie stopped him. Only people who didn't need money turned it down.

He stepped out of the water and lay along the horizontal trunk of a coconut tree to dry off in the sun. The island had gotten into him; he knew every single plot, every detail. He buttoned up his shirt, pulled on his pants. And then he headed down the ghostly path of Pointe

Marianne one last time. "Hurry up! Only one hour!" He had to badger himself to keep moving. There was no changing the past; the best he could do was confront it.

His feet led him to the church, its door ajar. He slipped inside, inhaled the scent of incense under the dust. The altar was still covered by a yellowing cloth. The crucifix hadn't been moved; it hung from an iron hook. Jesus was bleeding. Five wounds. What would Father Larronde make of all that? What would God? Why had God let those men do this?

The day was starting to wane. Through the one stained-glass window came a ray of orange light: Marie's color. She had been so beautiful that night. Gabriel walked out of the church and headed to the cemetery. The banyans beckoned him to push open the gate. Despite his efforts, the brambles had overrun the graves. If the new occupants didn't tend to the space, the cemetery would soon be a jungle. At Thérèse Ladouceur's headstone, he knelt. He'd worked to engrave the text in the basalt. The uneven letters betrayed his lack of experience. It didn't matter. Even the English and the Americans could read these words:

Here lies Thérèse Ladouceur
Mother of Josette and Marie-Pierre Ladouceur
Grandmother of Suzanne and Joséphin
Forever children of Diego Garcia.

The next day, Sunday, November 18, 1973, Gabriel boarded the ship, as did the Mollinarts. The luggage was piled up in a reserved cabin. After accompanying them to the pier, an American officer gave them a military salute. From the upper deck, they leaned over the railing. A strip of white sand, coconut trees. There was the landscape and what it contained.

Gabriel started. "Marcel. Look!"

In the distance, soldiers were walking their dogs on leashes: German shepherds, fox terriers.

Mollinart shut his eyes. "I can't. I really can't." He headed to the steerage, where Geneviève had already settled in.

Alone among the sailors, Gabriel looked one last time at Diego Garcia, dry-eyed. The island was no longer the one he'd known. All it left in his heart was a crater.

January 1971

The profile was more hunched. The smile less striking. But even in the darkest night, Marie would have recognized her. The harbormaster agent had been right; it was three in the afternoon, and a woman was making her way up the harbor. Josette.

Her heart pounding, Marie stood up. Not dead. Deep down, somehow, she'd always known. Her sister. Not dead! Time seemed to stand still for a moment—she was incredulous, afraid of being wrong, but it was absolutely her. An accident? A shipwreck? Mollinart had lied; her sister was there, before her. She shrieked and rushed like a distraught woman. When Josette recognized her, she almost fell. Then she started running as well. They hugged so hard they could barely breathe. After so many years, her body, her voice were here again. It was unreal. Nights upon nights of anguish, and now, suddenly, so much happiness that it hurt. They touched, reassured each other through all sorts of gestures that the other wasn't a mirage, heaven had graced them for once. There was too much for them to say, to take in, to behold.

"Let me look at you!" Was it her sister or Marie who'd said those words? Marie had no idea anymore; she ran down Josette's heavyset features: her smile, the rings under her eyes deepened by prayer.

"Alala!" Angèle gasped as she joined them. She crossed her hands over her belly. A true miracle! "My Josette Tasdebois, in the flesh!" There were more embraces, more laughs, more tears.

But as she came upon Suzanne outstretched, Josette grew alarmed. "Ayo, what does she have?" And when she noticed Marie's bloodied dress, she clapped her hands to her mouth.

"Not serious for me." She didn't have it in her to say more; she just showed her the bandage. Angèle explained everything to Josette: the accident, the horrible gash that she'd had to get sewn up. Suzanne was having trouble breathing but managed to open her eyes briefly. She must have heard them talking about her.

Josette declared, overenthusiastically, "Makine will have such a party for you!"

Hearing the name of her cousin, she blinked. Was Makine there?

"Not here on the harbor," Josette explained, "but that way, not far."

Marie wanted to know: Where exactly was that "not far," and what was it like?

As they walked, their bodies weighed down and aching—Marie carrying Suzanne, Joséphin in Angèle's arms—Josette talked. Their trip to Mauritius had started off well enough. A tranquil journey despite seasickness, the children as excited as a horde of flies. The arrival at Port-Louis had made an impression on them. Everything seemed so big, so modern. Christian was over the moon. Everywhere there were cars, buses, mopeds. Mountains of fruits and vegetables! At the bazaar, there was an entire corner just for meat. Chicken, beef, lamb, pork, and lots of it. Farther off was fish, just as fresh as on the Chagos, and farther still were flowers, plants, spices. A paradise. She even saw stalls of gleaming jewelry. Nothing like Diego Garcia. Nothing like their own arrival a few hours earlier, Marie thought.

With the envelope that Mollinart had given them, they'd started buying things, but the temptations were so numerous that by the fifth day they'd spent it all. The other Îlois hadn't had much more self-control. Without money, they couldn't live in Mauritius. They had to pay for lodging, for food—in no time they were back at the harbor.

"The next boat for Diego Garcia, when will it come?"

The man at the harbor, a fortysomething fellow with a kindly face, shook his head. "I'm sorry, lady, there's no more boats."

"What do you mean, 'no more boats'?"

It was all over. They couldn't go back home.

"I don't understand."

Oh, how many times she'd said that! I don't understand. Why? What's going on? You aren't allowed. Orders. The man didn't have any other words to use. "The islands up there are closed, ma'am. Everybody has to leave them." That word, *everybody*, had horrified her.

"I cried. Yes, I cried so much." Every day, she'd come back to the harbor. "At first I was sure a boat would come soon. Not a single one came. But I kept waiting for you."

Several times she'd nearly given up. But she'd kept the faith, and God had finally seen fit to reward her patience.

⋈

Under her feet, Marie could feel small stones, asphalt, shards of glass. It wasn't the sand mixed with earth of Diego Garcia. After they'd walked forty long minutes, the pretty buildings were well out of sight. Modernity had fallen away, replaced by run-down sheet-metal shacks. Red earth, gutters full of standing water with clouds of mosquitoes buzzing above, nauseating odors, potholes in which sullen dogs huddled, trash piled up in the doorways, an old cart with only one wheel left. A slum. Josette and the others were living in a slum. Joséphin pulled a face. She couldn't have put it better. *Here we are.* Her sister made a vague gesture. *This is it, the Charrette camp.*

A hobo tottered out of the first shack by the road. Marie narrowed her eyes, turned to Josette, and gave her an imploring look. But her eyes weren't fooling her. That hairy man, who she'd once known to be so robust and devoted, that man who belched as he stumbled through the trash, was Christian.

That stretch was so hard, Mama. Those first five years after we came to Mauritius. A hell. You were spared nothing. When I recount it, when I describe it, people don't believe me. The vicissitudes of fate on our wearied shoulders. For them, all that is practically unimaginable. Those lucky ones. Mollycoddled by what their lives have in store for them, protected from the very first. Born in the right place at the right time. They can't accept that other people don't have stars as lucky as theirs. Over the years, I've come to learn how to parcel out my tale. I measure out the misfortune in relation to each listener's sensibility. Hawking my wares of pain: one sou for the pail, ladies and gentlemen, just one sou.

I was so afraid, Mama. Afraid that you'd give up, that your strength would give out. Afraid that I wasn't enough for you. I swallowed all my wishes so I didn't weigh you down. I did what I was told. I made myself invisible. I wanted to vanish. I had daydreams about playing on the beach and nightmares about bloody accidents. Being done with it all. We think about death when we're little. So much. So often. Those grown-ups who forget have killed the child within themselves. But I haven't. I was five, ten, and my soul was a wounded animal's. The more I hurt, the less I showed it. Hide, little boy, curl up in a ball somewhere, don't make a sound. One day, maybe, the light will come back.

November 1973

Ghosts in the shapes of toads, coffins, hills. As he pulled away the drapes covering the furniture, Mollinart stirred up heavy dust that made them cough. Geneviève opened the boarded-up windows. The wooden floor squeaked. It would take a day or two for the Moka villa to regain its splendor, its odor of furniture polish with subtle notes of honey, its opulent sitting room, its immense dining room, its comfortable bedrooms adorned with paintings and religious icons. An army of maids was toiling away already. The residence was surrounded by a huge garden that was astonishingly well maintained compared to the house, with a fountain hidden deep within.

"The gardener did right by us." Mollinart sighed. "I'll owe him."

"We should have asked the nénènes to look after the interior as well," Geneviève quipped.

"You didn't want them to! You were so sure they'd steal your trinkets."

Gabriel had had a front-row seat to the couple's bickering for months, for years. How much longer would Mollinart go on with this? Going on was a challenge for both of them.

"Here's your bedroom," his friend said as he opened a door at the end of the hallway. He pulled off the white sheet covering the armoire, tapped the bedspread: it needed a proper beating, but besides that, the room was ready for him. Gabriel thanked him. In any case, he didn't plan to stay long in Moka. Mollinart helped him carry in his bags. "There ought to be linens in the armoire." He pointed to a door on the right. "You have a washroom. Make yourself at home. If you need something, just ask." Mollinart set a hand on his shoulder. Silence. "We'll find them, I promise you."

Gabriel lay down for a few minutes on the dusty bedspread. As it had years earlier when he'd come to Pointe de l'Est, his body was reeling. The motion of the sea was still deep within him. Mauritius. This burdensome feeling of being a stranger at home. The shelves in front of him caught his attention. He slipped a pillow under his head. The classics he'd studied at school: Molière, Dickens, Coleridge, Hugo. All of Hercule Poirot and Sherlock Holmes. A few history and botany books. He shut his eyes. *Find them.*

The next day, Mollinart set up his phone line again. The nénènes had overrun the house, dusting and washing and tidying. One of them let out huge bursts of laughter every so often that deteriorated into coughing, her stance often reminiscent of Josette's. The telecommunications employee picked up the receiver one last time: "It's good, it works." Mollinart clapped his hands in excited approval and took a bill out of his pocket. The balance the British had withheld had been paid out by the American lieutenant as they'd boarded. Gabriel had stuck the envelope with five hundred pounds at the bottom of his knapsack, pushing it deep with his fingertips.

"I'm going to call my friend at the Foreign Bureau first," Mollinart declared as he sank into a soft armchair, the phone set on the side table. "Stay here."

Gabriel sat down beside him. By sheer luck, the friend was the one who picked up.

"Now, tell me, I'm wondering what the latest is about the Îlois. You don't have any information, do you?" The interlocutor clearly had plenty to say, because Mollinart was nodding, hanging on to every word. "Ah, very good . . . Yes, I would imagine so." He twisted and untwisted the coiled wire around his fingers. "Nothing? But . . . the British . . ."

Gabriel raised his hand to ask where they were. Mollinart held up a finger, signaling for him to wait. Where was Marie? Joséphin? Suzanne? As the conversation dragged on, his throat clenched tighter and tighter.

"Next Tuesday? But of course. Yes, yes, I'll let Geneviève know. Agreed. Thank you very much. See you Tuesday." Mollinart hung up, looking distraught. "They're living in a slum. Past Cassis."

After making its way down the Port-Louis seafront and the palm-lined Place d'Armes, where families were taking strolls, admiring the government buildings and the statue of Mahé de La Bourdonnais, after going past the Royal College, where boys in white-and-navy-blue uniforms were heckling each other, the taxi dropped them off on a soulless street. Gabriel paid the driver, who made an illegal U-turn and sped off. The noise and bustle of where he'd grown up bothered him more than he'd expected. He recognized everything. He didn't recognize a thing. Before long, the pretty houses gave way to more run-down areas. His white shoes were soon soiled, the road turned into a path dotted here and there with potholes full of trash. Electrical wires dangled all around. He pressed on, his stomach in knots. A cluster of blackbirds took flight as he approached, whistling sharply.

After ten minutes, he saw a half-overturned cart in the canal. That was it. In that heap of sheet metal and mud. The English had ripped the Îlois from their land and left them here? He went in. Deep puddles were everywhere in the courtyard. It had rained the whole night, and the drainage wasn't working properly. The slum was calm. Nobody to be seen, just a few scrawny chickens. He shouted a hello but got no response. Nine in the morning. Maybe it was too late.

He shouted again. "Marie!" In one of the shacks, he made out some movement. The shelters didn't have any doors, just a curtain at best. A shadow filled an opening.

"Who's that there?" A gravelly, unwelcoming woman's voice.

He stepped forward. "I'm looking for Marie. Marie-Pierre Ladouceur." Just saying her name, her whole name, sent a shiver down his neck.

The woman came out. Heavy hips, a large belly. They stared at each other. Angèle. She wavered. Should she welcome him or not?

"Angèle, it's you!"

She gave in, rushed to him to hug him tight, immediately pulled back in uncertainty. "Come in."

He sat down on an overturned crate serving as a stool.

"When I shut my eyes, I see my wonderful shack from Diego. Here . . ." She waved vaguely, letting the sentence die out, before pouring some water over a bit of tea.

"Where is Marie?"

"At work. In the fields."

Well, but of course. After copra, she'd be working in sugarcane. "What about you? Don't you have work there?"

She shook her badly combed hair. "No, I work in the big white people's houses. Every other day. I'm not as strong as them young'uns."

He nodded, forced himself to sip at the already-cold tea. "How is Joséphin?"

Her face contorted; it wasn't clear whether she was crying or laughing. "Joséphin? A good little thing. Handsome, nice. He helps his mama. Together they sell rainwater at Saint-Georges Cemetery."

"Joséphin's working? He's not in school?"

Angèle hawked up some phlegm and spat it into a hole dug into the ground. Gabriel stiffened in disgust, but she seemed not to notice. "No." She emptied her glass and gargled to clear her throat and spit again. *"Ayo mo papao,"* she said.

He tried not to puke. The weak tea, this aftertaste of dirt, misery all around. "What about Suzanne?"

Angèle choked, coughed, coughed again, each sound rasping. Again that expression that could have been laughing or crying. "Suzanne? She's better, I'd say!" The coughing fit started up again, and he was sure she would suffocate. He got up to thump her back.

She stopped him with a wave of the hand. "Gabriel. You listen. Marie . . . it's over. She doesn't want to see your face. Never again."

The words chilled him to the core. "Why?" he whispered, even though he already knew the answer.

"You knew! You knew, and you never said!" she yelled, capping off her declaration with a curse.

Shame seized him anew. Angèle was right. "Life back then was too sweet. Marie was so happy." He didn't know what else to say, his eyes riveted to the hole in the ground.

"It's over. She hates you."

He stroked his chin. The sheet-metal walls undulated. Angèle's face grew hazy.

"She. Hates. You," she said, punctuating each word with a pause. "Now. Go. Never come back. You hear? Never!"

He stood up in a daze. "But what about Joséphin?"

Angèle pushed him out. "Enough about Joséphin. Not your son. Why pretend? God, that boy's not yours!"

January 1971

The day after they came to the camp, Suzanne was in convulsions. On the mat Josette had spread flat, the girl's arms and legs stiffened, and her whole body twisted and turned. Marie looked for a bowl, some water, anything. But to no avail. She tried to soothe her daughter's paroxysms, which only intensified.

"Josette!"

Her dozing sister opened her eyes wide in horror. "What?"

"I don't know, I don't know!"

Suzanne was bent over double, her back an arch of bone and skin.

Josette stood and dragged Joséphin outside. "I'm coming right back!"

The bandaged hand was flapping around, too. Lord! The smell filled her nostrils. Swollen, putrefying flesh. A diabolical fruit. The thread that Angèle had used to sew up the wound had dissolved in the skin's swelling. Makine tiptoed over. The gangrene horrified her. "Ayo, Makine, go! Get out of here . . ." The little girl didn't move.

Suzanne's jaw was clenched. Disfigured. "My darling, my little coconut . . ." It was Marie's fault. She never should have asked her to go milk the neighbor's mule. Her daughter wasn't accustomed to it—the leathery teats, the tinplate bucket. So sharp. But their goat's milk had dried up. Joséphin needed to be fed. Why had she asked her daughter instead of going herself? Oh! The Lord was making her pay for Gabriel's lie. And now Suzanne was being possessed by the devil.

Josette burst into the shack, accompanied by a man Marie didn't recognize, about forty years old with a thin nose and likable features. Marie's eyes landed on his two intelligent pupils, and she decided to trust him.

"Gaudry Depaz," Josette said by way of introduction. "A friend."

He had a bottle of alcohol in his hands. He took a cloth and soaked it in the liquid to dab at the suppurating gash. More of those horrible gestures, this endless torment.

"Mommy?" squeaked a small voice.

"Not now, Makine!"

The pain was so great that Suzanne's mouth opened wide, but no sound came: even that was too much for her. Gaudry examined the cloth: it was stained with blood and pus. "I'll try to get a doctor." He disappeared right away.

Marie called out after him in gratitude.

"That Gaudry," Josette said. "A good fellow."

He'd come from Peros Banhos. Josette and he had made the trip together on the *Mauritius*. He was a serious man who worked a great deal. His shack was at the other end of the camp. "When Christian goes too far, I hide at his place."

Marie sighed, her hand still on Suzanne's forehead. What had happened to Christian?

Josette shrugged. "He gets drunk." Added, "He's got too much sagren. It's so much worse than plain old sorrow."

Around nine, Suzanne finally fell asleep. Marie set her by the back wall, where it was quiet. All she could do was hope that Gaudry Depaz found a doctor. The room was dark. She poked her head out and saw Angèle trying to play with Joséphin. Her son came and clung to her. "Hungry, Mamita." Of course he was hungry. They hadn't eaten a thing the day before, apart from a banana. She rummaged in her belongings, found the containers of peeled coconut. The fruit's aroma was heartbreaking. What they were about to eat was a bit of Diego. Joséphin swallowed the shavings in a matter of seconds, unaware of how precious what she was giving him was. She shut the container.

"Why isn't Suzanne saying anything?"

"She's weak. Have to leave her alone." Marie unearthed a manioc biscuit, which he downed in two mouthfuls. "Josette, do you have any milk?"

Her sister took a basket outside to look through it. By sheer luck, she still had some powder. With some water, it would be perfect. The mixture couldn't do Suzanne any harm, either. She looked at her daughter, still asleep in the half darkness.

In a metal cup, Josette wet the white powder with rainwater and mixed it with her finger. Joséphin grimaced.

"No, you don't! You get this. Pinch your nose—drink this." Her stern voice scared him, and he gulped down several mouthfuls before she cut him off. "And your sister? You drink it all, and there will be none for her." She found a spoon in her belongings and went over to Suzanne, cup in hand.

Her body was stiff and contorted as she slept openmouthed. The convulsions had worn her out. Marie gently slipped a hand under her head to raise it. The shadows masked everything. "Here, my sweetie, a bit of milk." She gave her a spoonful, letting the mixture drip down her throat. "Some strength, darling."

The milk was slipping in, but her frozen body didn't react. It was only on the third try that Marie realized.

The spoon fell to the ground.

They knew, and they didn't speak up.

They could have helped, and they didn't.

They bled bodies and minds dry. Their indifference was a crime.

They're powerful, Mama, these ghostly shadows that haunt the palace. Men who sleep on two pillows at night. Servants of the state. Crowned heads.

The only crowns we had were those of our dead.

November 1973

A ring, two rings. Like a coin tossed into the air, your future engraved on one side: heads you win, tails you lose.

"Hello?" A woman's voice. Heads.

It wasn't Évelyne.

Sitting by the side table, Gabriel gripped the receiver. The woman on the line was named Georgette. The live-in nurse, clearly. He collected himself.

"I'd like to speak to Miss Évelyne, please."

"Miss?" The woman seemed taken aback. "Oh, you must mean Mrs.—Mrs. Miranville?"

"I . . . I had no idea. Might you have an address or a number I could dial?"

The nurse hesitated.

"Let me reassure you, I'm her brother."

"Oh, Mister Benoît? Ah! Your father will be so happy when I tell him you're back."

Gabriel nearly choked but managed to get down the numbers that Georgette was reading off laboriously, and then he hung up. He didn't wait another minute before picking up the receiver again and dialing the number.

The ringing seemed even shriller now.

"Hello?"

This time, all the uncertainty vanished in a flash. He took a deep breath. "Lizard?"

She was wearing heels and black darted pants under a pastel-pink blouse. Her hair, braided into a tidy plait, perfectly framed her forehead, offsetting her painted lips. Coral red. They stared at each other. Gabriel had played out this scene in his head a hundred times. With the first embarrassed moment now past, he drew closer, said, "Hello, Lizard," wrapped his arms around her as he'd done since she was ten, placed a hand on her shoulder as he leaned in for a loud kiss on her cheek. He hadn't imagined all this: the beige carpet, the Havana-brown armchairs, the huge porcelain vase, the doilies under the trinkets. The lipstick. His sister, unrecognizable.

The movement had been instinctive, even so. He let go of her and pulled her tight, but she was distant, so distant that he didn't dare go through with the cheek kiss. He looked her over again. Évelyne sat in one of the chairs and invited him to do likewise. The squeaking leather. The shoes sinking into the carpet. His sister was angry with him. Every woman he loved was angry with him. *She hates you!* Évelyne crossed her legs. A teen rebel had been left to fend for herself, told to make her way alone, and years later, upon his return, here was a married woman who'd become a stranger.

"Lizard . . ."

"There's no Lizard anymore. Stop it with that ridiculous nickname."

He absorbed the blow.

"You're back late," she continued. "Far too late."

"Not by choice, believe me. I was trapped on Diego Garcia."

"Trapped? Now that's a bit much."

"If only! It's a long story, you know."

He sensed that he'd piqued her curiosity. Évelyne had always been a bit of a romantic. She slipped off her shoes one by one and, barefoot, went into the kitchen to get two glasses. He heard some noise, another woman's voice. When his sister returned holding a pitcher, a nénène was following with a tray. "She wants to help no matter what," Évelyne complained. "I said I'm fine, Rama!"

"Ma'am, this is my job. Your job is to relax." The Indian woman bowed, set glasses, ice cubes, and boiled pistachios on the table, and left after another bow.

"She's terrified of losing her job if I do something in this place. And there's already two of them in the kitchen. Thank goodness Félicie isn't so zealous."

Gabriel smiled. "You're so bourgeois now, sweetie."

Évelyne furrowed her brow, but despite her attempts to look serious, she burst out laughing.

$$\text{\fontsize{20pt}{24pt}\selectfont X\kern-0.5em X}$$

She'd gotten married in April 1970 to Alain Miranville, a middle manager high up at the Mauritius Commercial Bank whom she'd met at a fancy fair in Beau-Bassin.

"He's not much of a looker, but he's charming enough. Beauty isn't everything—you know that, right?"

"Évelyne . . ."

"And there's nothing wrong with him that a proper setup can't fix, as they say."

"I never figured you for that sort of woman."

"I didn't, either, but what do you know? He did come into this nice house not too long ago. Both his parents died in some accident."

"Poor guy."

"Poor little rich guy, you mean! He's an only child. Although . . . he nearly got robbed by those slimy cousins of his. Good thing I was there. If I weren't, he'd have lost it all. Rich *and* stupid, that's what he is. That's all I wanted."

He nodded with a chuckle. "What about your Higher School Certificate?"

"Oh, I failed. Just barely." Her features darkened.

"You can take the exam again. You should give it another try."

"That's what Savita was saying. But I don't have it in me anymore."

"Savita! How *is* she?"

"Fine," she said. "Independence has been good to her family. Her father found a job after years of unemployment. So she's still in school. She's doing great. But Alain doesn't know that we meet up. Indians are still Indians, independence or not."

Some things never did change, after all. Politicians were selling a dream they didn't even believe in. A rainbow nation? Sure. Mauritius's communities stared at each other stonily, ready to shoot at so much as a blink.

"It'd be good to see her one of these days."

"Of course, Gaby. All in good time. Have a taste of Rama's lemonade, won't you?" She poured the cool drink into the glasses.

Évelyne rubbed her bare feet on the carpet. "That father of ours had a stroke in his sleep," she said quietly. "I didn't find him until the morning. The time it took to call for help . . . Doctor Lesage didn't think he could save him, but, well, there's life in the old dog yet."

His sister's disdain made him smile. He let her go on: paralysis, the nurse, Benoît's silence; her attempts to keep an even keel on such stormy seas.

"When did Ludna leave?"

"A month after you did, I think. I never did understand why. She told me she was leaving of her own volition, but I have a feeling he dismissed her."

Gabriel tensed up. If it was anyone's volition, it was very much their father's. He changed the topic. "The live-in nurse mistook me for Benoît, on the phone."

"Oh, him. A Christmas card, an Easter letter, and that's good enough for him! He's set up a practice in London, apparently. General medicine . . . You weren't one to write much, either." Her words landed like fists.

"I did write to you! All those telegrams you never answered. Over a dozen. The last one was . . . when the Americans came . . . Did you not get any of them?"

She shook her head. Set down her glass.

"Hold on—the Americans?"

He took his shoes off. It was time. He needed to tell her about Diego Garcia. Show her the truth.

December 1973

Another Sunday at the Saint-Georges Cemetery. Marie and Joséphin were back beneath the withered flame tree, wilting under the heat. The week had been hard. Nicolin, a textile worker in Floréal for two years now, had gotten into a brawl that had turned deadly. There was no use insisting it was an accident; the judges had their minds all made up already. The sentence had just been handed down: Melrose. The prison. An utter disgrace.

"No more Nicolin, no more son for me." Josette had unleashed her fury on Christian. "It's your fault! There's never any money. But when you want to drink, oh, there's money! Fine example, that!" She'd kicked him out, spewing all sorts of venom.

Marie could understand. She'd turned her hurt into fury, too. Ever since Suzanne's death, everything in her had shriveled up. Her heart, her body. She wasn't getting her period anymore. It had to be shock. Despair. Joséphin tried to make her smile. Always a soft spot for her. A kind word. He helped her as best he could, but still, looking at him made her lungs burn. His little face revived Gabriel's. But Jean-Joris was the father. Jean-Jo. Jean-Jo! That name didn't mean a thing to her anymore. He'd left the camp with a few others, Henri included, to live at Pointe-aux-Sables where life was no better.

Gabriel had known what they were waiting for. She envisioned him again at the pier, beside Mollinart, eyes downcast. The end of the supply ships, the threats to the plantations, that picnic on the beach that she'd never forget, the night before Christian and Josette left—it all haunted her thoughts. She was sure of it: he hadn't come because he knew that the Tasdebois family wouldn't be coming back from Mauritius; he knew that the Chagos had been sold off. He was ashamed. If only he'd told them, they could have done something. They'd have made plans, rebelled. Wouldn't have let themselves be starved out. Suzanne wouldn't have had to go and milk the mule. She'd still be alive today, her dog in her arms. Between two stretches of cutting cane, Marie had realized that the rest of her life wouldn't be enough to curse Gabriel. And yet all she dreamed of was seeing him again.

Joséphin was having a good time throwing pebbles when a cinnamon-skinned, lightly freckled woman came through the gate. She was radiant in her yellow dress as she set hibiscus down on a grave at the end of the path. Marie squinted. She was a new one. Something about this lady nagged at her. Her youth. Her beauty. Her round cheeks. A young woman whose life was footloose and fancy-free.

Joséphin walked over first. "One sou, ma'am, just one sou for the pail." The woman looked at him funny, knelt down before him. Marie walked over. As usual, sympathy got the better of her. The lady pulled out a coin and slipped it into the boy's hand. But this time, he couldn't hold back his words.

"Oh, oh! Five rupees, Mamita!"

Marie, embarrassed, started thanking the lady.

"Wait," the woman said. "You . . . Do you live by here, with your little boy?"

Usually, people didn't ask questions. They did their small bit of charity and then left. Marie didn't talk to Mauritians, not one, not ever, apart from a few friends in the sugarcane fields.

"Yes, over there," she said, waving her hand vaguely. She wasn't going to go into particulars about the Charrette camp.

"You have a bit of an accent," the lady said. "Where are you from?"

"The islands up there," she said quietly. "The Chagos . . ."

"Aha! Diego Garcia?"

The pail slipped out of Marie's hands. How could the woman have guessed?

"You know about Diego Garcia? Have you been there?"

"No, unfortunately. I've just heard about it." The lady fanned out the flowers. "They're so pretty, aren't they?"

Marie nodded, then realized she'd spilled the water. "Joséphin, bring another pail here."

He set off.

"Oh, there's no need! It's all right, I watered them before coming." She rubbed her nose as if to get some dirt off.

Marie waited. A funny feeling came over her. This fancy lady who was so nice actually seemed nervous. She had the look of someone with a favor to ask.

"I'll just come out with it: What's your name?"

"Marie-Pierre. Everyone calls me Marie."

"Well, Marie, I have a problem—let's say it's an issue. I've just gotten married, and I'm looking for staff for my house. Cleaning, ironing, cooking." She smiled. "Is that something that would interest you?"

Angèle had done cleaning. Marie still recalled how much it disgusted her. People shoved a sponge in her hands and made her clean the latrine. No, quite honestly, she'd rather deal with sugarcane that scraped her skin. "How much?" she asked anyway, to be polite. When she heard the number, she was sure it was a terrible joke. It was three times her pay as a harvester.

"It's not too little, is it?"

"No, no, it's a lot," Marie blurted out.

"Oh, that's wonderful! Do me this favor, please. My husband is so insistent, but I can't find anyone. If you'd like, you could stay in the little house out back. It's very pretty, very comfortable. You'll be happy there with your son, I promise you."

Marie was letting an angel pass her by. This offer was practically sent by fate, a fate that usually put her to the test. At the Charrette camp, there was her sister, her niece, her friends. At the Charrette camp, there was defeat and sagren. Joséphin's small footsteps hammered the dirt of the path; the new pail hung from his arms, his face scrunched up with effort. Her little one was so old already. What did she have to lose? She shooed away that memory of Angèle and nodded at the woman.

January 1974

In the purple-hued sky, bats were swarming in clouds, flitting around each other, flapping their wings in search of bugs. Their seemingly erratic movements belied perfectly planned trajectories.

Mollinart cracked a peanut in his teeth. "Pretty, isn't it?"

From the verandah, the view over Moka was crystal clear. Le Pouce Mountain stood out from the pink scrim of the sunset tingeing the rocks and fields gold. This corner of Mauritius was one of Gabriel's favorites. The red land, the hills, the sugarcane fields. In the distance the town of Ripailles was discernible; farther off was Crève Cœur.

"Well, enjoy it while you can." He crushed a new handful of peanuts. "I'm getting divorced."

"Huh?"

Mollinart nodded. "That's why Geneviève isn't here tonight. She's off to Europe. 'To recover.'"

Gabriel couldn't believe it. "Were you the one to . . . ?"

"But of course! It was all me. I couldn't take it anymore. The marriage never really took, in any case. Lately she's gotten it into her head that I've become a Commie. Never dealt with such a pain in the neck." He threw back his head and let out a laugh. "To think that she was the one to pass along all those secret documents."

"Geneviève?"

"Oh yes! Her father was old chums with a British MP, apparently. Used to be Labour, close with Wilson, and then turned Tory after some political betrayal. Eye for an eye, tooth for a tooth. That friend got a real kick out of sending me those papers."

"But why?"

"To blackmail Wilson, I'd reckon. Make sure he didn't throw any more spanners into the works. That hustler had his eyes on a plum post. Even though he was a nobody." Mollinart shook his head. "Geneviève could have at least gotten me that. Well! Don't leave me to enjoy my newfound freedom all by myself, will you?" He poured Gabriel some more whiskey before stubbing out a cigarette. Then he offered him one. "So, our Îlois? It's a disaster, isn't it? To think that those British were promising us a warm welcome . . . 'It's all ready for you in Mauritius!' How many times I heard that." He struck a match. "Three million. Three million pounds for the Chagos. In the government's pocket. Our government, needless to say. And the Îlois don't even have proper housing."

The smell of tobacco wafted in the air, attracting a few flies. One of them perched on Gabriel's glass. He swatted it away.

"What about Marie-Pierre? She still hasn't figured it out about your sister?"

Gabriel shook his head distractedly, still stunned by the number he'd heard. The Mauritian government had sold the Chagos off to the British. Literally sold. It wasn't just a matter of power and the island's independence. Three million pounds sterling was involved. He was so beside himself that he got up and paced around the verandah.

"Marcel . . ."

"Yes?"

"Someday it's all going to have to come out."

Marie had been working at Villa Talipot for a month now. Évelyne had been keeping the secret for a month now. She updated Gabriel every week. Marie and Joséphin were enjoying themselves in Pamplemousses; they'd settled into a rhythm.

"What about Suzanne?"

Évelyne had seen a little girl at the gate here and there. Marie didn't let her in, but they traded a few words and kissed cheeks. She had to be working already, the poor thing. The thought stung Gabriel. She was only eleven. What could she do apart from odd jobs like sweeping and washing? That she'd healed had been a miracle, but he'd have liked to do more for her.

"Lizard, couldn't you possibly . . . ?"

"Oh, Gaby, no. I'm already doing plenty. I can't take on the girl. Alain blew up at me when I came back with your wife and your son. I had to put up a real fight to keep them, and that was without letting on about them. So I can't. I'm sorry about Suzanne."

He understood. "And enrolling the boy?"

"I've taken care of it. I promised you I would, and I kept my promise. Next week Joséphin's starting school at Sacré-Cœur Primary."

When he told his sister about what had happened to the Îlois and his own forced stay, she'd forgiven him for his silence, his cowardice. His absence. Spared him further agony. Évelyne was his mainstay. Gabriel lit a cigarette and went back to his desk. There were still a few papers to mark. An analysis of Coleridge's "Rime of the Ancient Mariner." The Royal College students were smart enough—sometimes he wondered if they weren't smarter than he was. He owed this teaching job to Mollinart's contacts, not to his own literary skill. "English teacher, how does that sound? I haven't got anything better to offer you, in any case," the headmaster—a friend of Mollinart's—had said.

For eighteen hours a week, he taught, sticking as close to the textbook as he could: grammar, literature, and conversation. To think he'd once have given everything to be able to study in London. He didn't recognize that teenager, that dreamer, that little boy anymore. When he was done with his grading, he headed to the kitchen. He cracked two eggs over a hot pan, added some salt and pepper. He ate the meal standing up, put the pan in the sink, and went to lie down on the couch.

This apartment, too, was thanks to Mollinart: eighty square meters in Port-Louis on a street that was quiet apart from the neighboring church's bells—a living room, an office, a bedroom, a bathroom. He fell asleep without a thought.

Illness had been doing its job. The least that can be said is that it didn't fail you. You were weak, Mama. Unrecognizable.

A week before your death, I went with you to Grand-Gaube. You wanted to see the sea, savor its scent one last time. Take its sheen with you. Bettina was so exhausted by her pregnancy that she stayed in Port-Louis.

That day, there was a light breeze among the filaos. And nobody on the beach. At the other end of where we were, far off, so far off, was Diego Garcia.

You put your hand on mine. Your bones, I could feel every one of your bones. Oh, that touch, Mama, your hand already so cold—there was no warming it again. My body went just as cold.

You were looking straight ahead. You were squinting to see our invisible island. You weren't crying.

The week after that was a long descent into darkness. One morning, I left your bedside for a minute to buy some flowers. I wanted to give you some anthuriums and hibiscus, a little bit of beauty. And you picked that moment to pass away.

But I know it was really that day, Mama, when we were looking at the sea, that you said goodbye to me.

March 1974

Several months had gone by since she'd started working at Villa Talipot, and Marie was finally starting to feel alive again. She and Joséphin slept on two clean, comfortable beds. A table, benches, an armoire, a nook for cooking, another for washing. Latrines just for the staff at the end of the yard, with modern plumbing. The house elicited gasps of admiration from visitors: furnished tastefully and cool at all hours thanks to shutters that let in fresh air.

Ti Madame, as everyone here called her, had proved to be fond of Marie. She lingered in the kitchen, made jokes. Marie had more admiration for her with each passing day. It'd been so long since she'd laughed like this. Ti Madame had real personality, and there was something reassuring about her beauty; her face exuded vivacity tempered by a sweet look. She was a mixture of grace and masculine self-assurance. She was the sort of woman Marie wanted to be like. Ti Madame could throw a rotting fish on the table and say, "Please, won't you make something out of this? My husband's invited his old aunt to dinner." Joséphin loved her, and she took care of him: pens, notebooks, picture books—the boy was properly spoiled. It was thanks to Ti Madame that he was going to school. But every so often, for no good reason, Marie froze up. The sickness she'd first experienced at the cemetery came over her again. A dark, vile feeling that only grew as she felt even more thankful and grateful to Ti Madame. She had to be jealous of her youth, her striking happiness—all that life had robbed Marie of.

She finished the vanilla rice cake and started on the pâté en croûte. Alain Miranville was celebrating his birthday today and had his friends and family over. On Diego Garcia they'd have all gone to the western side for a big family picnic. After a trip on the dugout canoe, they'd have caught an octopus or two and some red snappers, cooked them, and then gone for a dip in the lagoon. She stopped, a hand in the mixture. Why not? Why shouldn't she head to the beach the next day with Josette and the kids? She hadn't gone for a swim since she'd been wrenched from Diego—not once. The idea transfixed her: she had just about forgotten how water felt.

Joséphin was already jumping up and down in front of the bus when Josette found them at the Victoria station. Makine ran over to them, every bit as excited. They boarded and huddled together on a red imitation leather seat that was all scratched up. Their weight pushed some yellow foam out of the seat's guts.

A big Indian guy squeezed into a uniform headed over to them. The bus had them bouncing at every turn. The ticket inspector fiddled with the device on his belt, pulled out several tickets, and proclaimed, "Five rupees."

"Isn't it four?" Josette said.

He turned to Makine and asked gruffly, "How old?"

"Ten years old," she said as proud as could be.

He repeated, "Five rupees."

Josette crossed her arms in annoyance.

"Kids nine years and up have to pay," the man spat out. "Five rupees."

Marie's eyes met her sister's as she started grumbling. "Ayo, sir . . . Eight, ten, no difference. She's little, this one!"

The inspector's face got even darker. "Papers."

Josette sighed. She didn't have any. Nobody from the Chagos did. Marie pulled out the extra rupee, and that was that.

Trou-aux-Biches. A huge beach lined with filaos. The color of the water was the same as on Diego Garcia, a vibrant, impossibly pure turquoise. How could the sea be both so transparent and so blue? Marie inhaled the salty air, drank it down in huge gulps. She relished the iodide, savored the sea and its air like a banquet. The sand was blindingly white. Under her feet she could feel the deliciously stinging burn. Really, how had she gone all these months, all these years without this? For half a second she felt like she was back home—nothing had changed, life was simple, peaceful, and Gabriel was holding Suzanne by the hand. She walked up to the water. Gabriel had abandoned her. He had to have returned to Mauritius. Not once had he tried to find her. "Go swim!" Josette yelled at her. She turned and looked at her sister, who'd gotten the kids settled in the shade. *Go in.* Josette was right. Driven by an upwelling of joy, she pulled off her clothes and, wearing nothing but her T-shirt and her underwear, dove into the sea.

All the memories her body held surged back into consciousness the moment she made contact with the water. She sank back into the slow movements that gave her a place in the world. Her hair streamed over her nape; she felt every cell of her skin anew, every fiber of her muscles, every one of her bones. She reclaimed herself, her broken self that had survived, as if after a long sojourn outside her body. She dove again. In the coral, so many creatures had taken up residence: needlefish, sea urchins, starfish, shellfish. She parted her lips to take in a bit of salt water, then resurfaced. The salt was harsh on her throat, unpleasant. But essential. She glanced at the beach. Josette was chattering away with the children. God, where was Suzanne?

Marie swam for a few long minutes, her back to the shore. The feeling of going to meet the horizon filled her with faint joy. She kept going, cut off from the world. The sea turned green, then dark blue. When she noticed, an inverse vertigo overcame her. She could make out the chasm beneath her body, the yawning fault amid the abyss. Ten meters deep? Twenty? Down below, unnerving fish followed a choreography she couldn't understand. No matter, she had to keep going. If she kept swimming, she'd reach Diego Garcia at last.

When the first cold current licked at her belly, she ignored it. But the second icy swell brought her back to earth. She turned to the beach; the humans there were black specks on a white swath. She'd gone much too far out. Dipping her head below the surface, she opened her eyes despite her fear. Darkness had swallowed up the underwater precipices. She did her best to come back to the surface. Her arms were starting to hurt; too many years of not swimming. She returned to a breaststroke and was soon out of breath. Then she realized: she was going against the wind, and the waves were picking up.

She tried to overcome her worry, shifted direction ever so slightly, found a crosscurrent and stuck to it. She was making better headway, but the shore wasn't getting any closer. Eventually she noticed a yellow buoy fifty meters away and aimed her sights on it. *Clear your head, don't look at anything but that buoy.* She made a few breaststrokes, her legs going in circles. The buoy wasn't fifty meters away; it was much farther. Her shoulders were hurting. She had to keep at it, but she wasn't in the lagoon's protective realm. In the deep swells, anything could happen. She thought she saw a shadow glide ahead. Massive, unsteady. She shouted: "What was that? Josette!" Tried to get a grip on herself. She'd never heard of shark attacks in Mauritius. There weren't any sharks, there weren't any sharks, there weren't . . . But when the shadow broke the crest of the waves not far off, she shrieked. And the buoy was out of reach! She kept going with all the strength she had. There weren't any sharks . . . After several long minutes of effort, the buoy finally drew near. She thrust out a hand and grabbed at it, gasping. Her arms were barely able to move; her legs weren't responding anymore. She curled up around the buoy like a starfish, looked all around. The shadow was gone. But then she spotted it, hidden in the water's midnight blue. She turned to the shore, so far, so far off. Unfurled her body, let herself float on her back to regain strength. In the sky, a lonely cloud scudded toward a thicker mass, racing to join its family.

After taking a big breath, she went back to swimming and didn't let herself stop. Her arm muscles were stiffening, her heart was pounding, but the real enemy, she knew, was fear. She had to forget the shadows still gliding around her. Not think about what was below her, in the dark depths, not think about a thing. Dazed and determined, she swam, swam, kept on swimming, and when her feet finally touched sand, she stopped, stunned, her rib cage run through by a thousand invisible knives. She let herself collapse on the sand, half-dead. The sun embraced her with its fire.

From where she was, she couldn't see Josette and the kids. She'd drifted so far. She slowed her heartbeat with drawn-out breaths. Let herself lie on the sand. Then, when she felt ready, she made her way down the shore, alternating between walking and swimming. There was nothing left to fear now.

The silhouette of her sister, standing beside Joséphin and Makine, her hands shading her eyes, watching the sea, finally stood out against the sunlight. She'd succeeded. Full of pride, Marie dove one last time and popped up in front of Josette, a huge smile on her lips.

March 1974

Sacré-Cœur Primary was a few minutes from Villa Talipot. A railing atop a low wall separated the schoolyard from the street. Anyone peering over it could see children hunched over their notebooks. The building consisted of five classrooms on the ground floor, all of them overlooking the schoolyard. Gabriel remembered his own school, with its religious decorations—wooden crucifix, Virgin Mary in plaster, handprints in paint, coloring-book pages messily filled in. Had things changed all that much? Back then, everyone had sung "God Save the Queen" in the morning; they'd lined up in twos to salute the Union Jack as it was raised. These days, the kids sang "Motherland" and shouted at each other in Kreol in the schoolyard. The four-colored flag fluttered in the air.

He was haunted by a desire to see Joséphin. For months, he'd been mulling over Angèle's words, going over them again and again in his mind. Marie hated him. Joséphin wasn't his son. The harshness of that confession. Jean-Joris. But a sire wasn't necessarily a father. Who had rocked, fed, carried, and soothed Joséphin? Who had helped him to grow, had been there for his first steps?

One morning when he didn't have classes of his own, Gabriel decided to stand in front of the school. Recess was usually at ten o'clock. He walked to the wall and hoisted himself up to the railing. Through the open windows, the murmur of children floated from a classroom: multiplication tables, recited in English.

"What are you doing?" A teacher leaned over to a small Creole boy who was fidgeting.

"He's bothering me!" the boy protested.

His desk mate elbowed him. All faces were turned to the teacher.

"I want you to speak English, please."

What was the point of independence? Kreol was always seen as a lesser language.

In the neighboring classroom, the children looked younger. On huge sheets of construction paper, they drew or colored pictures. Gabriel tried to make out the heads, looking for the darkest-skinned ones. To no avail. The bell finally rang. The children yelled, chairs scraped the floor, the sounds of zippers and backpack buckles reverberated, and they spilled out into the schoolyard. There had to be a good hundred and fifty of them. There was no way he could pick out Joséphin in the crowd. Gabriel's hands clenched around the rails.

"Can I help you?" The icy voice made him jolt. A nun in a light-colored habit looked at him sharply, a wooden cross hanging from her neck. Everything about her indicated that she was the head teacher. "Do you want me to call the police?"

"Oh . . . Forgive me, it's just . . ." *My son*—the words didn't escape his lips. He jumped down from the wall, ashamed and annoyed to have been caught, and headed off, practically at a run.

On his way home, he stopped at a greasy spoon serving fried noodles and polished off a whole bowl with an empty gaze. Could he do this some other way? Go back to school, politely introduce himself as the father of Joséphin Ladouceur, say that he wanted to see his son, wait for the head teacher to decide whether he was telling the truth or not. *Some identification, sir?* Then she'd see. *Gabriel Neymorin? There's nobody named Neymorin here.* At best she'd ask him to leave; at worst, she'd call the police. He should go back. The damage had been done in any case.

School lunch started at noon, so he had time. He lingered in the neighborhood, bought some *makatias coco* from a street vendor. Oh, how he loved those. He buried his nose in the packet, let the aroma fill his nostrils. The brioches were soft and golden, as round as communion wafers. Their centers were a sugary coconut paste, with a deliciously grainy texture that provided a perfect amount of crunch. Gabriel walked back to the school, chose the other end of the wall, and climbed up to the railing. When the bell rang again, his heart almost leaped.

The kids were swarming, gathering into groups for different things. Some sat in a circle to eat their sandwiches, jabbering as seriously as adults. Others put down their lunches to go play hopscotch or jump rope. There were shrieks, shrill laughs, sometimes sobbing when kids skinned their knees. Suddenly a face caught his eye. The boy had ebony-black skin and frizzy hair, and more than that he was standing on his own in the schoolyard. He opened his lunchbox. Nobody was sitting with him.

Gabriel's head felt like it was spinning.

"Joséphin!" He barely got the name out. He gripped the railing and stood all the way up. His movements sent the makatias coco flying to the ground. "Joséphin!" This time it was a yell.

The boy looked up and finally saw him.

"Come here, Joséphin!"

The boy walked over slowly.

His son had gotten thinner, longer, as if stretched out. Gabriel was ready to climb over the railing, but the boy didn't come any closer, just stared at him from a distance, as if he were seeing this man for the first time. Gabriel could feel the clamminess of his sweaty palms. Impossible. Had he forgotten him? Had Joséphin forgotten him?

"Don't you remember me, kid?"

The boy shook his head.

"It's me. Father. Your father! Joséphin, have you forgotten Diego Garcia?" A sob was rising in his throat. His son didn't recognize him.

Joséphin dropped his sandwich and ran to the other end of the schoolyard.

Turbulence. Some passengers are stirring. Fastening seatbelts, groaning, glancing this way and that. What if death were here in the cabin? Them, us, me, today? The end of the Chagossian delegation.

In the carpeted aisles, the flight attendants are joking, and their laughs reassure those seated. I don't have a fear of flying, myself. Only of boats.

A soft voice comes over the intercom, announcing that, once we are no longer experiencing turbulence, dinner will be served. I'm planning to save the cheese and dessert for lunch tomorrow. Once you've experienced poverty, you never forget it. The present is so fleeting; only the future counts. If there was one, I'd also stow the miniature bottle of wine.

March 1974

Since dawn, the whole place had been bustling. The Miranvilles were hosting a reception that evening—the director of the Mauritius Commercial Bank and his wife would be having dinner with them. Ti Madame had laid out a battle plan. She'd gathered everybody—Rama, Félicie, and Marie—in the kitchen to go through the menu.

"For appetizers: fish in aspic with capers. Then two mains: king shrimp in red sauce with heart of palm salad and roast venison with sweet potatoes mousseline." She paused. "I told my husband that it was too much, but he was insistent. For dessert: frosted pineapple bombes. They've already been ordered from La Flore Mauricienne—perfect." She crossed it off her list. "Coffee, liqueurs, and of course petits fours, canapés, and so on and so forth."

Ti Madame really was something else; Marie loved that gesture she was in the habit of making, a light twirl of the finger that suggested how silly she found this whole spectacle.

But they did have to get down to work. Rama pounced on the hearts of palm, which were easy to prepare, and left Marie to deal with the king shrimp. Of course. Ever since she'd shown up, the Indian woman had been giving her the evil eye. She had to see Marie as a rival, and all the kindness that Ti Madame lavished upon Marie only made matters worse. One day when a vase shattered in the lounge, Rama had pointed the finger at her. "Not true! I didn't break nothing!" Marie had a feeling Rama had been the one behind it.

Madame Miranville had looked at the porcelain debris and shrugged. "Oh, I didn't like it anyway." And she'd asked Rama to clean it up. Marie still felt mortified.

There was a salad bowl full of king shrimp. Marie set to work peeling and deveining them, then throwing the shells and heads in a pot with some oil at the bottom, some spices, and some *satini cotomili*. The stock would be the base for the red sauce. There was no time to waste.

Around four in the afternoon, Joséphin came home from school. He was looking withdrawn, wary. In class, the other students mocked his accent, gave him all sorts of trouble. "You're Black, you smell!" He didn't understand all this cruelty being heaped on him.

"Forget about them, sweetie. They'll say that, but you're the smartest of them all. They're jealous. Just listen to the teacher, don't listen to them!" That was the only thing Marie thought about: him succeeding. Being able to go to school was a privilege, so much so that she hadn't dared to mention it to Josette. Makine worked. She was just a child, but that didn't matter. During the week, when she left the small Pamplemousses restaurant where she was a dishwasher some days, she came and said hello to Marie at the villa. Through the gate, Marie gave her bread, cakes, candy.

"Any news, at the camp?"

That day, Makine wasn't smiling. "Every night they fight. Mommy is tired of Daddy. Yesterday he bashed her."

"Bashed? Ayo, Makine! Don't you tell me that!"

Her niece exhaled. "He saw Mommy with Gaudry. Never bashed her before. But yesterday . . ."

Marie recalled Josette's words. *Don't ever tell Gabriel. Not a thing!*

Makine couldn't hold back anymore. "I'm tired of him, too. Yes, Auntie, I wish he was dead."

"My girl, I don't like words like that."

Her niece wouldn't back down. That was the truth.

"All the truth in the world, that's no honey for throats," Marie said reprovingly. She slipped Makine a small coin before she left, shocked by this news. Christian was jealous. Christian had turned violent. She would go back to see Josette on Sunday and bring her not just a ration of rice and sugar but a bit of herself.

"Mamita." Joséphin's tone was plaintive.

"Not now, my boy."

The venison was cooking, but she needed to finish making the sweet potato mousseline that Rama hadn't bothered to prepare, of course. Marie mashed the orange flesh with a fork, added some pepper and chili. All that was left to do was to put the concoction on the stove when the guests finished their apéritifs. She walked past the laundry room for some cool air before putting on a perfectly ironed black dress. Rama and Félicie were wearing the same thing—their evening outfit.

Around six, as the Mauritius Commercial Bank director and his wife were making their way into the lounge, Joséphin slipped into the kitchen again.

"You! Didn't you hear me? I told you to stay in the little house!"

Félicie was removing the fish in aspic from the mold and setting it on a beautiful platter.

"I need to finish making dinner, Joséphin. Go and play, please."

"But I haven't eaten."

Marie wiped her forehead. Joséphin was in the habit of having a snack when he got home from school; she'd completely forgotten to make him some tea and biscuits. She grabbed a banana from the basket, opened the refrigerator, and took out some yogurt, then handed both to her son. He sat down to peel the banana.

"They're done with their apéritifs," Félicie warned her.

Rama, who was in charge of serving them in the lounge, came into the kitchen. "Oh, that beggar's still here?"

Marie gritted her teeth and ignored her, while setting the red sauce on the stove to warm up. "Eat, my boy."

"I'll bring out the mains," Félicie announced as she hoisted the fish in aspic.

Cries of admiration came from the other side of the wall.

"Mamita?"

Marie glanced at her son. Too busy.

"I saw Daddy this morning."

What? Daddy? He had to be dreaming. "Joséphin! Enough!"

But her son wouldn't be stopped. "Really, it was Daddy!"

A wave of dizziness came over her. She had to sit down.

"He came to find me at school. He even got up on that wall."

Marie's eyes looked skyward. Everything was swimming. A beauty mark behind his ear, a hooked nose. Suzanne sick. All of them on the beach. All of them on the Pointe de l'Est! Joséphin, my little coconut, my little Jo', good and Black, good and strong, a good zilois.

"Are you okay, Marie-Pierre?" Félicie was hunched over her.

Gabriel was in Mauritius. So close. His skin. His arms. On the other side of the wall, the soiree was still going. She tried to get a grip on herself, but the prospect of happiness, of maybe finding happiness again, was too much. She'd forgotten that, her heart clenching, her guts wrenching.

"Marie, next course," Félicie said sternly as she took out the heart of palm salad.

Marie's hands were trembling as she filled the serving dish with king shrimp and made her way into the dining room.

At the table, Ti Madame had the bank director roaring with laughter. The mood was lighthearted, intoxicating.

"Ah! Now that's a proper red sauce," Alain Miranville shouted. "Just the way my nénène used to make it!"

Marie served, taking care not to stain the tablecloth.

"My wife's got a knack for finding the best help."

Ti Madame stiffened; there was a hint of ice in her glare.

"And she knows her business! Without her, I'd have lost this house."

"Alain." Ti Madame's voice was sharp.

"You're the daughter of Léon Neymorin, after all," the director said approvingly.

Ti Madame was rigid. Her fork banged on the china. Marie rushed to get back to the kitchen, her thoughts a jumble. The daughter of Léon Neymorin. An odd little idea had gotten into her head, and she couldn't shake it.

In the kitchen, Joséphin was finishing his yogurt.

All the pieces of the puzzle were starting to fall into place. Ti Madame. That odd sense of recognition she'd felt that first time in the cemetery. Her being hired so quickly, her nice salary, their privileges, the little presents for Joséphin. Him being sent to school. Nausea rose in her throat.

She made her way into the room, bearing the bombes lacquered with coconut milk. Alain Miranville was guffawing at the bank director's words, while Ti Madame was chatting away with the wife. Évelyne Miranville-Neymorin. It was her. Gabriel's sister. Their eyes met. Marie didn't understand everything just yet, only that it was her—it had to be her—who'd orchestrated all this. The cemetery . . . the meeting . . . He'd humiliated her, abandoned her. Fobbed her off on his sister. And now she was a miserable domestic servant. "Marie?" Ti Madame's voice wasn't haughty anymore. Even her husband wasn't saying anything, Marie shakily set the dessert on the table and placed the knife and the cake server to the side. Professional to the last. Nénène to the bitter end. She stared at the lips, the eyes, the forehead of her boss. His features in hers. Skin the color of milk tea. Silky hair. A slightly hooked nose. She stayed put. Let the gold-plated betrayal wash over her.

It all happened so fast.

No more talk about your father, you hear?

She'd dragged me to the little house where we were staying. A sheet, our belongings in it, fast—it wasn't her first time. Ti Madame tried to reason with her. *Marie, this isn't what you think it is. Gabriel only wanted to do right by you. Would you like me to call him?*

I remember being so surprised. Gabriel. How did Ti Madame know my father?

My mother wouldn't calm down.

Nothing to say to him. You keep your family.

Ti Madame, Évelyne, Auntielyne. I don't recall when I connected the dots. Not right then, that's for sure. You were livid, Mama. You didn't explain a thing. You even left without the month's pay.

Outside, there wasn't any bus anymore. It was dark.

We're going to walk, Joséphin.

I was sobbing. I didn't want to go. It was so nice at Villa Talipot.

Hush. Our dignity, we got that.

We finally got to the Charrelle camp, the metal shack, the braided mat, the roaches. Angèle tried to soothe me. You didn't hug me that night, Mama.

Your father, well . . . Your father!

You were going in circles.

And I was stuck between two impossible loyalties.

March 1974

Gutters full of mud. Dust. Power lines at ground level. The old, busted cart without any wheels. Gabriel was in the slum. Ever since the phone call the night before that had sliced through the evening, Évelyne's voice had been hammering in his thoughts. "She knows everything, Gaby. She figured it all out. She left with Joséphin."

He felt hollow. He'd anticipated this moment as much as he'd feared it. There was no going back now. He was ready for the worst from Marie. About Suzanne and Joséphin, about being forsaken for so many years. He was ready. He wanted to see them again, plead for their forgiveness.

A warm light bathed the camp; in an hour, the sun would set. Silhouettes popped up here and there, along a metal wall, a shrub, or a shack, some recognizable, others unfamiliar or impossible to identify. But Marie—he could pick her out at a glance; that he was sure of. A shrill whistle went up as he walked; someone else picked it up farther off. Shadows appeared and disappeared before him, and then he saw her.

Her hair was cut short. Her hips narrow. Her feet bare as always. The same woman, even after enduring so much. A whittled-down, weathered beauty. Gabriel met her uncalm gaze, and his chest almost exploded.

Marie stood in front of him. Her whole body seemed to heap scorn on him; she was ramrod straight, in a warlike stance. "Some nerve you've got coming here," she spat out.

All his excuses went up in smoke. Wrath massed on that mouth he'd peppered so many times with kisses.

"I . . . I wanted to talk to you."

She took a step, walked past him without a glance. "Let's walk."

The roles were inverted. Years ago, she'd been the one to follow. He thought he could make out the head of a little boy behind a sheet of metal, but he didn't linger. She was already headed toward the road.

"Marie, I've thought about you day and night. Not an hour has gone by that you haven't been with me—your skin, your smile. You might not believe me, but that's the truth. I've woken up at night shouting your name. I was going mad, terrified by what the British were planning to do, trapped. It was impossible to leave Diego to be with you; there were no boats, not for us in any case. But the Americans could come and go as they liked. As soon as I could come, I did. I swear."

She held up her hand to make him stop talking. Far off, the sugarcane fields rippled under the wind. Marie kept on walking, her eyes on a point straight ahead, silent.

"And Joséphin! I couldn't leave him like that. Évelyne told me how sweet he is, how smart. Doesn't he deserve to go to school, to have a better life than in this . . . this dump? What's past is past, Marie, but that's my son. I'd give everything for him. For you. For Suzanne, too. I think of her as my daughter, my own flesh."

A stony silence was her only answer. He felt powerless. When they came to the foot of a jacaranda tree, at the edge of the field, she stopped. With the last few days' breeze, the pale mauve flowers had fallen, scattering a lilac snow on the land. She tilted her head up to him, revealing two huge dark rings under her eyes.

"Are you proud of yourself? You think you're a good father? Great. Maybe you should give some thought to your daughter, too." She set her hand on the jacaranda's trunk.

Gabriel's head was spinning. He could barely get any air into his lungs. Yes, his daughter, his little Suzanne, right there in the hole, under the dirt covered with fresh flowers.

He couldn't breathe.

I had a sister once. She liked animals, running races on the beach, little rice cakes. I was three. I don't have any other pictures of her in my head. No photos. Cameras weren't a thing on Diego Garcia.

I've forgotten her face. Did Suzanne have a smooth, round forehead like our mother? Dimples in her cheeks? The only image I have left of her is a body contorted under a sheet.

She was always chewing me out because she loved me. That's what you used to tell me, Mama. What I know is that we played together with Mérou. We collected shells. We made sandcastles to stomp on.

What kind of brother was I to her? For three years I was her little brother.

January 1971

Suzanne.

The funeral.

When she realized that her daughter wasn't breathing anymore, Marie let out a long, silent scream. A pain unable to work its way out of her lungs, her throat. She was sure she had passed out. But as she heard Josette's sobbing, and then Angèle's, and before long the whole camp's, she realized she wasn't unconscious. Everything that was happening was right there, utterly real. Even Christian realized and was blubbering, his fist clenched and his belly tight. When Gaudry Depaz arrived, maybe an hour later, along with a doctor who'd taken pity on them, he'd fallen to his knees before the small body. Marie was stock-still, paralyzed by suffering.

Women set the stiffened, contorted corpse on a mat in the middle of the room, went to gather a few flowers on the roadside, lit candles, whispered prayers. The doctor had made his diagnosis. "It looks like tetanus. The infection must have spread rapidly." He crossed himself and left.

"Hail Mary, full of grace," murmured the mouths around Suzanne.

A more distinct voice filled the hut's stale air. It was Angèle, intoning a song from Diego Garcia. The same one, possibly, that she'd sung for old Félix. Josette added her voice, as did Gisèle, then Makine and Becca, and all the other Îlois gathered around her. The soul of the Chagos intertwined with that of Suzanne, as if to show her the way forward.

Slowly, Marie joined the chorus of women. The melody was a wave, a gloom, a purification—singing felt like swimming, confronting the sobs of backwash.

Nobody slept that night. Silence, shot through with whispers, surrounded Suzanne. Joséphin sat vigil at his sister's bedside; nobody had been able to pry him away from the hut. Marie felt like her little girl was playing a horrible trick on them. Any minute now, she might open her eyes, bound to her feet, start playing with Mérou, tell her stories, splash her brother as she jumped into the water. The image gutted her. How could Marie accept that the flesh of her flesh would never do anything again, not ever, with her joie de vivre?

The next day, Gaudry came at nine in the morning with a man in black. A deacon who worked at the next parish over. "My condolences, ma'am. I'm praying for your strength in this ordeal." She thanked him with an unthinking nod. "Father Larronde has settled in the Seychelles, so I'm standing in for him." She felt grateful to Gaudry. Father Larronde was indeed from Mauritius, and it touched her that he'd remembered their beloved clergyman, but soon all she could think of was her pain. The deacon leaned over her girl and traced the sign of the cross across her icy forehead. He pulled out his rosary, began his prayers—the chaplet was like a final goodbye.

"My Father," Josette said with a sigh, "she needs to be buried."

But where? Marie was overcome by sobbing again. They were going to put her girl in the ground. Trees and flowers were in the ground. Roses and mango trees were in the ground. But Suzanne? The deacon waved his hands apologetically. The Saint-Georges Cemetery wouldn't be an option. To be buried there, they would have to buy a plot, and the price was far too high. The only possibility, alas, was the mass grave. Marie shuddered.

Even on Diego Garcia, such burial grounds didn't exist. Her girl in a pit, absolutely not. She'd sooner dig a grave with her bare hands at the edge of the field! And that would have been her first choice under other circumstances. The deacon looked embarrassed. "That's not allowed by law; you could run into trouble."

That was the last straw. Trouble? She could run into trouble? What sort of trouble could possibly top having been wrenched from her island, sold like a slave, thrown into the misery of a slum, and betrayed by the man she loved?

"My girl is dead. Eight years, that's how young! Forget trouble."

The deacon stepped back.

On the corrugated metal topped by a woven mat, a white sheet draped over her, Suzanne was carried out by Henri and Jean-Joris, finally keeping their word. Marie, her aunt, and Josette at her side, walked right behind, with Makine and Joséphin trailing. Slowly the Îlois formed a procession to the edge of the sugarcane field. The red earth was blazing. Gaudry had found a jacaranda tree and dug the soil at its foot. Marie approached. A hole. A void. She imagined it was big enough for two.

In the middle of the dirges, ever so carefully, ever so tenderly, Suzanne Ladouceur returned home to the earth.

IV

The plane is over Egypt. Soon we'll be past Africa, and we'll reach Europe. Where the world as we know it, as we bear it, was invented.

My best memory of the old continent is also the cruelest one. November 2000, the High Court in London. My mother was starting to get weak. Her hair knotted under a wrap, her gaze unwavering despite her small glasses; she'd claimed to be too afraid of flying to come. In fact, she was pushing me into the future, passing on the torch to me.

Our defense was solid. I had faith in the lawyer this time. Rightly so.

After a long trial, the High Court ruled that the depopulation of the Chagos was "unlawful" and in blatant violation of the Charter of the United Nations. It granted us the right to return, at least in theory, to particular islands of the archipelago. But not Diego Garcia.

Of course, the other side appealed. Of course, the whole matter was kept in limbo. There would be more waiting, always.

September 11th. The war in Afghanistan. The free world in upheaval. Panic widespread. The Diego Garcia military base turned into a massive aircraft carrier for B-52s. Nuclear submarines crisscrossing the bay. The sea turtles fleeing the Indian Ocean.

Our return visit was canceled: suspended. Nobody knew what was happening anymore. There were bigger fish for the Americans and the

British to fry. And now Mauritius, suddenly emerging from a long slumber, was opposing the United Kingdom and insisting on sovereignty over the Chagos. There would be so many more struggles, protests, marches. What buoyed us was the dream of returning home. I believed in it; God, I believed in it so much!

The last slap in the face was June 2004. Two Orders in Council from Queen Elizabeth. Decrees that overturned the High Court in London's decision. Access to the Chagos was now, and forevermore, forbidden to commoners like us. Our hopes were dashed.

The verdict was based on a feasibility study. What feasibility? Who was sent out to do it? Repopulating the archipelago is impossible, the study claimed: too expensive, prejudicial to the environment, and above all, as if that weren't enough, apparently it would be dangerous for us Îlois because of rising sea levels.

Our lawyer, Robin Mardemootoo, made the news with his reaction: "If sea levels are rising for the Chagossians, they're rising for the American military, too. The environment? Generations have lived there in harmony with nature. We can't say that much for the military armada at Diego Garcia." His conclusion was withering: "If the Chagossians had been white, they'd never have been forced out like this."

January 1975

"We make a mistake once, and we spend the rest of our lives fixing it. Trying to! Because we know it'll come to naught." Gabriel was looking for his packet of Gitanes, his lighter. "That's my life. Want one?"

Évelyne's puffy face evinced her fatigue at this overlong conversation; she shook her head.

He inhaled the tobacco smoke, spat it out into the navy-blue night. "My mistake's always been staying quiet. I'm making up for it with you, Lizard."

As he uttered those words, shame flooded him; it was with Évelyne that he'd started lying, betraying, hiding. To protect her, not to hurt her. And suffering had come all the same—from afar, by other means, not that it mattered, because it always came. A light came on in the distance, blinked a few times, and then vanished. He held a hand to his temples. In his head, the vise was tightening, as torturously as it had for months now.

"You should rest, Gaby. You're worrying me." Évelyne sighed. "I do wonder how you get on with teaching at this point. Don't your students complain? Don't your colleagues say a thing?"

He snickered as he stubbed out the butt. "I show up, I assign classwork, I read from the textbook, I correct papers, I give them homework, and that's the hour done. I do it all over again with the next one, then the one after. I keep going without thinking about what I'm doing, what I'm saying. I just keep going." He lit another cigarette—Évelyne tried to stop him, but it was too late. "I can't take it anymore."

The way he said that tiny little truth caught him by surprise. A lifeless voice, as if a fact they'd avoided for far too long was finally crushing them all. He was at the end of his rope. Drained of all energy, all hope. His body floated in a limbo. He kept on walking, talking to people, but it was another self talking, another self walking. He didn't believe in anything anymore.

"Marie . . . at least let me see Joséphin. I wanted to help you, that's all, send him to a good school. Is he still going to school? Marie, please. He's so little, he needs a dad. I'm sorry, Marie. Please let me have a minute. I want to see him, so that he knows that I love him."

Ten times, a hundred times Gabriel had gone to the Charrette camp over the months. In the morning at dawn, before she'd left for the sugarcane fields, at night when she was back from work, on Saturdays, Sundays. He'd tried everything: remorse, anger, pleading, logic, love, religion. Ten times, a hundred times she'd refused, forcing him to go back alone, torn, to his pathetic, sad job.

"You've lost weight, Gaby. You're smoking, smoking, smoking. You're crying. You aren't sleeping. You need to get a grip on yourself." Évelyne thrust her chin out authoritatively.

"Lizard!" he said with a trace of awe. "Do that again."

"Do what again?"

He smiled, looking off. "Do that thing with your chin again."

214

She jumped up from the chair and crossed the verandah. "Gabriel, I mean it."

"I do, too," he said. "You look just like her when you do that."

"Like who?"

"Mama."

She froze. Her body tensed, as if she were wavering between giving him a kiss or a slap. Finally, she said, "Stop it." Then she went and sat down.

"You know what the problem with dead people is, Gaby?" she whispered after a minute. "It's that they're never really dead. Their ghosts are more alive than you and me."

He let the thought settle. That was it. That was exactly it. Suzanne was, in Marie's eyes, more alive than he was; his mother was more alive to him than Évelyne because she wasn't there. How odd and unsatisfying human beings were.

"Look at yourself," she said. "You're picking the wrong battle, Gaby. The dead, the real dead, I mean the living who are suffering, are the ones who get up every morning crying for the night so that the day will be behind them, so that sleep will carry them away from pain. They're the ones who really need us." Gabriel could feel her eyes blazing. Évelyne grabbed his cigarette and stubbed it out in the yellow marble ashtray. "That's enough smoking for you."

Marie's face came in horrible waves. *He's not your son! Go!* She was yelling, her hair like snakes aghast, stunned by sudden light. Joséphin. So proud of him at first. He looked at the baby, thinking, *Look, that's a piece of me, some mark of my time on this land. I haven't lived in vain.* Then: *Even if he isn't mine, he's close to me.* But Joséphin today was a stranger. His son might not be dead, but he was as good as a ghost.

"And while we're on the subject of fathers," Évelyne continued calmly, "I know you don't want me to talk to you about the one we've got, but just listen. He isn't well."

On the vault of the sky, the stars were a fine white dust. "I hope he dies."

"Someday you'll tell me. You know I'm mad at him, too, but the hate you've got . . . I don't get it, Gaby."

He wavered. In his memories, Ludna had been sobbing for years and years.

"Is it because of Mama?" she asked quietly.

"You say he really isn't well?"

She sighed and didn't press the matter. The bomb needed to be defused. "He wants us to meet with the lawyer."

"Us?" He lit another cigarette that she didn't have it in her to grab.

"You, me, and . . . Benoît."

"Oh, Benoît?"

"Yes. He's expected to arrive next month."

His cigarette was burning away: a light-bluish ash scattered over his shirt.

"Gaby! There's an ashtray right there!"

He could feel the heat spreading to the pads of his fingers; he dropped the butt in the slab of veined marble. "Leaving London to talk about inheritances—now, that's to his taste."

His sister nodded. Benoît had never been close with them, not even when they were kids. Haughty, pretentious, he was the worthy son of their father but in no way the male protector that in happy families—but did such figures exist in those?—they called a brother.

January 1975

With her imaginary pencil, she sculpted letters in the air, shaping edges in the night, perfecting curves, here a mountain, there a beach, to get around her embarrassment. A big M, a little a, a big M again, little a, little n, the way Gabriel had taught her—her hand, a handprint in the sea urchin chalk.

Had she really lived those hours spent with Gabriel? That madness at the moment of leaving the island? Her mother's grave, so far, so far . . . The cemetery had to be overrun by brambles by now. Or maybe those men who'd grabbed the island for themselves were tending to the graves so as not to bring the dead's curses upon themselves; raking the path, weeding the grasses, wiping the gravestones as smooth as a baby's cheek with a cloth. What did Diego Garcia look like now? How could the sea be changed into anything other than the sea? The beach into something other than the beach? When she cast her thoughts on it, it was her eternal island that came back to mind, the sensation of water on her skin, the Pointe de l'Est pier, her village of Pointe Marianne, the plot, the smell of copra and iodide. Not the prison the British and the Americans now ran. Did they even see the beauty of her island, at least?

Its purity? She dropped her invisible pencil on the mattress and shut her eyes. So much squandered.

"Joséphin's stuck unhappy." Angèle was peeling manioc on the table of her little hut. When she didn't have any courage left, Marie took refuge at her aunt's house. She unburdened herself in silence, barely saying a word, scared for her son. For months now, every night as he was being tucked in, Joséphin had cried. Marie pulled the sheet up to his shoulders, told him a story, some fairy tale from Diego Garcia. Sometimes she just whispered the Lord's Prayer. The moment she left his bedside, he broke out sobbing. She came back to soothe him and couldn't let go of his hand until he fell asleep. January was always hardest. The memory of Suzanne, being torn from their island, all of it came back to her in horrible gusts. A heavy stone weighed on her lungs; for a bit she was sure she could hear her ribs cracking, snapping one by one like rubber bands stretched too tight. Her body was frozen. The pain drained her. Blood didn't flow between her legs anymore, not even a little. She felt empty.

"I'll say this, my girl," Angèle declared as she pushed away the manioc peelings. "Your son needs a dad. It's not good, that sagren of his." The accusation was cutting. A bad mother. Her aunt's eyes were downcast. "Gabriel never threw out the little boy, not even when he was told Joséphin was Jean-Jo's."

Marie exploded. "Two years he doesn't say a thing, and when he gets back to Mauritius he doesn't come to me, he sends his sister. Makes me her nénène!" She clicked her tongue. "Horses bite rock. But goats break their teeth."

Angèle gathered the manioc skins in newspaper. "I think he wants to help. We're poor as dirt, and he's not."

Marie didn't reply; she turned her head and fixated on a detail: a chipped plate on the crate in front of her. She was in the habit of doing that when her emotions got to be too much. Concentrate. Push away the sadness. Angèle wiped her forehead with her sleeve. The shack reverberated with the sound of the knife chopping manioc into small cubes.

"That wrath of yours, my girl, it's your fire."

Angèle was spot-on. Marie drew on that fury for the strength she needed to get through the day. She needed to be angry at Gabriel. The chipped plate bothered her, everything got hazy: the table, the crate, the little wooden shelf, the mat on the floor. But, unexpectedly, it was Angèle who broke out in tears.

"I'm sorry, I'm sorry!" her aunt finally said. "Gabriel came, came here . . . Long, long, long ago."

Marie was stunned, jerked back. Surely she couldn't have heard that right. But her ears weren't lying. Her brain had heard those words right.

"You were in the sugar fields," Angèle went on. "First thing when he returned to Mauritius, Gabriel came here. I found him thin, you know? He wanted to see you, kiss Joséphin. He only saw this mess." She paused. "He was asking about Suzanne. I couldn't tell him. My stomach was all knots. Still is. I told him lies. He paid for the others." Her sweat brought her damp fingers up to clasp her throat slowly. "I said Suzanne was better . . ."

Marie was reeling. And to think that she'd been expecting Gabriel then, that she'd still believed in him!

"Then I pushed him out. *She hates you!* That's what I said. *Don't you come back! You betrayed her!* That's what was in my heart. I'm sorry, my girl."

Marie got up. That was existence in a nutshell: a long string of truths and lies that could bring your life crashing down with a word, a yell, a bit of silence.

The imaginary pencil went back up in the darkness, tracing words of apology, of caress. Calls. Marie would have liked that: to know how to write for good. The little that Gabriel had taught her was now sleeping in a nook of her memory. Reading had gotten hard again. *Mama* was the word she remembered best. She hoped that one day Joséphin would know more than she did. But for now there was no more school, no more classes. She listened to his breathing, moved by the breath of this baby she'd managed to keep alive for seven years. The tears were heavy under her eyelids, and she turned to the sheet metal that served as a wall.

For months, my mother stood in the way. She refused to let me see my father. I had to stay hidden in the shack every time he came. I could hear yelling, pleading. I thought it was my fault. My godmother soothed me as best she could. She put sugar in my tea and cooked me karays of *kat-kat* manioc, a mixture of roots, spices, and little bits of pork, bought at half price when the market was closing for the day. That taste in my mouth is associated with heartbreak. With sagren. I don't eat it anymore.

February 1975

The sky was darkening already. Between the old palm trees of the Place d'Armes, the wind slipped through with threatening whispers. Gabriel shut his book. At his feet, single-file rows of ants were headed in the same direction. Suddenly he understood. A cyclone. "Don't just sit there!" a man already starting to run yelled at him. Clouds were massing over Port-Louis, growing more and more electric. Gabriel didn't wait a minute longer. He'd barely gotten moving when the view started to get hazy.

The downpour suddenly pounded at his shoulders, heavy and cruel. On the road, things were rolling: a few crates that a street vendor had abandoned, a shoe, a bicycle wheel. A gust forced him to stop—to crouch down so that the wind spared him. To try to keep going. The asphalt was almost liquid, and the water seeped into his shoes, his socks. No time to waste now. Gabriel kept going, bent over. Under normal circumstances he would have reached his apartment in five minutes, but the wind was to his right, making progress nearly impossible. A dog flew past in front of him; his owner stuck out his arms and just barely caught him. A cyclone! He crouched down again to keep going, practically crawling over the sopping ground. The rain was driving through his clothes, his skin. He could barely see a meter ahead.

By sheer determination, he finally got to his place. Everyone with a roof of their own was already huddled under it. The building's door opened, the wind rushed in and slammed it open. He pressed his back to the panel to lock it—first lock, second lock, done! Soaked to the bone, shivering, he reached around unthinkingly for the light switch: the electricity was out. He could barely make out the stairs in the darkness. His sopping clothes stuck to his body.

The wind grew harsher. The rain pounded the roof. He got upstairs and took refuge in his apartment. He'd never really had to rummage through the jumble of his little nook; he scrounged up an oil lamp, some candles, unearthed a few bits of cardboard, some thick tape, some rags, and started boarding up his windows. The icy caress of water running down his neck startled him. He realized he still hadn't taken off his clothes. He changed, rubbed a towel all over himself, and came back into the living room. A weak light outlined the furniture. He looked for tin cans in the cabinet, pulled out three or four. Tuna and corn. He kept rummaging. Cookies. The wind was now howling, making his windows bang.

Joséphin.

How could those shacks in the Charrette camp withstand it all? They wouldn't. But Joséphin. Going outside was too dangerous at this point. So he had to wait and pray to God.

⋈

Two days. Two long days shut in his apartment. The cyclone was unrelenting. Water poured in despite the thick walls, and there weren't enough buckets to catch it all. Not enough pails. The image of his son selling water at the cemetery was gut-wrenching. Back then, Évelyne's words had been precise and terrible: *Your son looks like he's six going on sixty.* Giving up on him wasn't an option. Marie hadn't understood this very simple fact: he couldn't abandon them.

Her anger swept everything else aside, had made her mean. The young woman of the past, smiling and lively, had given way to a gorgon. Keeping two people who loved each other from meeting, from talking? That was nothing short of cruelty. All he felt for her was rage, and sometimes this rage shifted into hatred. But that night the sky was raining down on the land to rip it open, to bring about her death. Imagining Marie buried beneath it, with Joséphin, was worse than being there.

On the third day, an unreal calm fell on the island. The lashing wind quieted; the rain no longer hammered everything. Gabriel went down to the lobby, opened the door, carefully, before pulling it wide open. The street was gutted. The power lines were touching the water. But through the mist, the sky was blue. Fragile, deceptive. They'd just entered the eye of the cyclone. The calm would be momentary, the end worse still. Gabriel had, at best, thirty or forty minutes before the storm resumed. He ran. The prospect that something, anything, might have happened to his son sent all caution flying. He sprinted back up to the apartment; grabbed a bag; stuffed it with two blankets, some canned food, and the last bottles of mineral water he had; and set off at full speed. From his place to the camp was half an hour by foot. He was risking everything. But it was the death of others he feared, not his own.

Outside was desolation. Along the road were overturned cars, trees bent over, branches strewn everywhere. Corpses of dogs, which stirred up painful memories. Above him, the azure was a yawning maw, like a drop of blue on the white canvas of the sky. He tried to go faster, spurred by the thought that if he died there, caught by the cyclone, he wouldn't have even seen Joséphin one last time.

The sky was starting to darken again as Gabriel came down the final stretch. The red earth had turned into mud; the water gushed out of flooded gutters. The rain resumed all of a sudden. *Faster, faster!* He crossed the canal. Third shack on the left. He hadn't forgotten. Dashed under the curtain twisted by the wind. In the middle of the room was a lopsided table. To the right was a board that was supposed to serve as a bed. Darkness swallowed up the hut, but he could make out, crouching in a corner, Joséphin and Marie. They were there. Joséphin! He heard himself shrieking. His son dashed over and jumped into his arms.

Marie drew near. Her hair was undone, her dress cut above the ankle. Barefoot, as always. Her eyes were wide with shock.

"Daddy!"

He let the warmth of those two syllables envelop him, burn him. It had been so long. His son smelled like sugar and fear, his skin exuded a bitter aroma, but this bitterness was wondrous, it was the odor of life.

Suddenly, the winds turned violent again, unleashing a heavy rain. A mournful groan filled the shack.

"Have to protect the entrance," he shouted.

Marie didn't move.

"Anything here to reinforce the walls? Fast!"

Finally she came out of her torpor and handed him a chair.

"That won't work! A board. Do you have a board?"

He turned to the bed. Under the foam mattress a board served as the base. He set it in front of the entrance and plugged the hole. Joséphin shivered.

"I'm here, my little coconut. Daddy's here."

He could feel Marie's gaze on him, but in the darkness he couldn't read her face. She hadn't sent him away. Death was closing in on them, and she knew it.

"The eye of the storm is already moving away," he explained to his son. "That means it'll be over soon." But the truth was that the worst was yet to come.

He took out the two blankets and gave one to Marie, the other to Joséphin. "I brought a flashlight and some food. Let's get under the table."

Marie shooed Joséphin in first. She was about to crawl in as well when a huge roar tore through the sky. A cry ran through the camp.

"Someone's hurt!" Marie shrieked.

Gabriel put his hand on hers. Immediately pulled it back. "It's just the wind."

They didn't get to dwell on that thought before another sound like an explosion made them jump. He reflexively pulled them in close. Marie pressed against him.

The gusts whistled past, and Gabriel, terrified, felt against his skin the skin of this woman he'd loved so much, took in her warmth, the memory of her, her long-forgotten softness. She buried her head in his neck. When he shut his eyes he could feel, fleeting yet forever, a kiss under his ear.

February 1975

He looked haggard, his hair a mess. When Marie, deep in the shack, curled up tight, noticed Gabriel, she was sure she'd seen a ghost. Joséphin hadn't felt the same wariness; he'd run over to him, and this sudden burst of utter happiness had borne her along as well. A step. He'd come. Despite the cyclone, he'd come. She was at a loss for words now that Angèle had told her the truth.

Another step. She didn't have any strength left. Gabriel before her, hugging Joséphin. The past framed his avian silhouette. Outside, the world was collapsing in a welter of metal and water. He'd pulled her into his arms. There'd been that kiss, as shy as their first time.

A step back.

He pulled away abruptly. "Under the table, now."

He crouched down beside them. The cyclone was roaring, outside, inside, within her. They were there, all three of them, brought together by the mad sky—animals nestled against one another, practically a family. Marie grabbed a leg of the table, clutched, clenched, and forced herself not to think about anything anymore.

She had no idea how many hours went by like this. Joséphin's tears dried; Gabriel held him tight without a word. Suddenly all was quiet. The winds died down again. The rain subsided. Marie let go of the table leg; the pain in her fingers grew like a cramp.

"It's over," Gabriel declared as he got up.

Joséphin and Marie followed suit. Once he'd removed the wooden board blocking the entrance, light flooded the shack, forcing them to shade their eyes. The sun was shining anew on the Charrette camp.

The huts were ruined. Here and there, sheet metal lay, floating in puddles the size of basins. An acrid smell, a mixture of burning and decomposing bodies, stung their nostrils: drowned rats, belly-up or stuck in the mud. She'd never seen such a sight. On Diego Garcia, there were no cyclones. The equator protected them.

She turned to Gabriel. "Have to find Josette."

Her sister, her niece, her aunt . . . How could any of them have held out?

"I'll go with you," he said, taking Joséphin's hand. Under his feet, the clayey earth sloshed around.

Josette's shack was damaged. Because it was down the slope from Marie's, the waters had flooded it. Makine was curled up on the bed. At the back, Christian was rocking back and forth wordlessly. In shock. Marie noticed some sheet metal stuck in the ground. She realized. A sheet had been ripped out by the wind and had landed upright, not even a hairsbreadth from Christian. He could have been beheaded.

"Where's Josette?"

Her niece still wasn't talking; Marie took her in her arms. Gabriel, in turn, helped Christian up. The bottom half of his body was soaked, and the smells of dirty water and mud mixed with that of a body that had let itself go.

"It'll be okay, it'll be okay," Gabriel repeated. But it wasn't okay.

"Makine, say something! Where's Josette?"

The poor thing was unable to speak. She must not have had anything to drink, to eat for two days now.

"Gabriel, she needs water!"

He dashed out.

"Makine," Joséphin whispered, poking at his cousin gently the way he used to with Suzanne.

"Oh, thank the Lord!" Those words came from Josette. She ran over to Makine, with Gaudry tailing her.

The girl's only response was "Mommy!"

Gabriel returned then as well, his bag over his shoulder. Josette looked surprised, but he held out a bottle, some fruit, a bit of chocolate, and she didn't ask questions. Makine took a long gulp of water.

"Slowly," Gabriel said. "Your tummy will hurt if you drink too fast." He took the bottle out of her hands to give Christian a bit, too. He was still dazed, letting out small yips every so often. "Where were you, Josette?" he asked.

Her sister looked at the ground. Marie turned around, met Gaudry's sheepish eyes.

"And Angèle?"

She sighed, indicated that she hadn't seen hide or hair of her.

Gabriel picked Joséphin up again, setting him on his shoulders this time. "Let's go find her. And you"—he was speaking to the other four—"stay here." He left.

Marie let him. She didn't have any strength left.

As she took in the ravaged slum, utter discouragement fell over her: the little they still had was now gone. It would have to be rebuilt from the ground up. Everything destroyed by the cyclone needed to be thrown out. They'd have to find furniture, utensils, clothes. Clear out the gutters. Clean up the land. And with what money?

"Angèle!" From the other end of the camp, her aunt was making her way, hunched over and clutching the calf of her leg. She let out a groan as she saw Gabriel and collapsed into the mud.

Marie raced over. "Angèle, get up, don't lie . . ."

Her leg was bleeding. Glass shards. Marie tried to pull them out of her calf.

"Godmother," Joséphin whispered sadly.

"It's okay, my little coconut, it's nothing at all. Give me a hug."

He did.

"Not too deep," Marie announced in relief. "But best you stay in the hut. Lie there." With Gabriel's help, she accompanied Angèle to her place. "We'll be back soon, promise."

Her aunt got up on her elbows. "Gabriel . . . forgive Marie. It was me. I was the poison witch." She collapsed onto the bed, her face wrenched by a grimace.

Marie saw Gabriel furrow his brows. "Later, Angèle."

Later she'd tell him everything.

In the middle of the camp, two women from Salomon were hunched over a body. Marie crossed herself once, then again. A gesture. A word. The others didn't even have the strength to talk. How could she help them? Gabriel looked serious. He no longer had the charm of his nineteen-year-old self, but gravity had given him new depth. His weary eyes exuded a dark light that was attractive, like a mark misfortune had left on his skin. There was beauty in disaster. She recognized it.

They retraced their steps. Gaudry was already emptying the pails of muddy water, while Josette was throwing out the belongings that couldn't be salvaged.

"Joséphin, go help Auntie," Marie said, before gesturing to Gabriel to come with her.

Marie pulled over the table under which she'd taken refuge and leaned on it, her feet in the mud. Part of her dreamed of a kiss from Gabriel, a caress, a proper reunion; another part didn't expect anything anymore. They'd been apart for months while they'd both suffered from the same hurt. They'd found each other just when everything separated them.

"You heard Angèle's words?"

"I think," he said.

She took in the musty air of the shack, found it too much, far too laden with catastrophe.

"The poison witch . . ."

"What does that mean?"

"She lied to us."

Gabriel's head jerked up. She didn't know where to even begin. "Angèle says she pushed you out one day. I didn't know. I waited for you, yes. I prayed to heaven to see you. She pushed you out while I waited for you."

He took a few steps into the shack.

"When Joséphin said you were there, when you saw him at school, I was happy, yes, I was so happy. And then I learned about your sister. Oh, Gabriel! The hurt when I learned who I was nénène for!"

Shrieks came from outside. Little by little, the Îlois were discovering the extent of the damage.

"All Angèle's fault," she said. "She was so unhappy. Nobody forgot you with Mollinart at Pointe de l'Est, you know."

He stared up at the sky, and she didn't go on—what use would it be? What use was it to stir up unhappiness again?

"Mollinart and me . . . We were pawns in their hands," he whispered. "If you had any idea how much I regret it. Oh, there aren't words for it."

His grief matched hers, and she held out her hand.

He jumped. "I can't."

Her hands closed in on empty air.

"What you did with Joséphin, Marie, it broke me. I put up with so much. Jean-Joris? Really? But that doesn't matter. He's my son—he'll always be my son."

She stammered, "Because Angèle lied! I didn't know, no."

"We've all behaved badly," he said, cutting her off. "Angèle, Mollinart, me first of all. But you got that innocent soul mixed up in it all."

That was the last straw for her. She broke out sobbing. "I'm desperate. Forgive me, Gabriel, please, please." She reached out again to stroke him.

He grabbed his bag. "Don't you see? It's like you sent me an invitation to a ball, but it already happened. Do you understand, Marie?"

He walked out. She followed him, distraught, saw him hug their son in front of the ruined shacks.

"I'll be back tomorrow, little Jo, with some food and some things. I'll come back every day." Joséphin clung to him, lost. "Do you understand, Marie?"

No, she didn't understand. On Diego Garcia there were no balls, nobody sent invitations, they just met on the beach, they made a fire, they ate, they drank, they danced a dance that brought everyone together, never pushed them apart.

Gabriel left without even a glance back.

Why are you fighting, Joséphin? It's been going on for fifty years now. Your sleeplessness, your broken back, your headaches, no respite, and you still believe, but why do you believe? You'll never win. They're stronger than you, they'll crush you, the United Kingdom, good god, and America, don't you realize? What chance do ants have against giants? And you've sent your wife into that whole mess, soon your daughter, too. Leave Pierrine alone. She's got a life of her own; a father's battle is all of two minutes. Why fight when you haven't got a chance? Your mother fought, your aunt, your godmother, all the adults! That's something, sure, but that was another time. Do you really want to go back to the Chagos, to the wild, fishing, crabs, being far away, cut off from the world? Is that the future you want? Busying yourself with the dead in the cemetery? Playing Robinson Crusoe? Enough. Drop it. Just smile for the picture and hold your fist up high. Good, that's a strong symbol. You've given it a good try, Joséphin, you've done everything you could. Who could hold that against you?

No. I made her a promise. I'm never going to give up.

February 1975

Amid the black rocks, snared in fishing nets, shards of boat hulls and uprooted tree trunks dotted the beach.

"I have to wonder how this old thing held up." Mollinart's little house at the northern end of Mauritius had weathered the deluge, no doubt because the storm had mostly pummeled the heart of the island. They sat in the shade of a veloutier tree. Since his divorce from Geneviève, Mollinart had fled the city and settled in Grand-Gaube, on the coastline. A tiny building with no superfluities—almost no furniture, no decorations. Infinity for a horizon.

"Look," he said, pointing straight ahead. "See it?"

Gabriel squinted. Apart from a few canoes that had survived, he didn't see a thing.

"It's there, right in front of you."

He blinked, looked again. No. Nothing. The sky was milky blue; peaceful.

"The Chagos," Mollinart whispered with a half smile. "Straight across, right there . . . By the way, did you hear that Gervaise formed off the coast of Diego Garcia?"

Gervaise was the name of the cyclone. Who'd decided to give women's names to storms? Gabriel shook his head: he'd had no idea. Mollinart pulled a leaf off the veloutier and rubbed it between his fingers.

"And what about your family? Any damage?"

At Évelyne's a bit of the roofing had been torn off, and they'd found the mermaid from the fountain broken in half, the girl's bust on one side, her tail on the other. In Beau-Bassin, apparently only the big mango tree had been touched. That beautiful giant, torn out in the middle of the courtyard. A fallen monument. Gabriel had remarked that it'd have been nicer if it had been the old guy rather than the tree. Évelyne hadn't laughed. She'd just recalled that Benoît would be in Mauritius at the end of the month.

Mollinart threw the leaf mush straight ahead and picked up a branch of coral, which he started rubbing with his thumb. "Six dead, yes?"

Gabriel nodded. "And seventeen hurt. Nobody bothered to give them shelter. The slum's in ruins."

"You know what I think? The government's never going to help the Îlois, not until they're forced to."

"Forced how?"

Mollinart dropped the coral to light a cigarette. "Want one? Well, the Chagossians are going to have to file suit. Against the British government."

The smoke unfurled in the wind.

"Against the British government. The Chagossians?"

"Yes, Gabriel! Only the law can right the wrong done to them."

Now he could see it: the illiterate, uneducated Îlois against lawyers for the British crown.

"Marcel. How do you expect them to do that? With what money? With what help?"

"I've got an idea. You're good at checkers, sure, but have you ever played poker?"

✕

"Oh! It's you, number two." Slumped in his chair, Gaëtan Duval was poring through a file with an adviser, who left right away. A firm handshake.

"Number two?" Gabriel smiled instinctively.

"You were Léon Neymorin's younger son?"

"Ah . . . Yes, that's exactly right."

"I heard that Léon was poorly, I'm sorry. Well, life isn't a bed of roses. All right then, don't just stand there, come have a seat, let's see." A bottle of wine was on the table, already uncorked. "Have some Bordeaux. I think you'll like it."

He took the glass Duval offered him, thanked him, and tried to clear his head, but the man was so imposing. Gaëtan Duval. His father's idol. The head of the Mauritian Party. The man who would save the island from independence, unite the Creoles, keep the Indians from coming to power. The king!

"Well? My friend Marcel was saying you wanted to talk to me about the Chagos. Did you work there a long while?"

"Seven years, sir. From 1967 to 1973."

Gaëtan Duval let out a whistle. "Seven years isn't nothing. And those years in particular."

And those years in particular, indeed. He set his eyes on the blue banner adorning the wall. *Don't forget,* Mollinart had warned him, *he's got incredible charm. Don't let yourself get pushed around the way I did.* For years Mollinart, like his father, had helped to keep the Mauritian Party in good shape; he believed in the king, in his uprightness. *I poured thousands of rupees into it. The day Ramgoolam named the national unity government, Duval agreed to be his minister. I still haven't forgiven him.*

The wine was good, even when warm. Before him, Duval waited, his shoulders squared. Gabriel started talking. "I don't know if you've been to the slums at Cassis, Pointe-aux-Sables, or Rochebois, sir. Some

Îlois are living there, nine to a room. They don't have toilets. They're starving. The children are uneducated. Ever since the cyclone, it's only been worse. Six dead and seventeen in terrible shape."

Duval waved his hand in annoyance. "Yes, it's a sad story. Another horrible consequence of independence."

"Indeed, sir." It was time to make his move. "I have confidential documents in my possession. They're all evidence that Prime Minister Ramgoolam negotiated the detachment of the Chagos, to his advantage, with the United Kingdom in 1963. I'm going to show you one, just one."

He slid the sheet of paper to him; it was the copy of the document attesting to the secret financial agreement. Three million rupees paid by the British to Mauritius. Duval was cautious. Not a word. Not a smile.

"Mauritians aren't aware of all this yet," Gabriel went on, "but what if they were? People read the papers. They listen to the radio." He stopped there, awaiting the reaction of the man listening to him.

Duval sipped his wine slowly, ever so slowly, before suddenly asking, "What do you want me to do about it?"

Mollinart's words reverberated in his head. *You know what Duval said during the anti-independence meetings? "I don't like the British, but I love their pounds sterling in my pocket!" That's what brought him and Ramgoolam together. Their love for money.*

Gabriel stood up. Put the compromising document back in his bag. No fancy words, no hemming and hawing, just a simple, realistic request.

"I want to bring suit in court against the British government. Ask for damages plus interest for the Chagossian victims. On my own, I can't do a thing. I don't have contacts, a network. And I don't even speak for the Îlois. But if you help me, we can find a way to inform the Mauritian population of what really happened when the country became independent. A year out from the new elections."

Duval set down his empty wineglass. There was a gleam in his eye. "We need to protect those poor souls, you're right. I'll help you to call on the British courts. But for that we'll need a Chagossian." He was already saying "we."

"A Chagossian?"

"Yes. You can't act on your own behalf. Only a direct victim can do so legitimately. You need to convince a Chagossian to play that role. Someone strong. Probably a man." He didn't let Gabriel respond. "Well, this Bordeaux is wonderful." He refilled both glasses. "A man," Duval continued. "With a woman there'll be too many emotions, tears, sobbing, and my baby this, my baby that. Judges only want one thing: facts. I'm a lawyer; I know this."

Gabriel forced himself to smile: of course, of course.

"Once you have your Îlois, I'll find you a reputable law firm in London. Wait! I have a friend who can help us. I'll call him right now." He opened a notebook and started dialing a number energetically. Gabriel settled into his chair. "Alex? Oh! Hello, Alex! How are you, my friend?"

In a perfectly fluent English, Duval summed up the situation to the man on the line. Gabriel imagined Alex at the other end of the world, still in a bathrobe, sitting in front of a cup of tea in the breakfast room.

"What's the name? Sherdon, you say? Okay. Where are they? Yes . . . Good. Thank you, Alex. Whenever you want . . . You are very welcome here in Mauritius." He hung up and gave Gabriel his notes. "The Sherdon law firm in London. The best lawyers, my friend says. Here's their address. Alex Bradley is a specialist. He handles my affairs in England. If you should ever need it, he can represent you over there— you have my word." He was almost laughing now. "Now do tell me, my friend. Why would you do this? I mean, I understand that these people's hardship is touching—it's touching for me, too—but for you it seems like . . . ah, like an obligation."

Gabriel had expected this question. *All I have to do is tell him the truth, that I have a Chagossian son.* Mollinart had shaken him by the shoulder. *That's insane! Don't say that! A mistress if you want, but not a child!*

"I'm in love with a Chagossian woman."

Duval's smile was roguish. "I knew it! That's our answer. *Cherchez la femme.*"

He got up, signaling that they were off and away. Gabriel slipped the address of the law firm into his pocket.

"Keep me updated. I'm with you, my friend. And as for this information, you can wait until I've alerted Marcel. Nothing can get out until you have my green light. Are we in agreement?"

The gleam in his eyes had hardened. Duval walked him to the door and set a hand on his shoulder. "And don't forget to pass along my good wishes to your father. I'm very fond of him, always."

February 1975

A week after the cyclone, work in the sugarcane fields hadn't resumed. The harvest ruined by Gervaise had left them in arrears. Marie spent her days at the Charrette camp trying to clean and fix and rebuild what she could, both at her place and at others'. Gaudry and Josette had managed to dry out the ground by opening up the roof completely to let in the sun. The two of them were now open about their relationship since Christian had gone insane. The poor man wandered among the shacks, a childish smile on his lips and not a thought in his head. Death, which had come so near with that flying guillotine, had done a number on his taste for alcohol and violence. He was a sorry sight. As for Joséphin and Marie, they were helping to clear out the houses, driving out rats and the crows attracted to the remains of the animals still stuck under the rubble.

"Daddy, what's that?"

Gabriel was holding a metallic bed frame that he plopped down at the entrance to the shack, out of breath. "Your new bed. I also got you a mattress." Joséphin and he headed back, returned with a rectangle of foam still wrapped in plastic. Marie walked over and thanked him, but he froze. A chill. A silence.

"You could put the bed at the very back on one side, for a bit more space, yes?" Gabriel's voice was measured again.

She nodded. What other option did she have? For a week now, he'd kept his word, had come every day to see Joséphin—but he was keeping his distance with her. He took out the table, the chairs, and the paltry belongings that had survived the cyclone to make some space, turned the bed frame on its side to get it inside. "One down." He did likewise with the mattress. A bottom sheet, a top sheet, two pillows that he'd already brought over. The bed almost looked like the one from his past life; the image stung.

"Thank you, Gabriel," she repeated.

He brought the table back in, and the chairs and the tchotchkes and belongings and utensils, before wiping his forehead. "Now I need to talk to Gaudry," he said. "Do you know where he is?"

They found him hammering nails into boards. A shelf for provisions. Josette was busy gathering the laundry she'd rinsed several times in the river's brown water.

"Gaudry," Marie piped up. "Gabriel wants to talk."

"To me?" He was shocked. He dropped his hammer on the ground. In the distance, Christian stared at them momentarily, as if suddenly he'd come to his senses. Then he burst out laughing and went back to wandering.

)(

"If I say yes, but I lose the trial . . . Why bother?"

"Don't worry, Gaudry. You're not risking anything. At best everyone here will get some compensation, will be housed someplace better, will have Mauritians and British people paying attention to you. At worst nothing will change."

Josette was following her man's lead: if he smiled, so did she; if he furrowed his brows, so did she.

"The big courts, though . . . Complicated, yes?" Gaudry stammered. "Lawyers, barristers—that takes money."

"It does. But that's not your problem. It'll be paid for by the Mauritian opposition. I give you my word that you won't have to spend a rupee."

Gaudry let out a breath, and so did Josette. She was crazy about him, just like she'd been about Christian before. It was hard for Marie to get her head around. The upright, sturdy man from Peros Banhos was such a contrast to the violent drunkard who'd hurt her sister so much; between the two men, it wasn't even close.

"I'll need the signature of a Chagossian to bring the writ to the British lawyers. If it's not you, Gaudry, it'll be someone else." Gabriel stretched his words out. "But if it's you, it's better. I'm told that you're the best one. The pillar of the Charrette camp."

Gaudry's bright eyes landed on Josette, who started giggling like a teen girl. "Okay, I'll sign. But how? I don't write."

Marie's eyes met Gabriel's. There was a pause.

"All you have to do is draw a cross, or to make a thumbprint with some ink. You will be the face of the Chagossian cause, Gaudry. It's a huge responsibility. You need to understand."

Hope hung in the balance. Marie, too, could be the face of the Chagossian cause. On Diego Garcia she had pulled together her belongings in an hour and left her island among soldiers. She'd survived the crossing, been heaped together with all the others in the overheated hold, her daughter dying in her arms, her son uneasy against her belly, her blood soaking her skirt, this blood that didn't flow anymore. She'd found her sister on the harbor quay, gone through the hell of this slum, humiliation, sagren. She felt all the fury that was needed to fight for their rights. But she didn't dare to say a word.

"I accept," Gaudry declared, thrusting out his chest.

Gabriel shook his hand. Marie looked away. She was one of the few in the camp who could have signed with her name.

X

As she made her way back to her hut, she noticed a pickup truck at the edge of the camp. She shaded her eyes.

"Oh! The Catholic relief service, at last," Gabriel announced.

A team of four or five people were handing out containers of water and foodstuffs. The people were thanking them, some throwing them in their bags, others barely able to move.

"Look over there," Gabriel suddenly said.

In front of them, a thin silhouette was hunched over a wounded man. A priest.

"Is that him?" Marie couldn't believe her eyes.

"It is."

Father Larronde. Father Larronde was there. It had been seven years at least since she'd seen him. The last time she'd uttered his name, she was burying Suzanne.

"Come along." Gabriel tugged at her arm and headed toward the cleric. "My Father?"

The old man looked up. There was a second of uncertainty before a glimmer of recognition shone in his pupils. "Remember me? Gabriel Neymorin. We traveled together on the *Sir Jules*, many years ago."

"Yes, yes, my son, I remember." He held his arms out. "And here's Marie-Pierre Ladouceur . . . , my girl." He smiled as he took her hands. He hadn't forgotten her.

She was suddenly overcome by emotion. She could feel his patchy beard, as soft as a duvet, on her skin. "My Father . . ." Her voice cracked. She wanted to tell him about Suzanne, about Joséphin, about Diego Garcia, but she couldn't get a word out.

"So you were forced out of the Chagos, too."

"I beg your pardon?"

"Ah, Gabriel, I lived in the Seychelles for nine years. My last ministry. There, too, there were Îlois. Mostly from Salomon, and Peros Banhos. Deported."

Marie sidled up to Gabriel. She needed to feel him close to her; Father Larronde's wrinkles were weighed down with too many stories, too many memories.

"When did you come back to Mauritius?"

"Back in December. My health's not what it used to be. I'm not so hale and hearty these days. I've had to be in the hospital a few times. But with this cyclone, I couldn't just sit by." He shook the crucifix on his chest. "To do something for the weakest, that's my mission on this earth."

He was taking a few steps toward them when Christian bounded up. Father Larronde stumbled, and Gabriel just barely caught him. Marie sensed his uncertainty; Father Larronde didn't want to believe it, either.

She confirmed with a sigh, "Christian Tasdebois."

The cleric's eyes were wary. Under that bent back, that filthy mop of hair, was the man whose wedding he'd officiated in the church on Diego Garcia.

"Alcohol went through him," she explained. "And with the cyclone hell, his brain's gone."

Father Larronde dropped his head. "I see, I see." He crossed himself.

Just as abruptly as he'd run up, Christian turned heel and dashed off.

"God is great, and His mystery is unfathomable, my girl. May the Lord in His mercy grant you all the strength to love and go forth."

He went off on his way, leaning on his cane. Every so often, shrieks and voices shook the air. Marie saw Josette rush out and throw herself at the clergyman's feet, Gaudry behind her, at a respectful distance. Her sister was waving her arms all around, yelling—she had to be telling him about Christian, Gaudry, Suzanne, too, maybe, their hardship, the efforts that had come to naught with the cyclone. They talked for a few minutes until she slipped her arm into his to accompany him. The cleric, Marie realized, had to be almost eighty.

"My children, we can't leave Christian in that state," he declared. "The good man he once was deserves our compassion." Two other members of the Catholic relief service joined them. "We'll take him with us, to the parish." The volunteers helped Christian, who was sitting in the gutter, to get up and led him to the truck. "I'm afraid that the justice of men won't be able to right your suffering." The clergyman sighed. "But rest assured that divine justice will come."

Joséphin, who had been quiet thus far, finally reached out to Gabriel.

"Who's this little one?" the priest asked with a smile.

Marie spoke up first. "Our son."

The road home is such a long one. Long and uncertain. Paved with ordeals, duels, and silence. I'm feeling so tired all of a sudden. If the United Nations doesn't rule in our favor, what authority can we turn to? Who beyond the International Court? Who beyond the whole world?

When nightmares sneak up on me at night, that's what comes to mind. The limit. Our limits. Is there a point in a life where we say, *That's it, I'm stopping there, it's over*? At what moment do we know that there's nothing left to do but tip the hat, say thank you, sir, thank you, ma'am, and leave?

If nothing has been solved in this whole matter before I die, I'll come back to haunt the hallways of these courts. With my bare bones I'll dig through the earth until I reach the Diego Garcia cemetery again. And then, at last, I'll be able to rest.

March 1975

The writ ran three pages, not counting the appendixes: *This is why we are issuing a writ against the Attorney General, for the Secretaries of State for Defence and for Foreign and Commonwealth Affairs. We are claiming damages, aggravated and exemplary, for intimidation, deprivation of liberty, and assault in connection with our forced removal from Diego Garcia and subsequent events. We are exercising our rights as citizens of the United Kingdom and asserting that the authorities behaved unlawfully not only in deporting us from the Chagos but also in forbidding us from returning there.* Gabriel had made a few copies for distribution. Nobody at the Charrette camp could read it, but he knew the value of a printed text. Some would pin the document on walls, or what served for them, like a trophy.

Even Mollinart had done as much. "The shot's been fired, Gabriel! Now it's time to take the next step."

After it was read, the Îlois clapped. Marie had pulled her hair back, framing her prominent forehead and her large eyes. Her two dimples. Gabriel sometimes felt like he was going weak at the knees. Gaudry, touched at being thrust into the limelight, floated around as if the case had already been won. Angèle asked for a bit more water. Gabriel acted as if he hadn't heard. He'd barely spoken a word to her since Marie had revealed everything.

Josette headed toward the water pump in the courtyard. She gave her aunt a glass with some brown particles swimming in it. That was the best they could do. Rebuilding was going so slowly.

Gabriel turned to the slate board he'd recovered from the high school. He wrote a word on its left: *Justice*. Drew a star under it. On the right: *Opinion*. Drew a sun under it. Between the two he drew a double arrow. "There. We've started here"—he pointed to *Justice*—"our first official action against the United Kingdom. Lawyers, magistrates, courts, and so on. To strengthen our case, we need Mauritian opinion to be behind us." He pointed to the sun. "The Mauritians don't know your story. Those who've met you think you're beggars, nothing more. They don't know that you were unfairly exiled from your homes. They need to have all that explained to them, so they're aware, so they're angry." His index finger met the curve of the double arrow. "Soon there'll be new elections. If the people demand accountability from Ramgoolam, he'll do something for you. Even if it's just to be reelected. Starting by settling you someplace else, for example."

A loud *yes* rang out in the audience.

"The next step," he said, borrowing Mollinart's words, "is to organize a sit-in. We have to protest."

Fifty or so Îlois. Placards adorned with slogans. It was time. Marie had put on a white dress and pulled her hair back with a brightly colored headband.

"Are you sure you don't want to come?" Gabriel had asked Mollinart over the phone. His friend had orchestrated everything from Grand-Gaube but refused to emerge.

"I've seen too much, my boy. And my presence could send the wrong signal. I'll be there in spirit."

Sunday. The church bells were tolling in the distance. "Everybody got their Sunday best on? Let's go!"

Slowly, they formed a procession to the Port-Louis city center.

Joséphin was walking in front of them. "Daddy, am I really allowed to yell?"

Marie burst out laughing, and Gabriel couldn't hold back a smile. The high spirits were buoying them all. It was time to fight, to stand up to the enemy and show their faces. They'd been trodden underfoot for too long. They were done suffering in quiet.

After forty-five minutes of walking, they reached the buildings of the British high commission. Marie cupped her hands around her mouth. "Ladies! Up front, here!" Josette, Angèle, Makine, Gisèle, Becca, and others huddled around her. That was her idea: that the women and girls be in front, to keep the police from stepping in right away. They didn't attack women. The men got going again behind them, and Gabriel hoisted his son onto his shoulders. He was seven and starting to get heavy. With all the strength he had in his little body, Joséphin yelled, "Give back Diego!"

That set everyone off. Marie struck the first note of a song she'd thought up in homage to Suzanne. "Me, I was eight . . . Me, I was eight in the Chagos . . ." Her voice was buoyed by those of other women. In the back, a few ravannes accompanied them. "I won't forget, I'll never forget, Mommy." They sang, and Gabriel felt borne by the wave, love and rage both, something like a revolt, so thoroughly intertwined with the air he breathed. When the song died on her lips, Marie started chanting the slogan again: "British! Give back Diego!" The violence of her yell. A cannonball shot out of her mouth, her fury intact. The women joined in chorus. "Give Us Diego!" And the women repeated, "Give Us Diego!" She raised her arms to the heavens, her fists clenched. "Chagos be my only home! Mauritius be my misery!" All—men, women, children—answered with a growing clamor. The ravannes upheld the condemnation, piquing the curiosity of passersby.

Suddenly, he saw them. With their light uniforms, their kepis. The police were rushing Marie and the women at the front of the procession. "You've got no business here. Go!"

There were five or six of them. But rather than retreat, Marie pressed onward toward them. Nothing seemed to scare her. "British! Mauritius! Thieves and partners in crime!" She pulled away from the group. A scout, a guide. "Give Us Diego!" the women behind her chimed, almost humming. A policeman put his hand on her. "Let me go!"

Gabriel's blood boiled. He put down Joséphin and rushed over to help Marie, but another policeman grabbed his waist. Another policeman had pulled out his truncheon. Marie didn't back down.

"You have no business here. Go back home!"

Go back home? She grumbled. That was exactly what they were asking for! That was what they were being told they couldn't do. Bent under the policeman's weight, Gabriel peered up at her. She almost looked like a giant. Her hair rose up to the sky, furious. Her feet were like tree roots.

She poked her finger in the policeman's stomach. "It's your government's fault that we can't go home! Home, that's Chagos for us. Diego Garcia, Peros Banhos, Salomon!"

A mob gathered around them. Gabriel tried to wriggle free of the policeman's grip, but to no avail; he was being pulled by the shoulders out of the circle. Around Marie he could see lights, like camera flashes.

"You want to fight, we'll fight! I'm not scared of the police! We'll yell until we can't anymore!" she declared. "You hear that? Until we can't!"

Fury seethed in his belly, and he could feel it pounding up and down his body. The policeman grabbed her arm to quiet her, but she only yelled louder. Another policeman came as backup; she fell on purpose, brought them crashing down as well. Angèle, despite her bruises, rushed into the fray, followed by Josette. Nails sunk into skin, truncheons hitting back, yells, bites, the women were fighting against the uniforms. "Give Us Diego!" The men knew not to fight; if there was any violence, they would be locked up straightaway, but the situation had deteriorated so much that they jumped in. "Chagos be my only home!" Marie was headbutting the police, kicking them. Gabriel did likewise and suddenly managed to wrest himself free of the henchman. He ran over to her. The policemen hadn't been able to calm her down. She was stronger than them. She was invincible. They had no idea that her strength came from afar, from the day a woman named Thérèse Ladouceur had agreed to let her live her life barefoot. She thundered, scratched, punched; she was the storm, she was every cyclone, the sea in turmoil, the indignation of an island. She stretched her torn skin out to the ocean, she was shattering every idol with her machete and casting them, bloodied, down on the shore.

Gabriel knew he would love her forever.

March 1975

THE ÎLOIS PROBLEM

BLOWS TRADED BETWEEN POLICE AND PROTESTORS

There were four arrested and three wounded in the confrontation that broke out yesterday morning on Chaussée Street in front of the British high commissioner, between the members of the police forces' Riot Unit and some 50 Îlois protestors.

After demonstrating in front of the building, the protestors overran Les Jardins de la Compagnie while chanting slogans like "Ramgoolam sucère di sang," "Anglais volères," and "Séle solition: révolution."

Once they reached the British high commissioner, the protestors held a "sit-in" that blocked road traffic along Chaussée Street.

Around noon, the Riot Unit members attempted to drive the demonstrators back to Les Jardins de la Compagnie. However, they were un-

Marie stared yet again at her picture on the front page of *L'Express*. Barefoot, clad in her sundress, she was fighting off five policemen around her. The photo had perfectly captured the moment.

What she liked about the article wasn't the slogans they'd chanted—"Bloodsucker Ramgoolam," "Thieving Britishers," and "The only solution is revolution"—but the photo caption Gabriel had read and reread to her:

Stopping the Îlois: Easier said than done.

He'd distributed a dozen copies of the paper throughout the slum. Their trophies.

"Mamita," Joséphin had trumpeted. "You're a celebrity!"

She'd burst out laughing and kissed his forehead. It was true that all anyone saw in the picture was her. But that wasn't the most important thing. She turned to Gabriel. Her eyes shone.

In the house, Bettina has a whole cabinet devoted to the Chagossian struggle. Books, boxes, three or four thick binders holding photocopies, documents, press articles, blog posts, photos, transcripts, letters of sympathy or encouragement for the cause. She works the old-fashioned way, cutting out newspaper clippings patiently, slipping them into plastic pockets, playing at being an archivist, not letting anything slip past. I don't have half the patience she does.

One day, when I was especially discouraged, I asked her why she went to all that trouble.

She looked at me with a smile. "For after you? So that Pierrine can keep on going with this endeavor. So she'll know where she came from."

March 1975

"He's coming." Peering through the window, Évelyne was torn between excitement and fear.

"Are you sure it's him?"

"I am." She'd gone over to see Gabriel in his Port-Louis apartment a few hours earlier. Benoît was supposed to meet them before they all went to La Jalousie. "How long has it been? Eleven years?"

Twelve years and three months, he thought, but he didn't say it out loud. He'd have liked to be wholly indifferent; that pretentious, spoiled brother who had been the apple of their parents' eye and the bane of Gabriel's and Évelyne's childhoods. The mere thought of seeing him again had ruined his sleep for the last several nights. Doctor Benoît Neymorin. A degree from Cambridge, sure, but not a single letter, not one phone call.

Footsteps on the stairs.

"I'll go get the door," Évelyne whispered.

He squeezed her hands hard, the same way he did every time his sister had needed to be reassured when she was little. He didn't pretend. He didn't force a smile or any politeness; he said as little as he could.

The door opened.

Benoît, a good deal heavier, almost bald, walked into the room. A faint smirk played on his face. Off-putting. Gabriel would have liked to stay put on the sofa, his arms purposefully crossed, but good manners got the better of him. He stood up. Neither of them was sure how to act. Benoît finally stuck out his hand, as he must have with his patients. Évelyne was wordless. Gabriel went to get three glasses and set a bottle of juice on the table. Cigarette.

"Don't you know you shouldn't smoke?" Benoît said in that tone that always annoyed Gabriel.

"Funny, you've just shown up, and I'm already wishing you'd leave." Gabriel spat the smoke out.

Évelyne glanced at him, pleading with her eyes.

Benoît snickered. "The years go by, but you stay as stupid."

"All right, are you happy now?" she cut in. "Is this reunion as much of a failure as you were hoping it would be?"

Gabriel winked at her: okay, okay, he'd keep his mouth shut from now on.

Benoît seemed amused.

She turned to him. "Tell us a bit. How are things in London?"

He sipped the mango juice, shifting in his seat. "It's wonderful. You'll have to come one day. The city is wonderful."

Gabriel didn't miss that Benoît seemed to only be saying that to Évelyne.

"Do you have a practice?" Évelyne asked.

"Yes. With a secretary and about fifty patients. I have to say no to practically everyone."

"Oh, those poor things," Gabriel said sarcastically.

"That's enough!"

It wasn't worth the trouble. Évelyne wouldn't have any luck. This little family reunion was completely useless. And the worst awaited them at La Jalousie. Gabriel got up. If he didn't leave for Beau-Bassin straightaway, he'd lose all his courage.

"We should go," he said, grabbing his things. "Now."

✖

When the cab stopped in front of the big white gate, he felt like a huge bucket of ice water had been splashed in his face. Sobered up. All of a sudden. La Jalousie stood before him, as it always had been: the prettiest house in all of Beau-Bassin. By the gate, trading a few words with the street vendor, his mother awaited him under her straw hat. She hadn't moved, not in all those years since she'd passed away. She was still there, smiling. "Hot, hot . . . Hot makatias!"

Évelyne and Benoît went through the gate. The ghost of their mother turned to dust again. Gabriel climbed the basalt steps, unease in his belly. Inside, the hall was as clean as always—the smell of wax and honey. But the huge birdcage reminiscent of the Arabian Nights had disappeared. In its stead was a huge void. Where were the birds? The lovebirds, the finches, the parakeets?

"We're here! Georgette, it's us," Évelyne shouted.

Benoît ran a finger along a piece of furniture, checked for dust. In the lounge, the chairs were still there, with the same leather upholstery, the same cloth to rest their heads on, the same huge arms that his sister liked to sit on. The little pedestal table in the back. The shelves. He recognized everything. He didn't recognize anything. It was a murky feeling, both gentle and violent. Time hadn't taken its toll on these things, and in this room of mahogany furniture, he saw his childhood frozen in these objects. But his life had taken too many turns; his memories were mere decoration now. This house—it was another man who'd been in it, lived in it.

"Hello, pardon, hello." A fortysomething woman, short and stout, with very dark skin was standing in front of them. She wore pink house slippers.

"Ah! Georgette, here are my brothers, Benoît and Gabriel."

She waved to them and beckoned them to follow.

"Ever since his stroke," Évelyne said, "we've had him in the big bedroom in the back. Well, Gaby's room. That's easiest for the help."

His father in his bed? In his bedroom? Gabriel stopped. How many superimposed lives would he have to confront in one go? On the door to the right was his parents' bedroom, where he'd found their mother inert, where he'd hidden as a little boy, the room not meant for children. On the door to the left was the bathroom, the shelf with the father's Brillantine, the high-quality shower—their entrée into modernity and the dream of the future. All the way at the back was his turf, but without the tableau vivant of the mango tree, his confidant, which had been ripped out at the roots—the aftermath of the cyclone. And with Benoît, who was walking calmly, as if he'd left the house, the city, the country just last night. It was too much for him. He couldn't. Évelyne glanced over her shoulder at him. *Please be strong.*

Georgette waited at the door, a gatekeeper to hell. His unease intensified. All the smells, all the sights and sounds of the house overwhelmed him with contradictory emotions: floor polish, vanilla, coarse carpet, roughcast walls, citronella, creaking floorboards, and above all the spiced perfume of his mother floating in the air, intact, as if to give form to her ghost. He hurtled forward.

Lying on the bed, his head wrenched to one side, his hands knit together like talons on his belly, his left eye twisting under a wide-open eyelid, the father welcomed them with a grumble.

Évelyne pulled the chairs up to the bed. "Benoît and Gaby are here!"

Neither man could bring himself to say a word. Even Benoît had lost his haughtiness. Gabriel clapped a hand over his mouth so as not to cry, so as not to throw up. Their sister crossed the room and leaned over the father; a kiss on his forehead, on his lips. The ravaged eye swirled in its socket, making the thin, whitish cover spin like fish thrown onto the deck of a boat. Gabriel could feel the effect. He wanted to shriek and run out, run away again. Where was the old, ignoble monster behind this sick being? *Enough of this horrible joke. Take off that mask. Show me your face, your hands. You want me to believe you've got those hands now? Where are the real ones, the ones you dug into Ludna's stomach and slapped us with?*

Benoît touched the father's body. A grimace on his lifeless lips: maybe that was emotion.

"I'll notify the lawyer," Georgette announced. She left and came back with a man in a gray suit with small glasses on his nose.

He tipped his hat, said, "Maître Doisnel, esquire," and then opened his briefcase and took out a pen. "Léon Neymorin has asked me to gather the three of you here so there are no disagreements on the day when, in the fullness of time, of course, your father leaves us and the matter of an inheritance must be raised."

The old man's eye spun in its socket again. In his language, it was a gesture that meant *Go on*.

"Very well. Monsieur Léon Neymorin here and present would like to bequeath to Madame Évelyne Miranville, née Neymorin, the house of La Jalousie, with all its furniture, linens, dishes, and decorations."

Évelyne wrung her hands.

"Monsieur will leave to Monsieur Benoît Neymorin his shares in his import-export company and all pertaining dividends, the title of chief executive, and the company's name, Neymorin Exports."

Benoît's eyes flared. Well, medicine or exports? He would have to decide.

"As for you, Monsieur Gabriel Neymorin, your father wishes to leave you his life insurance deposited in the account at the Mauritius Commercial Bank."

A long silence followed the reading of the document. Whereas Gabriel could see what the house or the company amounted to, the sum of that life insurance was wholly unknown to him.

"Could you furnish us with the valuations of these different bequests?"

Maître Doisnel turned to the father, whose lips were trembling.

"I . . . I will have to look into it, sir. I'm afraid I don't have those numbers with me. But I will convey that information to you as soon as I can." The lawyer cleared his throat. "Monsieur Léon Neymorin, last but not least, has added a final clause. He regrets that he does not have any grandchildren and promises the first of you who . . . addresses this regret . . . the amount of . . . Let's see. Ah! There it is. Two hundred thousand rupees."

Évelyne tilted her head discreetly at Gabriel. *No. No, Lizard. He didn't want to talk about Joséphin.*

Benoît caught them trading glances. "You two have something to say."

"I don't," Évelyne said. "But Gaby . . ."

The father rolled his eye back and forth several times.

"Papa," she said in a firm voice, "you have a grandson. His name is Joséphin. He's Gaby's son. Do you hear me?"

The lawyer pulled off his glasses. "How old is this child?"

"Seven," Gabriel said, shaken.

"Who is the mother?"

"Marie-Pierre Ladouceur. You don't know her. She's Chagossian."

With that last word, the father sputtered; a hoarse sound rose up from his throat and died out in a wild hiccup. Évelyne understood that he was calling her over.

"What is it? Hmm? What?" She held her ear to his lips, waited. And suddenly she blanched. Gabriel could already guess his words. His sister stood back up. "He's not in good form today. We'll talk tomorrow."

But the old man was forcing out an animalistic groan.

"I think monsieur is protesting," the lawyer said. "Madame, could you please repeat his words to us?"

She shook her head no. *No, no.*

"It's all right, Évelyne. Tell me."

Her eyes were downcast. "He doesn't want . . ."

"Doesn't want what?"

"He doesn't want to give his money to . . ."

"Yes?"

". . . to a little Mozambican."

Gabriel stared at the man outstretched before him. The man he could have loved as a father if he'd been a different man. His illness was no excuse. He'd been rotting from the inside out for a long, long time. For Gabriel, everything was clear now. He didn't expect anything from Léon Neymorin anymore, and this realization freed him from futile hope. He cleared his voice, and spoke.

"Mozambicans, as you call them, didn't always disgust you."

The bulging eye shook in its socket.

"They were something you rather loved, before, weren't they?"

A stifling silence fell over the room. The eye spun, spun. Gabriel tore the pen out of the lawyer's hands and brought the nib down to the father's forehead.

"Gaby!" Évelyne shrieked behind him.

"What? You don't want to know? All of you here, you don't want to know?"

The pen hovered millimeters over the skin. Benoît's hands were clasped in prayer; Georgette and the lawyer seemed stupefied. The blue nib sank into the wrinkled skin; the skin drank the ink hungrily—a tattoo.

Gabriel left the room, closing the door gently behind him, as if it were the bedroom of a dead man. On that horrid forehead he had written two words: *Pardon, Ludna.*

March 1975

The excitement had subsided. Despite the success of the first sit-in and the article in *L'Express*, the Îlois were still stuck in the slum. Gabriel had spoken with Gaëtan Duval again, had gone into their meeting with a downcast look. "The cyclone's shaken everything up. Mauritians have been seriously affected, too, and they . . . they're the priority for the government. They're the ones who vote. Not you."

These days, Marie put her head on his shoulder to console him. Ever since the protest at Port-Louis, Gabriel had softened. He let himself look at her properly, sometimes even smiled at her. She herself was taking things one step at a time, a gesture here, a touch there, aware that he needed to be tamed anew.

She was coming back from the sugarcane fields, where the work had finally resumed, when she saw Gabriel sitting in front of her shack, his head in his hands. She led him in, shut the little door he'd built for her.

"I saw my father," he began.

She remembered his panicked face the day Gabriel had learned of the stroke. But he barely ever talked about him. "How is he?"

He lay down on the bed. "My head hurts so much."

She put some water on to boil. "Gabriel . . ." She was insistent.

He turned to her, his eyes bloodshot. "I hate him. And he hates me back. He hates *us both* back!"

"Us both? Why?"

"Well . . ."

"Because I'm *ziloise*? Because I'm not schooled?"

"Yes. He'd say that."

She poured the hot water over some cumin and pepper. A recipe of her mother's for assuaging migraines. "Drink. It helps your head."

He stood up. "Marie. I've thought about it. I want to enroll Joséphin at Sacré-Cœur Primary again. It's too important. We have to give him every chance we can."

She squeezed his hand almost automatically. This time, he let her.

⋎

Joséphin was scared about how he would be welcomed back by his classmates: he'd been away for so long, and the classes were being taught in English.

"Sit in the front row and listen to the teacher," Gabriel told him. "That's half the job done there. I'll help you with the other half." He had faith in Joséphin.

The following Tuesday, Joséphin started walking to school again. His schoolbag looked too big on his thin body.

"Marie, what time exactly do you finish work?"

"At three."

"I'll come pick you up, and we'll go wait for him when school lets out."

The day went by quickly. Where the cyclone had flattened the fields, the sugarcane had rotted, but new stalks were already poking up here and there, and all the rest had to be cleared away to let them soak up sunlight.

"Hey, you! Are you sleeping or are you cutting?" Josette yelled at her.

Neither: she was dreaming.

At three o'clock sharp, as she finished throwing the sugarcane stalks on the pile at the end of the path, she saw the taxi. She kissed Josette's cheek and ran toward it.

"First we're stopping by my place, so you can rest for a bit," Gabriel announced. "Joséphin doesn't get out until four."

She nodded. Noticed the small nick on his shaven neck, the fresh smell of his shaven cheeks mixed with some lingering aftershave. White shirt, flannel pants. And her with her hands sliced up by the cane, her skirt stained with dirt, her skin sopping with sweat. Her feet bare. Like an old scene playing out.

"Twenty rupees, please."

Gabriel pulled a bill out of his pocket and waved the driver away. The building was in front of them, two stories of concrete covered with yellow plaster. He rummaged for his key, pushed open the front door. "I'm upstairs," he said quietly. His voice was different. She herself could barely speak. The fact of what would come next. She followed his footsteps—the *Sir Jules* on the horizon, a birdlike silhouette, a city man, of course. Another door. "That's the one." Her heart pounding.

Was the magic coming back, would they know how to do it again, would they do the right things, enjoy the same caresses? They moved slowly—refashioning time, preparing themselves for the reality of reuniting. Marie was afraid, but the fear was intoxicating, a fear she gave herself over to willingly.

Gabriel pulled her close.

Their mouths angled toward one another, taking each other in. He nibbled at her neck, her nape, her breasts. She brought her hands to her shirt, undoing the buttons one by one, and cast off the garment. He held her tight, running his tongue across her skin, and she hungrily sought out that small bit of skin under his ear, slipping a leg around his waist, clutching his back, letting her hair fall over his face. The bed was large. Their bodies found it, aching, eager. The rest of the world faded away. They did not talk. Making up for lost time, wasted time. Their love was a love tinged by regret.

Regret—oh, my life's had its fill of that. Hasn't yours? We all make our way through, of course, turn the hurts into other things, come up with excuses. And we hold on to our happiness and stoke fires. We make up our wandering. Our idiocy.

When Bettina wanted to introduce me to her family, she wavered for a moment, she who'd never wavered before. I thought it was because of me. Who else would it be? Her skin was the color of mocha, mine was a good, strong black. But I was wrong. She was embarrassed by her own family. Or rather, by the thought that I might worry.

What is it, Bettina? She took a deep breath. Whispered as she looked down:

My mother's sister married an Asian man.

When two cultures, two ethnicities mix, it's always too much or not enough. There's never a perfect balance. There's no recipe, no dosage to go by. No matter what you do, you'll always be seen as someone you aren't.

April 1975

Around four in the afternoon, as Gabriel was about to leave the Royal College, the administrative secretary came and found him in the teachers' lounge. "Monsieur Neymorin, there's an urgent call for you."

It was Évelyne. "He's dead."

He didn't have to ask who.

They agreed to meet at the Pamplemousses Botanic Garden, and she hung up.

⋇

The water lilies were in full bloom. As big as dinner plates, with jagged rims, the leaves formed a wide aquatic mosaic. The garden was magnificent this time of year.

"His heart finally gave out, apparently."

"What a shame that Benoît left already. Dying in front of his son the doctor, now that'd have been a pretty sight," Gabriel said.

"He's not a doctor."

"Huh?"

"Benoît isn't a doctor," she repeated coldly. "After you walked out, last week he had a ministroke. The one that killed him was really the third. He was starting to choke, so we all looked at Benoît. He panicked, didn't have a clue what to do. And then he copped to not actually being a doctor." Her smile was bitter. "Just a nurse. A male nurse at some hospital on the outskirts of London—no pay, no respect. There you have it."

Gabriel was gobsmacked. He'd have expected anything of his brother, anything but that cruel joke. What pride had driven him to make up that whole backstory, what madness?

Évelyne took him by the arm, and they walked around the basin. "And you've got your own share of things to tell me." Some visitors walked past them, headed for the palm grove. "Pardon? Ludna?"

He looked at his sister, noticed for the first time the fine lines at the corner of her eyes. He'd never been sure how to protect her. All the people he'd loved, he'd hurt. The road to hell was paved with such good intentions. He cleared his throat, mulled over his words, but it was the bluntest sentence that finally made its way out of his mouth. "He raped her."

Évelyne absorbed the shock.

"I happened upon them one day, in the kitchen. Ludna was sobbing, and he . . . he was behind her. On our breakfast table." The memory rose back up, every bit as bitter. "I think Ludna saw me. But he didn't. I don't know. I got the feeling it wasn't the first time."

His sister gestured for him to stop. They found a bench and collapsed onto it. She could barely hold back her tears.

"Is that why you left for the Chagos?"

"Yes. I couldn't stay in that house anymore. And I couldn't tell you, either. You were so young. Where could you have gone?" The tears forced their way out of his closed eyes. He set his arm around her shoulder. "There's something else I've never told you, Lizard . . ."

"Mommy doesn't love me anymore."

"What are you talking about? Of course Mommy loves you."

His little sister shook her head. "No, she doesn't love me anymore."

"Why would you say that?"

She wrapped her arms around his neck and clung to him.

"Lilyne, what is it?"

This girl! He had better things to do; the math teacher had given them three exercises to complete for tomorrow. He rocked her for a few seconds, his eyes riveted to the mango tree. The fruit would be ripe soon. He could ask Octavie to please make a tart, or maybe a sorbet. With a bit of grated coconut on top, it would be so good.

"Enough! You want to play with me, is that it?" He set Évelyne on the bed, picked up the banana-leaf doll that the nénène had made, and thrust it out to her. "Let me work now."

He went back to his desk. *If I have seven marbles in my bag, Paul gives me five, and I give him two, how many marbles will I still have for playing?* Why were math problems so complicated?

The little voice cut through the silence. "Mommy isn't talking anymore."

He turned to her. "What do you mean, she isn't talking anymore?"

"When I say something to her, she doesn't answer." There was a pause. "And she keeps her eyes shut."

Goose bumps rose on the back of his neck. "You wait here. I'll be right back." He made sure to close the door behind him.

His lungs were about to burst. The bedroom was at the other end of the corridor. His father was at the office; the nénènes in the courtyard. He'd never realized how long this hallway was. The walls were swaying. He clutched the doorframe for a second, took a deep breath, and then opened the door.

His mother was lying across the bed, inert. Her body was already cold.

He rushed to her side. "Mommy, Mommy." He took her hand, gripped it, found a paper clutched in it. And noticed right then the medicine bottles around her. Empty. She'd taken them all. He'd gone to buy them for her. "My dear Gaby, go see Monsieur Zhang at the pharmacy and get these for me." He'd done it; he'd obeyed.

Despite the tears blurring his sight, he forced himself to decipher the message: *To my dear children* on the front. And on the back, in sloppier handwriting, a few incomprehensible words: *I saw them . . . Have to set the birds free . . .* He'd put the paper in his pocket, hadn't touched the medicine. Once he was outside, death screamed in his head.

⋈

"I remember the doctor saying she had a heart attack. A plain old heart attack," Évelyne whispered as she wiped away her tears.

The father had rushed back from the office. Gabriel could still recall his stammering voice. "Where did those medicines come from?" When he'd confessed that their mother had asked him to go buy them, and that he'd done what he'd been told, he'd seen a black rage grow in his eyes; that day, hate had taken root in the father permanently.

"I have a feeling Mommy found out what he was doing with the nénènes," he said, "but we'll never know."

Évelyne was reaching into her bag for a tissue. "She's hardly blameless, though. You don't abandon your kids just because you've been cheated on. That's selfish, self-absorbed."

He opened his hands. "Maybe there was something else, Lizard."

"Like what?"

"I don't know. Revenge, maybe."

His sister got choked up. He kissed her cheek. "I need some time," she said. She pointed to the palm grove. For a few days now, all the visitors had been rushing to visit. The talipot palm was in bloom. "We'll go see it another time, okay?"

"Yes, another time."

Read me the Bible again, Joséphin, the passage where Jesus drove the merchants out of the temple.

And the Jews' passover was at hand, and Jesus went up to Jerusalem. And found in the temple those that sold oxen and sheep and doves, and the changers of money sitting: And when he had made a scourge of small cords, he drove them all out of the temple, and the sheep, and the oxen; and poured out the changers' money, and overthrew the tables; And said unto them that sold doves, Take these things hence; make not my Father's house a house of merchandise. And his disciples remembered that it was written, The zeal of thine house hath eaten me up. Then answered the Jews and said unto him, What sign shewest thou unto us, seeing that thou doest these things? Jesus answered and said unto them, Destroy this temple, and in three days I will raise it up. Then said the Jews, Forty and six years was this temple in building, and wilt thou rear it up in three days? But he spake of the temple of his body.

She smiled.

See, Joséphin? Not everything is for sale. Dignity cannot be bought. A country cannot be bought. Neither one's soul nor one's faith can be bought. Some things are sacred and must stay so.

May 1975

The fields stretched out before her and shone green, touching the valleys and hills. The sugarcane thrusting up to the sky was starting to swell with sugar—it would be pressed a few months later. Two sous per toise on Christmas, one sou the rest of the year.

"Oh, Marie, Marie, Marie!" Gaudry hummed in a fashionable séga rhythm. He gathered a heap and threw it in his huge cart, and immediately set off, whistling. Last year, he'd been named the season's "best sugarcane cutter," and he'd gotten a small bonus for it. She waved and went back to work. Work in the sugarcane fields wore her out more than on the copra plantation. Look straight ahead, swing the machete, ignore your sore arms, your blistered hands, your swollen wrists, your aching back. Throw the cane behind you, take a step forward. The leaves were sharp and cut into her legs beneath her skirt. Josette was better with her hands, went faster than she did on her portion of the fields, never forgetting to give her an encouraging word or glance.

Despite the offer Gabriel had made her to come live with him in the apartment, insisting that Joséphin would be better off there, Marie had decided to stay at the camp. She was wary of herself, of her overpowering feelings, of her wild moments of fervor. Suffering had become a landscape for her, serenity an impossibility. She took what life gave her, gently, cautiously, met Gabriel at his place at the end of the day, then came back to Cassis, her skin drenched with his smell.

One night when she was walking to the camp with Josette, she saw a crowd at the camp entrance. The Îlois were gathered into a tightly packed, roaring mass. From her plastic stool, Angèle waved them over. "My girls! Big news! My heart's bursting. We're getting money! The British give us *com-pen-say-shun*."

They both let out a happy shriek. "When? How much?" Marie clutched a hand to her belly. Finally, things were changing! "A British man just came . . . he went around the villages. Rochebois, Pointe-aux-Sables, and us. He's back tomorrow morning."

"Who?"

"A specialist man . . . lawyer . . . Ayo . . . Too complicated, *zenfants*. Gaudry! Come here, you explain."

Gaudry pulled away from the crowd and walked over, beaming. "We won!" He hugged Josette and lifted her off the ground.

Joséphin ran over and grabbed their legs. They'd won! "Tell us more," the boy said excitedly.

"Alex Bradley. A man from England. He says the British government wants to come to an agreement. They're scared of us! Ahahaha! Cowards, cowards, that's them. He says the compensation is six hundred fifty thousand pounds sterling!"

When she heard the number, Josette yelled. That much money! They could build houses, palaces, roads with that!

"When, Gaudry?" Marie asked. "When do we get it?"

He pulled off his hat to cool off, waved at another Îlois who was yelling his name. "Bradley says not long. Two weeks? A month?"

It was wonderful news. Life was only getting better. She couldn't wait to tell Gabriel. He'd promised to come the next day. She blew him an imagined kiss.

Around seven in the morning, as Marie was brewing tea for Joséphin, a man showed up at her shack. His skin was white, his hair so blond that it almost seemed white, and he spoke French with a strong British accent. The face of the soldier stopping by her hut popped up in her memory. She set down her metal cup and went to welcome him. Josette and Gaudry were behind him.

"Mademoiselle Ladouceur. I'd like to introduce myself. Alex Bradley, from the Sherdon law firm in London."

She shook his hand, embarrassed not to have washed her face properly. "Some tea?"

He nodded and they all went into the shack.

"I saw your photo in the newspaper a few weeks ago. You made an impression on me. Our government is genuinely interested in what's happened to you, you know. It's heard about your movement and would prefer to negotiate with you rather than go to court. I think that monsieur"—he gestured to Gaudry—"has already told you everything. The United Kingdom is ready to pay out six hundred and fifty thousand pounds as compensation for the wrong done to you. It's only fair."

The man spoke properly and spoke a great deal—she didn't understand everything. She ran a hand through her hair, trying to smooth out a rebellious curl. They'd done wrong by her, yes, and even if no money would ever bring back Suzanne, the thought of being able to offer Joséphin a better future was a weight off her chest.

"When does the money come?" Josette asked.

"Very quickly. In less than a month. To make it happen all you have to do is sign this document. I brought a paper for each of you."

Marie couldn't read any of it; it was all written in English. She asked Bradley about it.

"The letter says that you're accepting financial compensation offered by the British government. Look, here." He pointed to a line with a six and a five and four zeros. "You can see the numbers: six hundred fifty thousand pounds sterling, meaning forty million rupees. It's a big number, isn't it?"

Josette let out a happy laugh and drew a cross at the bottom of the letter.

"Oh! I'm sorry, ma'am, I'll also need your fingerprint. Your thumb," he said as he pulled out a small inkpad.

She pressed her finger on it, then did so on the paper, childishly, as Gaudry hooted and hollered.

Marie wavered for a second. She'd have liked for Gabriel to be there.

The British man looked around. "It looks like the February cyclone was terrible. I'm so sorry." The sheet-metal walls, the lack of electricity or toilets, the tap outside that barely drinkable water dripped from. Yes, she couldn't take it anymore. She took a pen from the man and with her nicest handwriting she signed: *Marie-Pierre Ladouceur.*

The lawyer gave her a copy. "This one is for you. Here." He stowed the papers in his messenger bag. "Mesdames, monsieur," he said, and then left.

$$\text{X}$$

The day in the sugarcane fields was without question the best one since she'd come to Mauritius. Everyone was singing, delighted by this good news they didn't dare to believe. Gaudry was strutting up and down the rows like a king. Joy, at last. They headed home a bit earlier than usual; Marie washed up, borrowed a bit of perfume from Josette, which she'd found under the seat of a bus one day, probably fallen out of some lady's bag.

"Just you wait, there's big news, really big news!" Josette was guffawing outside, pushing Gabriel inside.

Marie gave him a kiss, a real kiss from a lover; it was so sweet to meet his lips, hold his arms, feel his warmth.

"Well, that's quite some welcome!"

"Come in, come in quick."

She immediately thrust out the letter folded in half.

"What's this?"

She burst out laughing, told him to read it. He sat down on the foam mattress, unfolded the sheet. But the delight she expected didn't come. On the contrary. The more he read, the more his face blanched. To yellow, then to white.

He undid his tie and threw the paper on the table. "Tell me you didn't sign this."

His words were like a slap. Anguish, such anguish. She'd forgotten how much such a feeling could hurt. Of course she'd signed. And with her very best handwriting.

"Marie, who gave you this?"

Her throat was suddenly dry. The words wouldn't come.

"Who?" He was almost yelling.

"A man. A good sir from England . . . Alex Bradley."

His fist landed in his other hand. "And who signed?"

"The three of us, all three of us! But why?" She was shaking now.

"And Bradley was the one to make you sign that!" This was serious; she didn't know why, but it was very serious. She was rooted to the spot, waiting for the next blow. "Marie," he stammered, "you signed this document to get money, yes, but in exchange . . ." He fell silent.

"What? What now?"

"In exchange, you've agreed to give up all further litigation against the United Kingdom, and, even worse, you signed away your right to return to the Chagos."

Tell me you didn't sign this. Tell me you didn't sign this. Tell me you didn't sign this.

A letter in English. She didn't speak English; nobody here spoke English. Nobody, or almost nobody, knew how to write. Gabriel had blown up. "Dirtbags! Rotten to the core!" He'd pulled his arm back, like he was going to hit something. Josette, Gaudry, and Joséphin had watched him from the doorway, speechless.

"Money!" he'd yelled. "Their filthy lucre!"

She'd sat down beside him. Nothing was going through her head anymore. She was numb.

"We're not going to let them get away with it. I'm going to talk to Mollinart. There has to be some way to prove that you were misled. You didn't know what you were signing. Did he tell you that you were giving up your right to return?"

Marie clenched her jaw. "No. And not Josette, either."

All of a sudden, he clapped a hand to his mouth and ran outside. Marie fell onto the mattress. Above her head, the sky was black. Another storm? Then she let out a nervous laugh. No, it was the roof. The only storm was Gabriel's fury. She shut her eyes.

No.

She couldn't accept it. Not after everything she'd been through. Suzanne was looking down on her, Mérou held tight. Joséphin, too. Her baby. The umbilical cord wrapped around his neck. She'd fight back, with her teeth if she had to. Just let them do this? No, never.

This meant war.

V

It always seems impossible until it's done . . .

Was it him that Josette and you were thinking of when you started up the Chagos Refugees Group in 1983? Nelson Mandela? Our icon. He was rotting in jail in South Africa when our protests began. But you understood right, that we needed a flag, a structure to carry our voice. I was fifteen years old back then, in high school. You didn't think twice about making me part of the group, Mommy. You said that we were resistance fighters, that nothing was impossible. At the bottom of your bag, right by a card-holder, you had a photo of Madiba.

There's nothing original about invoking his name today, especially if you're Black and the opponent is white. But that doesn't matter. People who are rebelling don't need to be at the bleeding edge. They want to change reality.

I clung to his strength. To the simplicity of a message boiling down to: Do it. Do it, and you'll change the world. That's the movement that's led me to The Hague.

May 1975

Low tide. The rocks' curves a contrast to the orange-hued pools. Mollinart took in the sight, standing, his hands in his Bermuda shorts.

"Marcel!"

He turned his head.

Gabriel's stomach was still trembling in the wake of his vomiting. Marie had poured a bit of water over his face and neck. "War," she'd repeated in a monotone.

War. Cold war, colonial war, civil war, constrained war. War, pure and simple.

"We're going to fight, Marie. I promise you."

Gaudry and Josette had stood back, shattered. He'd run a lifeless hand over Joséphin's hair.

"I need to talk to Mollinart. I'll come back after."

Marie had stayed stock-still. A black sun blazed in his eyes. He'd borne that fire away with him—a motor, a drive.

"Terrible timing, sir." The taxi driver hadn't been wrong. Two hours to reach Grand-Gaube! More than twice the usual time. Cars honking everywhere, people yelling at each other, mopeds weaving wildly between trucks and buses. A hellish racket of noise, gas, and dust. The roads were always in terrible shape. Gabriel felt like he could boil over. He couldn't think through this alone anymore. What agreement could the British have made with Mauritius through the Sherdon law firm? If only he'd been there, at the Charrette camp, instead of teaching those stupid classes at school, instead of sorting out these administrative matters with the estate, the Îlois never would have signed this deal with the devil!

"Isn't there any other way?" Gabriel asked, at the end of his patience.

The driver's only answer was to turn up the radio. But that was indeed the question: Could another way be found? Gabriel sank into the seat, bent double by a new stomach cramp. So he had to wait, because there was nothing else to do. The road finally opened up and Grand-Gaube came into view.

"It's a catastrophe. The Sherdon law firm . . . They betrayed us. Bradley's in Mauritius, of course. He went around all the slums. With that." Gabriel gave his friend the copy of the agreement between the Îlois and the British.

As Mollinart scanned it, his forehead turned blotchy anew, the way it once had on Diego Garcia. "They dared to do that?" He reread the document. The letter shook in his hands. "A promise of how much? Wait, wait." He opened a drawer and pulled out a calculator. "With the number of Îlois deported to Mauritius, that comes out to a little under six hundred pounds per person." They looked at each other balefully. The number said it all. "Barely enough to buy some furniture. And giving up their islands on top of that. On behalf of *our* lawyers! I thought I'd seen it all, but this . . ."

Gabriel rubbed his temples. His head was in a vise, his neck hurt. "Now I understand why Gaëtan Duval asked you not to reveal the document involving Ramgoolam. He negotiated directly with the British. See, he's even worse than us."

Mollinart shook his head. "I'm sure the British government's toasting to both sides now. We've never been too wise. I wouldn't be surprised if it turned out Ramgoolam had signed a pact with Duval. Just a few months before the general elections." Mollinart got up. "You know I don't drink the way I used to, but what with all this I need something strong."

Gabriel raised his hand. "Make it a double."

The prison of ignorance. It was the Îlois' naïveté that all these men—the powerful, the politicians, the dignitaries—were profiting from. Gabriel was sure of it. How many illiterates were there among them? Marie had a few memories of their lessons back on the Chagos, but her memory was already playing tricks on her. It'd been so long since she'd made use of it. And even so, nobody spoke English. Impoverished people. Those who couldn't read or write were inherently vulnerable. And it was the richest who'd kept them from gaining knowledge.

"How much leeway do we have?" Gabriel asked. "Legally, we should be able to prove that they were misled and that they signed blindly, shouldn't we?"

"We should," Mollinart sighed. "But that means going up against the Sherdon law firm. Against our own lawyers! That's insane." He downed his whiskey; Gabriel followed suit and then lit a cigarette.

"I want Marie and Joséphin to be able to go back to Diego Garcia one day."

"I know, Gabriel. I know."

"Do you know what Marie said before I came here? That nothing could hurt her anymore now."

"Then she'll be stronger than them."

She had to at least believe that. To be strong enough to fight, to keep going.

"All right," Mollinart declared, "so the British want to mess with us? They're going to regret it. You're right: we'll rat them out."

"To whom?"

"I don't trust the Mauritian press any more than the British press."

"The Americans?" Gabriel ventured.

Mollinart opened the drawer again and pulled out an envelope. "I need to find the contact information for the *Washington Post*. But that won't be hard."

"You think they're more honest?"

Mollinart let out a snicker. "Honest? It's not a matter of honesty, Gabriel. Just of tactics. The *Washington Post* wouldn't let such a scoop slip out of their hands. With the Vietnam War, military topics are a hot-button issue. A base illegally formed on Diego Garcia—you can see where I'm going. What do you think? Just for starters."

Mollinart handed him a document that he'd never seen before. One last vestige of Geneviève's bequest. It was a secret letter from Denis Greenhill, a British diplomat, to the secretary Paul Gore-Booth of the Foreign Office, dated August 1966. Sent to determine whether Diego Garcia was a terrain immediately ready to be turned into a base or not, Greenhill wrote: *Unfortunately, along with the birds go some few Tarzans or Men Fridays whose origins are obscure.*

Mollinart tapped his fingers on the table. "The United Nations approved the creation of an American base only because there was no native population on the island. Meaning, in no time, the British turned the Îlois into seasonal workers. This note amounts to a preliminary challenge to the legal proceedings, doesn't it?"

Gabriel rubbed his temples; the headache wasn't going away. "Yes. I'd say so."

The idea wasn't half-bad, not that they had much choice. They needed to fight however they could.

In June 1980, a debate at the Assembly had outraged my mother. The old Mauritian bogeymen were blowing up in our face again. The opposition party, led by Anerood Jugnauth, wanted to include the Chagos archipelago in their definition of Mauritian territory.

The British response had been a categorical no. The British Foreign Affairs secretary had insisted that the BIOT was part of the United Kingdom and its overseas territories—that they could not deny the fact that Diego was legally British and that nothing could change that.

Their line of defense was unwavering: it was with Mauritius's consent that Diego Garcia had been, in their own words, "excised."

Prime Minister Ramgoolam, still in power, had been only too quick to agree and acknowledged that the British government had paid £3 million for them to give away Diego Garcia. A request was made in the Assembly to include Diego Garcia as a territory in the state of Mauritius. They could not do that for fear of being ridiculed, as Diego Garcia did not belong to them anymore.

Our lawyers warned us: that was and would always be the main argument of the British defense before the International Court of Justice. The

Mauritian government had officially recognized the detachment of the Chagos. That the opposition party was now in power changed nothing. Every government, no matter what its political stripes, determines through its choices the future of its people.

June 1975

She had picked out fragrant white flowers. Flowers she'd never have been able to buy herself.

"It's my gift to you, Marie, pick what will make you happiest."

When Gabriel handed the floral arrangement to her, she'd been half-certain that what she was holding was a wedding bouquet. But she set the flowers at the base of the jacaranda. Suzanne would have been thirteen years old that day. She'd grown up so fast; when she'd struck her pose—hand on her waist, impish smile—she'd looked like a young woman already. Marie spread her fingers on the trunk. The thin gray bark, burnished by time, brought her a small measure of consolation.

Do you know what they did to us, Suzanne? The trap they set for us?

She sat on the ground, leaned against the tree.

I should have kept up with my lessons. Learned English. Learned how to make speeches. I've been thinking, my girl. I have nothing to fight them with, no money, no degrees, no power. But this nothing is enough for me to fight with. This nothing is me. My body. My breath. When we're poor, that's all we've got: ourselves.

The idea had struck her one morning. A hunger strike. The weapon of those who have nothing else to offer.

"But you'll ruin yourself, Marie! A hunger strike? Do you know how hard that is, how much it hurts?" Gabriel had shaken his head over and over. "No. It's too risky."

She'd let him yammer on. Her mind was made up.

I'll hold out as long as it takes. I'm not afraid anymore. I signed to get some money, not to cut myself off from Diego Garcia forever. Not to kill myself. Do you understand, Suzanne? I'm ready. There's a moment, I hear, when a body becomes so light that it feels like it's floating. You stop feeling hungry anymore.

"You'll sleep at the house with Joséphin." Gabriel was firm. "I'm not leaving you alone on your mattress with what's in store for you."

At his place, so long as the strike lasted. All right. After that . . . after that, they'd see.

I've learned one thing, Suzanne: you don't have to dream big. You don't even have to tempt the devil. Life has too many twists and turns already.

In the night, while Gabriel was sleeping beside her, peacefully, a forgotten sensation woke her up. Like a ghost-memory. She opened her eyes, got up, and tiptoed to the bathroom. Yes. It was happening. She was getting her period again.

June 1975

Hunger Strike—Day 1. A simple piece of cardboard serving as a calendar, and a placard with it: *Give Us Diego!* They jostled at the fence of the Jardin de la Compagnie, facing the British embassy. A bit of dew coated the benches still.

Marie walked up to the bronze statue, examined the man armed with a pen. "Who's that?"

"Léoville L'Homme. Have you heard of him?"

She shook her head.

"A poet. The first Mauritian poet. A journalist, too. He fought for people of color to get the right to vote."

"That makes him family!"

Her words made him smile.

He stroked her cheek, lingered on her dimple as he recited: *"Lieux chers à mon enfance, ô quartier des Salines, / J'ai parfois le regret de vous avoir quittés . . ."* Spaces dear to his childhood, oh, Salines quarter, he felt regretful at times about having left them.

Marie clutched her strips of cardboard. "Salines? The Saint-Georges Cemetery is there, no?"

"It is." He didn't notice the implication.

A weaver took flight straight ahead, a straw in its beak, looking for its nest in the cherry plum.

"Say his name again?"

"Léoville L'Homme."

"Pretty. Just his name on a page, poetry, that."

"That it is, indeed."

She hoisted up the cardboard signs. "I hope there's more people by the embassy. It's too quiet here."

She walked out and headed confidently toward the building. He looked at her, alone with her slogans, her fierce head of hair, her bare feet. He watched her walk straight ahead, toward the British flag fluttering above the building, her cotton dress swishing around her legs, her back rigid; he watched her, so small in the morning light, and determined all the same.

And then: "You coming?"

The city was slowly waking up; a Thursday in the Southern-hemisphere winter. The streets silent. The employees, the workers, still unseen. Marie sat. Her radiant smile amid the cardboard. She was alone. The Îlois were supposed to leave for the fields, Joséphin for school; Angèle was still dragging her leg. "See you soon." The truth was that they still didn't believe it. The Sherdon law firm's betrayal had stunned them all. Gaudry, so proud at first, had sobbed for three days straight. This hero of the camp, trapped like a rat! Josette worked twice as hard without complaint, despite the blisters now covering her hands. Physical suffering was nothing compared to this shame mixed with despair, this sagren.

Only Marie had stood up, her eyes blazing. "I'm Chagossian! And I can't go back to the Chagos?" She was a sight to behold in her fury, and she did her best to mobilize her family, her friends, her neighbors. "We can talk all we like. The thing is to make them listen."

They all liked her ideas, but nobody had her courage. A hunger strike? That was unthinkable. Gabriel had to agree with them. She would do herself in for nothing; the government wouldn't get their hands dirty to save a little headstrong Îlois woman. Especially not if she was the only one.

"Tell her, Gabriel, please. Tell her I won't give up on her," Josette had pleaded with Gabriel. "But a day she doesn't work is a rice ration we don't get for Makine."

Marie glanced at the embassy. "Is the reporter coming?"

Gabriel sat beside her, the fence digging into his back. "Not today, Marie, I don't think."

He was supposed to alert the Mauritian press, but he'd gotten the cold shoulder. The 1976 election campaign was already making waves; dealing with the fallout from the cyclone was the focus of every debate.

"What about the American?"

Mollinart had managed to reach the *Washington Post* a week ago. "Just pick up the phone, call the editorial desk, explain with your best accent that you've got a very big story, and you're connected to a journalist right away," he'd marveled. "They're incredible! The guy is named David Ottaway. He's a correspondent in the Middle East and Africa. He's often traveling to report from the ground. I sent him a copy of Greenhill's secret note by airmail. He's supposed to call me back when he's read it. Let's cross our fingers."

"The Americans." Gabriel needed to buy some time. "That's in our sights. But we have to be patient."

"We can wait. I'm ready." She turned to him, looked at him seriously. "We have to keep faith."

X

The morning went slowly. People walked past them without stopping, barely glanced at her slogans. Marie didn't yell; rather, she stared at the faces of the British men coming and going from the embassy. Not just British, either: plenty of Mauritians, too, who wanted to get a visa, a passport, some sort of support. Around noon, she buried her fist in her stomach.

"Are you doing okay?"

Her belly was starting to rumble. "I want it to be quiet," she said.

Gabriel put an arm around her shoulders. One day, two days, let's say three days. But after that. How would she fare? It wasn't only her belly. Her head, too. Her thoughts. She had to resist the delight of biting into fruit or a bit of bread. It was against herself that she had to fight.

The afternoon proved to be just as dreary. Barely anyone, and this overwhelming feeling of loneliness. Around four, Gabriel suggested that they go home. This first day had left a bitter taste in his mouth. The strike had begun, but only for Marie. Nothing had happened. Without other people helping, she'd never succeed.

He went to the Charrette camp. He urged several Îlois to support her. Even if they'd have to take shifts for working in the fields, go by a random draw, anything! They couldn't leave her by herself. They had to protest with her.

That night, he waited until Marie had gone to bed before he went and, without a sound, standing at the kitchen sink, nibbled on a bit of pineapple.

The plane's starting its descent. The sky over Paris is cloudy, and the temperature is fifteen degrees Celsius. At the airport, we'll have to get our suitcases and head for the Gare du Nord. I hope we don't lose each other. The end is in sight. Or is it really the beginning?

June 1975

"Give Us Diego!"

The policeman held up his hand for her to be quiet. Oh, he could hit all he liked! She'd yell even louder.

"Thieving Britishers!"

The policeman's nails dug into her arm, but she didn't let go of the railing.

"You leave my sister alone, you!" Josette cut in, grabbed him by the jacket, ripping the cloth.

He drew his truncheon. "Let go right now!" But the truncheon hung in the air, and Josette sat down immediately, sticking her fingers through the railing. Marie followed suit.

"Give Us Diego!"

The policeman whistled for reinforcements.

Angèle, Becca, Gisèle, Corinne, Liseby, and Anna rushed over and surrounded the women, their arms interlocked in a human chain. *Hunger Strike—Day 3.* Her sister, her aunt, her friends—they had all come to support her.

Through the array of skirts in front of her, Marie could make out the bottoms of the policemen's pants, and below that, their shoes, which were by turns waxed, muddy, clean, worn. She focused on their movements: a step here, a step there. Her head was spinning, but she wouldn't pass out; the others were protecting her. She would make it through. Angèle asked to talk to the police chief. Marie held on to Josette, focused on her aunt's plastic flip-flops facing off against the leather soles.

"We don't have guns, we don't have nothing," she was grumbling. "And you pull a truncheon on us! I'm sixty!" ·

Marie and Josette traded glances. Since when had Angèle been sixty? She'd just barely turned fifty.

"I could be your mama, your grandmama!"

The shoes retreated. "I'm sorry, ma'am . . . but we're under orders . . ."

"Orders to hit your grandmother?" There was a pause, and the left shoe rose up, as if caught in midair.

Josette gave her a delighted nudge with her elbow.

"My niece here's on a hunger strike! How many days you skipped your afternoon snack, huh?"

Heel, toe. He stepped farther back.

"We're no animals! We defend our rights, that's all. You leave us be."

There were a few hushed exchanges, some groans, and then a whistle blow: the pants walked off. The chain of women broke, and Marie held her head to the fresh breeze. She leaned on the railing to pull herself up, and hugged her aunt while Josette gave her a tongue-lashing, laughing. "Oh, you're sixty now, huh? My old auntie!"

Calm settled again, little by little, and all the women found their place along the embassy wall, launching into their slogans every time people walked past. Passersby stopped, intrigued. Some recalled the Chagos affair from reading about it in the papers. Most were angry about it. Why hadn't they been told a thing? The matter of the Îlois had never been raised during the independence referendum. When wallets were opened, in an outpouring of feeling, Josette accepted the coins in a small pot—for buying markers, scissors, strips of cloth for making banners.

"How much?" Marie asked.

Josette counted. "One hundred rupees, almost."

That was good, but not enough.

"Gabriel says we can get five hundred Saturday."

He'd passed the baton to the women today—his sister wanted to see him.

"Give Us Diego!"

Around eleven, Marie noticed the smell of frying and spices. Her stomach gurgled. She was vomiting a clear bile that wrenched her guts. Down the road, a street vendor walked up to them. "Hot samosas!" She forced herself to shut her eyes, but it was too much: the smell of curry meat and flaky crust filled her nostrils, overwhelming her. "Samosas!"

"Ayo! Get him away," she said to Josette. The taste was already lapping at her palate, deliciously salty, the finely chopped meat, maybe a few peas, some bubbling oil. She felt dizzy.

"Drink," her sister ordered before walking off to the vendor.

Marie took the canteen. The water sloshed, but it wouldn't fool her stomach. Nothing seemed more desirable to her than that small hot meat-stuffed triangle. In the distance, Josette was talking to the vendor, who finally went off. The odor faded away, leaving behind the memory of hunger in her belly.

June 1975

The line in front of the town hall already stretched thirty meters, even though Gabriel had gotten up early to secure his place before it was officially open. What could all these people—men and women alike in suits, kurtas, saris—possibly want? He took his spot in line.

"It's been five months now that we've been waiting to get electricity again!" a woman with gray hair complained. "You hear me? I have to cook what we eat on a plug-in stove. My children are sick."

An Indian man with a craggy face was despairing over a lost harvest. "I don't have anything left. The government has to help!"

The same requests all around. For help. Compensation. A way out of their predicament. Marie and the others? They were lost in this welter of complaints.

After an hour's wait, he finally reached the welcome desk. "What are you here for?"

"To declare my child."

A smile brightened the face. "Congratulations!" She gave him a ticket. "Third floor, office number three. Salam!"

Gabriel headed for the stairs. The building exuded a smell of dust and concrete, of cleaning products. He found the office right away, pushed open the door. Two people in front of him. The imitation leather chair squeaked under his weight.

"Next person!" A short man with a mustache gestured to him. Gabriel handed him his ticket and watched it fall immediately into the trash. "I'm listening." The agent's voice was flat.

"I'm here to declare my son."

He slipped a sheet into his typewriter, evincing no emotion. "Your name?"

"Gabriel Neymorin."

"Mother's name?"

"Marie-Pierre Ladouceur. All one word, Ladouceur."

"Child's first names?"

"Joséphin."

"That's all?"

Gabriel paused. An idea had just occurred to him. "Diego."

"Joséphin Diego, okay. Child's date of birth?"

"December 17, 1967."

The employee's hands dropped to the desk. "That means the baby's seven years old already!" Gabriel stood there, silent. "You're declaring your son seven years late, are you?" He tore the sheet out of the typewriter.

"Ah, I'm sorry. I mean, I want to recognize him."

The agent inserted a new sheet in the typewriter. "Certainly. It's a different procedure, recognition. Always the same old story: I didn't know I was the father, and so on. Very well." He sounded irritated. "The current name of the child, then?"

"Joséphin Diego Ladouceur."

"Whom you want to officially recognize, is that it?"

"Indeed."

"So his name will be Joséphin Diego Neymorin."

Gabriel scratched his head. "Isn't there some way to keep Ladouceur? Neymorin-Ladouceur?"

The functionary stared at him.

"That's not an option, no. Which name?" His typewriter ribbon jammed just then; he cursed while shaking the machine, wiped the ribbon. "Nothing's working right today. Fine, the date of birth, we have that already. Place of birth?"

"Diego Garcia, in the Chagos."

The man looked up. This time, Gabriel saw genuine emotion. Embarrassment. Compassion, even. "Your son is Chagossian."

"Yes."

The man smoothed his mustache several times. "Unfortunately, I can't record him."

"How do you mean?"

"You didn't declare his birth in 1967?"

"No. But on Diego Garcia, nobody declared their children. There were no administrative services."

"I see. The issue is . . . In the eyes of the law, your son today isn't Mauritian. He was born between the referendum and when independence was made official, and everything changed in that time. He doesn't have any identification, I imagine?"

"No."

"Then he'll need to obtain citizenship first. That's another office."

"But if my son isn't Mauritian," Gabriel stammered, "then what is he today? British?"

The employee opened a bottle of water and filled two small paper cups. "Not that, either. You know, with this whole mess . . ." He waved his hand all around. "He's a citizen of the British Indian Ocean Territory. The BIOT. A British Chagossian, if you will."

Gabriel lost his patience. "My son is the citizen of a land where he doesn't have the right to live! So what is he, then? Stateless? Is that it?" He fell back into the chair, livid.

The staffer undid his collar. "I'm very sorry, sir. I heard about what they did to the Îlois, and honestly I think it's, well, vile." He paused. "You're Mauritian, so your son will be, too. There's just one extra step. Go to the citizenship office. In the other building. And come see me after. Oh, one piece of advice: go see a lawyer, too. Make a will, an official document, something. A safeguard."

Gabriel exhaled.

The man walked him to the door and shook his hand. "Put up a good fight, sir. That's all you can do."

After the guillotine blade of the two 2004 royal decrees, after new protests, a new hunger strike, we, we rootless beings, we stateless people, finally got British citizenship. It took more than thirty years. Why? What were you doing, all of you, in your offices, your administrations? Thirty years. Some people die at that age. But our patience was rewarded. We were finally granted an identity, and we were given the right to live and travel with a passport.

Some were angry at me. Our unity was starting to show cracks. British citizenship? The enemy's stripes? I was insane. I was selling my soul to the devil!

They didn't understand. This citizenship wasn't personal, visceral, original. It was strategic. It was a crucial means of defense. British people who kept other British folk from living on a British territory, that could be fought in court, that could be overturned. I certainly think so.

June 1975

How many days now? Nine? Ten? She didn't know anymore. But the miracle had happened. The metamorphosis. Everything was soft in her, fluid, agreeable. The headaches had gone away. She felt light. So nice, like she'd never felt before. She wasn't hungry anymore. The city was swaddled in cotton. There was no pain. Gabriel was there.

   People came to take pictures of her, ask her questions. She smiled, maybe answered, but what had she answered with? She couldn't recall. She was floating. It was like swimming in the lagoon, taking in the whole sky in her head, in her muscles. Waves in her belly, on her feet, under her eyes, waves everywhere. Time didn't exist anymore. She was a soul freed of a body.

June 1975

"Very good," Maître Doisnel declared formally. "First, please allow me to express my condolences for the death of your father."

Gabriel's eyes met his sister's.

"Now, as agreed, here is the estimated valuation of the different goods. The Neymorin company that your brother, if I understand right—his proxy is here—will claim in due time is valued at nine hundred and fifty thousand rupees. The family house at Beau-Bassin, known as La Jalousie, along with all its furniture, is estimated at one million rupees. That's for madame."

Évelyne nodded.

"As for you, Monsieur Gabriel Neymorin, your father has left you his life insurance, which amounts to—hmm—twenty-eight thousand rupees."

He was sure he'd heard wrong. "Twenty-eight thousand?"

"Let me double-check," the lawyer said. "Yes, that's correct. Twenty-eight thousand rupees."

He couldn't help it: Gabriel let out a huge, disbelieving laugh.

"Maître, that can't be possible," Évelyne protested. "A million for me, a million for Benoît, and not even thirty thousand rupees for Gabriel. Are you telling me that's legal?"

"It's all quite legal, madame."

"What about the two hundred thousand rupees set aside for the first grandchild?"

Doisnel shook his finger no. "Your father was firmly opposed to that sum being paid out to the son of monsieur and a Chagossian woman. My regrets."

"So where will that money go?"

The lawyer took the cap off his pen. "It will be sent in full to the Mauritian Party, as requested by the late Monsieur Léon Neymorin. I'll need to ask you for a signature here and here, please."

Évelyne's defeated face turned to Gabriel. "If you don't want me to sign, I won't."

He shrugged and scrawled his name on the bottom of the pages. "Don't worry. This way I won't owe him a thing. A single thing."

His sister was going to add something else but then she changed her mind and signed.

"Good. Perfect!" Doisnel concluded. He was already pushing back his chair to walk them out.

"Maître?" Gabriel said. "Can I speak to you for a moment?" He turned to Évelyne. "If you could give us a minute, please. I'll meet you outside."

⋈

"What did you talk to him about?" she said as they walked down the main path of the Jardin de Pamplemousses.

"Some legal advice. About Marie." He didn't go on; he was barely looking at the basin with lily pads.

"She's so brave," Évelyne sighed. "You think she'll be able to keep going? It's been almost two weeks now. I don't know how she does it."

"I don't, either."

Her courage astonished him. Every morning, she got up, saying, "It'll be today." Today that the British would give in, that the press would speak up about the Chagos, that life could start again. She washed up, did her hair, kissed Joséphin before he got on the school bus. Every morning she sat down in front of the embassy's railing, with her placards, her slogans, her tenacity. The watchmen now waved at her like a colleague. A little British staffer had even come over to congratulate her a few days earlier, in secret. "Hold on tight, they'll have to give in." But every evening, when she went to lie down, the situation hadn't changed one bit. Gabriel was desperate. The people who were high up didn't care about her health. Her vomiting worried him. She was getting dizzy more and more often. Bouts of shaking. They'd have to kick things into high gear before she worsened. The *Washington Post* was dragging their feet. Mollinart had tried to get in touch with David Ottaway again, but to no avail. The journalist was on a trip, he'd been told. The local news pages of *L'Express* wouldn't be enough. And he had been counting on his inheritance to start new legal proceedings, with lawyers worthy of their name this time. Twenty-eight thousand rupees!

"I can help you, Gaby. We'll split it. I'll give you half of my inheritance."

"You want to sell La Jalousie?"

She paused, embarrassed. "I . . . I don't know."

"If you don't sell it, consider it that you don't have a cent more than I do. The house is there. It's worth a million, but that's nothing but a number; there's nothing in your bank account."

She snuggled up to him, her damp little girl's eyes fixed on his. La Jalousie made him think of those mansions from fairy tales—at once welcoming and secure, haunted and dangerous. Just like human beings were: ambiguous.

"Keep it," he whispered. "It's our childhood home, Mama's home."

Évelyne set her head on his shoulder, didn't add anything. They stayed that way for a few minutes, silent, united.

Gabriel stirred first. "All right," he said. "It's a long ways off, that tree of yours, isn't it?"

In the heart of the palm grove, that was all anyone could see. The talipot palm. Évelyne's favorite tree. It was almost fifteen meters high. They had to crane their necks to admire the flower at its crown. A bouquet of silvery, vegetal feathers that swayed in the breeze. The flower in and of itself wasn't all that pretty, but it was rare, and it was the only one. It only bloomed once a century. After which the tree would die. He walked around the king palm to admire it from every angle. In a few days, the bloom would be over.

"Are you happy that you got to see it?" she asked.

He kissed her forehead. He should bring Joséphin here, he thought, before it was too late. A flower every one hundred years. "Very, Lizard."

Évelyne smiled. "Gaby . . ." Her eyes were radiant. "I'm pregnant."

They sat on a bench, not far from the talipot palm. His sister, pregnant. Had time really gone by that fast? Their youth gone, just like that? He could still see her playing pick-up sticks, carefully extricating the hardest one to reach. Life was catching up to them now.

"Alain must be beside himself with happiness," he whispered.

Évelyne clutched his arm and this time real tears were forming. At first he thought they were tears of joy, but his sister was trembling. She never trembled. She was shaky. Suddenly he got a funny feeling.

"What is it you want to tell me?"

She blew her nose hard. Tried to steady her voice. "It's hard, Gaby . . . Remember Savita?"

He did. Her Indian friend. The girl from Rose-Hill. But what did that have to do with this?

"Savita doesn't exist. She never has."

"What?"

"Savita's name is Ranjit. Ranjit Balasamy."

He grabbed her by the shoulder. "Hold on. What are you saying?"

"I'm the one who had the idea. To mess with Father. To get him ready for the idea that I was seeing an Indian man."

He couldn't believe it. He'd never guessed, never suspected.

"Well, that worked out pretty well! A Malbar friend didn't amount to anything in his eyes. But if he'd found out about Ranjit, he'd have disowned me, too, no question."

The picture of his sister as a little housewife, married and responsible, had seemed so perfectly satisfactory to him—wasn't that how all women ended up? How stupid he'd been. As if Évelyne could ever settle down, smooth out all the rough spots. Marie wasn't like that, his mother wasn't like that, and now, clearly, his sister wasn't. It'd have been easier for him to believe that, that was all.

"We've loved each other since middle school," Évelyne went on. "I've never told anyone. It's been almost ten years. You're the only one I ever imagined telling, but when I was going to, you left for the Chagos."

"But Alain? Why did you marry him, then?"

"To get out of the house, to get away from *him*, to stay acceptable, to make it look like something was happening in my life!" She took a breath. "Maybe I wanted to try to forget Ranjit. I was alone, do you understand?"

Gabriel tried to take in all this. His sister's loneliness was something he was largely responsible for. "So, your baby?"

"Ranjit's, of course." She smiled.

"Does Alain suspect a thing?"

"What do you think? The day he finds out . . . It'll be terrible. I'm fearing the worst."

The two of them were quiet.

"Ranjit comes from modest means. He's a dockworker at Mahébourg. But he's a wonderful man, you'll see."

"Will you move into La Jalousie?"

"Why not?"

She had her chin set in that amiable way that reminded him of their mother.

"An Indian man in the house. That'd really be showing him, wouldn't it?"

That it would. A feeling of pride suddenly lifted Gabriel's spirits, had him dwelling on a new pleasure. The day hadn't gone so badly after all; on the contrary, it was a day the likes of which he hadn't experienced in years—a wild, spirited day, a day of freedom.

June 1975

Her guts were ground up, her stomach collapsing on itself. *Hunger Strike—Day 16*. And this white arrow running through her head. At the foot of the railing, surrounded by a horde, Marie was having trouble breathing. "Chagos is my only land!" There had to be fifty of them, maybe sixty. Joséphin hugged her.

Angèle did, too. "You go, I'll take him to school. Stay strong, my girl. Hold tight."

She was hot.

Gabriel dabbed at her forehead with a damp cloth. "If you feel too unwell, you can stop. Do you hear me?"

She blinked. The British government still hadn't announced that they would reconsider their right to return to the Chagos. She wouldn't stop until then. She was in deep, too deep; they had to be the ones to blink first. Otherwise . . . they'd have her death on their hands. And the sagren of an orphan to tend to.

Time had no hold on her anymore. Faces slid past in a mad dash: Gabriel, Joséphin, Josette, Makinc, Gaudry, Angèle. Stay strong! Father Larronde and even Christian—a brainless smile that scared her. On a day of dizziness, she thought she recognized Henri and Jean-Joris, hustled along by Gisèle. Was it really them? She had no idea. The sweetest face remained Suzanne's. Her daughter visited her when the sun was at its strongest and humans hid in their holes. *Suzanne! Where's Mérou, my darling? I already told you to leave that dog outside. The pail. Take the pail.* Sometimes she forgot why she was there, clinging to this railing along the street, cardboard signs set around her, her belly caved in by some interior monster. Her body's last assault on her soul.

"Gabriel! We got it! We got it!"

A hubbub reached her ears, her head, and suddenly she felt a huge void beside her, like a chill. Gabriel must have gone to meet the voice. People were talking, talking. She could make out little bits. Names. Her head was hurting. So empty. Suddenly a paper was waving in front of her.

"Marie. The *Washington Post* article! It's here! We got it!"

She opened her mouth, hoping for some water.

"It says the Îlois were 'summarily tossed off their island to make way for a military base'—and Greenhill's note! They published it!"

Thirsty.

"Now everybody will finally know what's happened."

She tried to move, swallowed. Gabriel must have seen her because he slipped the water bottle gently between her lips. The water hurt; it made her belly twist.

"Sixteen days, my god. Marie-Pierre, can you hear me? It's Marcel. Marcel Mollinart! You have to hold on, Marie-Pierre. Just a little longer, okay? We're almost there."

She nodded. Okay. Hold on. A little longer.

June 1975

Sitting across from Joséphin, while Marie was already in bed, weaker than ever, Gabriel pushed away his empty plate. He hadn't been eating much ever since the start of the hunger strike, but he still ate.

"That chicken, Daddy, so good," Joséphin said, setting down his fork.

"So much the better, my little coconut. Come here." He took Joséphin in his lap. His son was getting thinner by the day, too, and a tiny dimple was starting to show on his right cheek; only the right one. Of Jean-Joris he'd kept maybe those round eyes, the big forehead, but there wasn't much other resemblance. Gabriel was convinced that there really was some mimicry at play here—some stranger could have slipped into the room and found them there together, the father focused on the son, the son focused on the father, and wouldn't have doubted for a second their relationship.

"I have a present for you. Be careful, it's fragile."

Joséphin undid the tissue paper delicately. A cry of wonder. In his little hand was a shell—the spotted cowrie. His son seemed not to recognize it.

"It's not just any shell. This one is magic. It's from Diego Garcia and belonged to your sister and your grandmother before you."

Gabriel had given it a shine several days earlier, and now the cowrie shell gleamed like it once had. Thérèse Ladouceur's grace. An inscription in the basalt. Hammer, chisel. Were the Americans tending to the cemetery?

Joséphin stroked the shell. "When do we go back to Diego, Daddy?"

The man looked at his son. Hugged him wordlessly.

June 1975

Twenty-one.

No strength left. Hurt. Many people. Sunday, maybe?

"Give Us Diego!"

"Gabriel?"

"I'm here, Marie."

The garden, Léoville L'Homme, the embassy. Just a little longer. Her belly screamed. Her head hung.

Twenty-one.

The railing behind her.

Joséphin; little hand in hers. Women's voices. "We'll fight to the end!"

The sudden sound of metal. The grate opening. Men. White. Well dressed.

"Ma'am . . ."

Light shoes.

"We wanted to tell you in person. The British government has agreed to reconsider the matter you oppose."

Everything was floating around her: the lights were twinkling.

"Enough words! Return to Chagos is okay?"

Dizziness.

"The document you signed is no longer considered valid. The proceedings are starting anew." Commotion, cheering. "Give Us Diego!"

Twenty-one. Hurt . . . Hot . . .

"Did we win?"

A hat tipping. "You've won this round."

Yells, yells, yells.

"Marie, you won!"

Tears. Gabriel. Heart pounding. Twenty-one! Around her everything was white. Huge. Cold. That has to be it . . . Snow.

Marie woke up amid hospital machines. Her head was pounding, but she could see Joséphin right away, and Gabriel, and Josette. Then came a deluge of kisses. "You won, Marie! You made them fold." She sat up in the bed. Part of her didn't want to believe it—she'd had so many hopes dashed. But the smiles and the light in Gabriel's face reassured her.

"It's true! We won!" Josette insisted, tapping her hands.

"Mamita! Look at this." Her son showed her the newspaper.

This time, Marie could barely recognize herself on the front page of *L'Express*. Weak, held up on both sides by Josette and Angèle, she looked old, on her last legs. She didn't even remember being photographed.

"I'll read you the article," Gabriel said, squeezing her hand. He cleared his throat and started:

"More than a photo, deeply moving proof that a woman on a hunger strike has finally reached the end of her ordeal. For her two friends, a finish line that can only be met with joy.

"The question bears asking: Is it necessary that already marginalized compatriots risk their lives for the legitimacy of their claims to be acknowledged?

"In any case, this is further evidence of the shortcomings of British colonialism."

Marie nodded, and this simple gesture reverberated through her whole body. She saw the tubes stuck in her arms, the slow drip of a bag full of liquid above her. Smelled the odor of rubber and bleach. So this was what a hospital was like.

"The Mauritian government will build us houses," Josette said. "And we get *com-pen-say-shun*, too."

"Which will be increased. We'll negotiate for it, at any rate," Gabriel added.

Marie inhaled. What about returning to Diego Garcia? When? Her eyes fell on Joséphin.

Tourists. They want to make us tourists, pilgrims, beggars. March 2006. To ease tensions, the United Kingdom finally granted us access to the Chagos. A weeklong "heritage visit." Which means three short walks and then back to Mauritius. They're dangling this little concession before us. "Us" meaning a hundred Chagossians. We'll have to decide who gets priority—sorry, we'll let you know once we've decided. Who's going, who's staying on Mauritius? Who gets to be first? The elders. Okay. Then who? Everyone who's been part of the struggle. Nobody will be compensated. Not many people—that's the important thing. In case we start getting ideas about unauthorized repopulation of our own islands. Josette, Makine, Angèle: they don't make the cut. The two of us, Mama, we tick all the boxes. We'll be on the boat.

Ladies and gentlemen, the Trochétia cruise offers three stops on three days for the three islands. First Salomon, then Peros Banhos, and finally Diego Garcia. We've been warned that it'll be a maximum-security affair: we won't be able to do as we wish. The island is "at the heart of the American military apparatus in its war against terrorism" and high-level suspects are interrogated there. Make of that what you will.

I want to throw a wrench in the British's plans, make them play by our own rules. On each of the islands, focus on cleaning up every place of historical significance, tend to the cemetery. And at each spot erect a stele, build a monument, engrave our history. They've agreed. It's not a choice.

A Grand Departure for a Grand Return is the headline for *L'Express*. How nice, how tempting. How I wish that were true.

July 1975

At the Charrette camp, the first inhabitants were already getting ready to move. Two weeks after the hunger strike ended, the Îlois were given the addresses of their transitional apartments—a gesture from the government as they waited for houses to be built. Some shacks were already empty. Others seemed to be midexodus. Belongings piled up everywhere, heaps of clothes, home goods, small furniture.

"You'll want to keep the sheets, I imagine?" Gabriel asked Marie, who'd given the bed frame and the mattress to Josette, who'd moved in with Gaudry and Makine at Pointe-aux-Sables.

Marie and Joséphin had decided that they'd settle down at Gabriel's place. He felt like the three of them could finally be a family. He'd bought a sleigh bed for their son, seen to the reorganization of his apartment. Évelyne had opened the doors of La Jalousie so they could stow their belongings. Relations between his sister and Marie were still somewhat strained, but they would improve over time; he didn't want to rush matters. The upcoming lunch would be enough.

"Yes! Everything from Diego Garcia I'm keeping."

After two weeks in the hospital, Marie was finally on the mend, even if she was still experiencing bouts of dizziness here and there, without any warning. Sitting on her plastic chair, she surveyed the upheaval.

Gabriel packed the pile of laundry into a suitcase when he saw something slip out. "Oh! You still have it!"

The writing notebook. Carefully tucked away among the sheets, it fell open to the page of capital *A*s.

Josette peered over. "All good?"

Marie nodded yes. "I have to start the lessons again, Gabriel. With Joséphin."

Their son was starting second grade in January, and both Marie and he were in agreement: Joséphin would be doing his homework.

"Tchak!"

Gabriel jumped.

It was Christian, his hand clenched tight as a swordsman's, his arm folded in half. "Tchak!" he repeated, even louder, his eyes bulging, delighted by his joke.

"Christian! Haven't you bothered enough people?" Josette scolded him. He strode off toward another group of Îlois, his feet dragging, his hand upright.

"Honestly. His spirit's no good," Marie whispered. "He shouldn't come back here, he's kicking up a cyclone in there."

It stung Gabriel to see him in such a state. Father Larronde had insisted that he go out and see people, and especially not withdraw into himself. The results hadn't been promising. Christian seemed to only be getting crazier, even, if at rare moments, a bit of lucidity shone in his eyes.

"The mess kit?"

"Yes, keep that, too."

Gaudry stepped out of the shack, a toolkit in his arms. "You need anything?"

"We're good, thank you." Josette yelled, "Christian! Come here."

The man staggered over and she gave him the toolbox. "Go put that over there for me."

He burst out laughing again and obeyed, with his face like a lost child's.

"That poor thing," Gabriel said.

"Why?" Josette said. "He's not nearly as bad these days as he was when he was drunk, believe me."

The cab headed down the path to La Jalousie. Despite himself, Gabriel looked for the mango tree at the far end. He wasn't used to that void. Évelyne was waiting for them on the front steps. Gabriel unloaded the car and tipped the driver.

"Put that down here, Gaby. We'll deal with it later. Here you are at last!" She kissed them both on the cheek several times, in high spirits, and complimented Marie. "What you did was incredible. Twenty-one days. It's impressive, you know. Where there's a will . . ."

"Faith," Marie explained, her head bowed. "Just faith."

Joséphin was already running inside, astonished.

"Come in, come in!"

Gabriel made his way through the vestibule, Marie at his arm, when he stopped dead in his tracks. In front of him was the birdcage from their childhood, with its dome like an Indian palace. Rusty here and there, but nothing that a bit of paint couldn't fix. "You found it?"

His sister nodded. "It was in the garage, apparently." Instead of birds, Évelyne had filled it with pretty flowers and big plants. "I couldn't see myself locking up parakeets or lovebirds. All that's in the past."

His sister was a wonder. Oh, how he loved her.

Marie slipped her fingers between the cage's bars. Having her so close by, right where his mother, in her long dress, had shared her sorrows with him so many years ago had him choked up.

"Come along now," Évelyne said gingerly. "Let's sit on the verandah while we wait for lunch."

They settled into seats facing the orchard, amid the cushions adorning the rattan chairs. Time could have stopped for a second, a life. Gabriel finally felt happy. It was a pure feeling, unencumbered by thought—a physical state.

Footsteps echoed on the tile. He turned his head, saw a tall man with dark skin. Gabriel was struck by his handsomeness. Alain Miranville didn't hold a candle to him. "Savita" had thick eyelashes. An honest, radiant face. A slim profile. He bowed. His hands were shaking. Évelyne was at his side immediately, just as moved. There was a silence. Gabriel smiled.

August 1975

The water on her skin was warm and regular. The lather covered her body. A cascade. She turned off the shower when the temperature started to cool, never tiring of this pleasure she'd dreamed of so often while in the slum. After pulling on a dress, she opened the door to let out the steam. In front of the mirror, she braided her hair and pulled it into a chignon. Rubbed her arms, her belly, her legs with coconut oil. Her pumice-scrubbed heels, usually so thick, now seemed so light. She wasn't ashamed of these two boats of hers anymore. She was proud of them, in fact. She walked up to the mirror, smoothed out her eyebrows. All that was left was . . .

"Joséphin!" Sitting at the table in Gabriel's living room, her son was busy coloring. "You have a yellow-colored pencil? Give me it, please."

Slowly, she applied it to her eyelids. The result was better than she'd hoped; the golden-hued wax offset her skin, illuminated her features.

"You're so pretty," her son said.

)(

On the Pointe-aux-Sables beach, the fire was already going. A séga Saturday, like in the past. Fish seraz, octopus that she'd caught that morning in the bay of Cap Malheureux, some rice, some bananas in coconut sauce. The three old slums were together again: Cassis, Rochebois, and Pointe-aux-Sables, to celebrate the new buildings and their petition being filed anew against the United Kingdom.

Father Larronde, whom Gabriel had invited, said grace over the grilled meal. Hungry flies were swirling around. Everyone crossed themselves, even Christian, who was aping gestures here and there.

Josette turned to Marie. "See, with him I lost a husband, but I got a son."

"Josette. No. One day you need to see Nicolin in Melrose."

Her sister's response was firm: absolutely not, end of story. Visiting the prison was out of the question.

Christian walked up to Josette. Nudged his head against her shoulder like a child.

Gaudry caught him by the shirt and yanked him back. "Get a move on, boy!" he said sharply.

"Oh, stop. You're jealous," Josette said sweetly, bestowing a queenly kiss on him.

Christian let out two sad hollers and then waddled off.

"Marie," Angèle yelled. "My girl, eat! Before it gets cold."

The plates were overflowing. Every dish was delicious; she tasted a bit of everything—"a little bit every so often, not a big meal every four hours," the doctor had advised—and savored every mouthful: the crunchy texture of the *camarons*, which were pearly on the inside; the freshness of the coconut chutney; the butter on the *farata* bread flowing down her throat; the chicken curry ever so slightly burning her tongue. The sauces ran down her fingers; the smells swirled.

By the shore, Gaudry was hammering sugarcane: with dessert, the fresh juice would be delightful. Christian sat beside him, a laughing smile on his face again, fascinated by his movements. Behind them were two huddled, slightly familiar silhouettes drinking beer: Henri and Jean-Joris. She walked over to them without fear.

"Hey! Marie the Beauty!" Henri shouted, genuflecting.

Jean-Jo gave her a loud kiss on the cheek, as if they'd only said goodbye the night before; she noticed that he had a finger missing on his massive hand.

"Our queen and pride, Marie," Henri said with a heavy accent. "Your strike, that . . . Jean-Jo never could have done it!"

He pinched the paunch of his friend, who protested weakly. They hadn't changed one bit, despite all the years and all they'd been through. Lighthearted, sympathetic, completely mindless. She waved amiably at them and left them to their jibber-jabbering.

On the other side, their feet in the water, Joséphin and Makine were trading *sirandanes*. "I throw it and it's white; it lands and it's yellow?"

"An egg!"

Gabriel, his feet bare as well, joined in. "It's got all its smarts in its nose?"

The two kids pondered.

"A pointer finger!" Makine shouted.

"Absolutely not."

"What is it, Daddy?"

He set his pointer finger on his nose, snuffled twice.

"A dog," Joséphin shrieked.

Nearby, Father Larronde was talking with Mollinart.

"So all that's over? The copra plantation? Really?"

"Dead and buried."

"And what about your wife?"

"Oh, her. I hope you won't be upset, Father, but I'm divorced now."

Angèle, who was passing by with a tray of cookies, raised her thumb high. The cleric furrowed his brow. "What God has united man cannot disunite."

Marie's eyes met Gabriel's, and they cracked up laughing.

"Some cake. You want some?"

She thanked her aunt but didn't take any; her stomach was already stuffed and hurting.

"But of course, my Father—just ask Gabriel. I swear to you that it's true." Mollinart was protesting. "Gabriel, didn't Geneviève steal the silverware the day we left?"

He nodded energetically.

"See! Now tell me, could I really live with a thief?"

Angèle was trying not to laugh.

"Even the Americans were shocked," Gabriel added.

Marie snickered again.

"Well, they've met their match in my wife."

"All right, who will dance?" Gaudry stood before them, a jug of cane juice in his hand. Christian was behind him, as faithful as a shadow. "Josette! You tell your dog: stop following me. I'm tired."

"Leave him be," Josette said. "See, he's nuts."

The night was falling gently, leaving the light concentrated in the fire and the stars. No moon. "Come on! Roll *matak*! Let's dance!" The ravannes warmed up. The first notes reached the beach, racing across the sea, scattering with the backwash.

Gabriel had an arm around Marie's legs. She knew that he could feel her bones protruding, nothing like the roundness of the past, but he didn't pull back.

"Marie, I have to tell you something soon. I went to the lawyer this morning."

His smile intrigued her, but he refused to say any more. When he gave her his glass of juice, she put her lips exactly where his had been.

The music picked up, launching into song, setting blood and muscles astir. She came over to the fire and started swaying her hips. Gabriel faced her. Danced with her. White shirt, light pants. All the elegance of a big Mauritian. But his movements, his bare feet were those of an Îlois. There was no mistaking it. His whole body now bore the imprint of Diego Garcia. A bird of the Chagos. She kissed him as their family and friends hooted and hollered. Beside them, Josette was twirling around Gaudry. Angèle was clapping. The séga was freeing them from all their sagren.

And that was when Marie saw him.

Christian, his eyes cold, stared at Josette dancing. In his hand was Gaudry's hammer. He didn't look like a little boy anymore. Not one bit. Clenched jaw, tensed muscles, like a wild beast. Marie wavered for a second. He couldn't possibly, but Christian was already running toward them. She shrieked. *Josette! Gaudry!* Gabriel turned his head. *Stop him!* He dashed over to get between the two and protect Josette. Held up his arms . . . But it was too late. Shock flooded his eyes as the hammer hit his forehead.

Gabriel collapsed on the sand.

In the Diego Garcia dawn, when the first rays of sunlight illuminated the military harbor—concrete, asphalt—it was him you thought of first. Gabriel. Your love, Mama. The gray-green vessels were arrayed before us, barracks, tents, another camp, but this one military. And you knew that where this ugly seawall stood there had once been a wooden pier, the one where you saw him for the first time in his pale clothes. But for me, what I saw was the hinterlands of violence.

The soldiers were waiting for us, hats snug on their heads, big smiles on their lips. "Hi, guys!" Tourists, I'm telling you.

My mother, like all the elders, was on her knees. In tears, kissing the ground. It wasn't the immaculate sand of the past, that milky white that burned soles. It was the bite of tar—a black, fatal kiss. The surface of tarmac, like a serpent's scales. We looked for it everywhere: the purity of lines, the brightness of past decades. The smell of sap. Instead was a heavy smell of Ferodo brake pads; that was the smell of civilization. The sea in the distance had lost its clarity, massive shadows swallowed up its belly. We were home, but this home didn't make much sense.

As expected, we were taken to the church and the cemetery. I followed you slowly, Mama, and at every step you took, the doors of time opened.

There was the plot. And there, the furnace. At first all I could see were the army buildings, all this concrete, these crude cinder blocks, but then, little by little, I recognized the garage where telegrams were sent, the path to Pointe Marianne, the coconut forest. I created these memories.

Hurry up!

The church, smaller than in my memory, was overgrown with vegetation. The whitewash was peeling off the façade. Inside, there were still a few pews, the altar, the cross hanging from its hook. Your bare feet met the coolness of the flagstones, and I did as you did, I took off my shoes, pressed my toes to the ground, and I took your hand. The tears were coming. The Îlois' voices, the accent of our lost, squandered happiness. I heard songs that didn't exist, nobody was singing, and yet I could hear them. "Me, I was eight . . . Me, I was eight in the Chagos . . ." My sister had a face again. Bright eyes, offset by long lashes, and she was holding out a little rice cake and laughing. How could I have forgotten that laugh? *Come along, little Jo, come along*. I walked out, floored.

The soldiers were still there.

Our worst shock awaited us a few meters off. The cemetery. The gravestones bore cracks. Overrun by weeds. No more landmarks, the stones worn down by erosion, beer cans, cigarette butts. I didn't recognize a thing. Someone cried out. In the distance were three pretty steles, white and adorned with British flags.

Monty, Timmy, Lucky
1993–2002
BIOT Police Dogs

Army dogs. Buried properly. Shrieks of fury rose up. The soldiers were suddenly less sympathetic, started gesturing for us to calm down. Yes, they took care of their animals. Didn't they have the right to? The dogs weren't in the same boat anymore.

You turned your back on them, Mama. You left them behind.

You were looking for something else. You looked. Amid the brambles, under scattered bits of white wood, no doubt remnants of crosses, you found the grave. The basalt was split in two. I slipped my hand in yours. I hunched down, and then . . . Oh, Mama! Our sobs mingled.

Ici repose Thérèse Ladouceur
Mère de Josette et Marie-Pierre Ladouceur
Grand-mère de Suzanne et Joséphin
Enfants éternels de Diego Garcia.

You were there, Daddy, your cigarette in hand, elegant as always. Your death didn't change a thing. You were there, with us, you cleared the path for us.

Justice doesn't come from laws or governments. It only comes from men, too late and too rarely.

August 1975

I could tell you that he loved you, that he wanted your happiness, that he felt real the day he held you in his arms, tell you that he wanted to understand why, why bad luck and bad choices happened, why nothing in life was simple. I could tell you about his features, his profile on the Diego Garcia pier, his lost gaze, his awkwardness. I could curse fate, God, Satan and his henchmen, the misfortune they brought upon us, point fingers at a good man driven mad by hardship, turn up my nose at jealousy, bad karma that never relents. I could cry, stab a knife into my heart, I could dive, let the sea bear me away, forget Suzanne, forget everything else. I could do better than that, though. I could revive his courage, his life, and his wrath to give them to you, my son. I could go on. I could shut my pain in a box and set it on fire. I could watch you, you my hope. My faith. I could keep on fighting. With the others. With all the others. And live.

On the table, the lawyer's documents were jammed into an envelope, with complicated words, numbers, orders. Mollinart would help; he'd promised to. One set of papers caught her attention. Inside was a single cream-colored sheet, folded in half. Marie opened it.

In the middle of the page, written in Gabriel's hand, was a name.

Joséphin Diego Neymorin

Something in her let go. *Look, my angel. His promise.*

Joséphin, bare-chested, looked. Only then did she notice, in shock.

On the back of his neck, half-covered by his hair, her son had a birthmark shaped like a cloud.

The Hague, at last. A perfectly pink sky coils around the Peace Palace; not a single cloud, not a single wisp of mist. I got up early after a sleepless night. Too nervous. *This case is a winning case,* our lawyer told us yesterday. The outcome of the hearing was one he had no doubts about: the Chagos would win. All it takes is a single cry of victory—*This case is a winning case*—for ice to run through my veins. I pull on my suit, my tie, pin our Chagossian flag to my lapel. Orange like the sky under which we'd been forcibly removed from Diego; black like distress; turquoise like the lagoon. In my pocket is the spotted cowrie I never left behind.

Around us, cars start to arrive. Behind the tinted windows are judges. Before the palace's gates open, security guards check badges and wave wands under the vehicles in case there's a bomb hidden beneath. I'm shaking: I can't look at the park or take in the corridor leading to the courtroom. But inside, amid the frescos, the stained-glass windows, and the blue-and-green carpet, the UN logo is almost glaring. In front of me is the dais. Fourteen empty seats in a long row, all of them terrifying, overlook the room divided into two sections. To the left is the United Kingdom; to the right is Mauritius and us, the Chagossians.

Suddenly a whisper rises up.

The Court!

We get up. One by one, the judges enter, stern faced. In the center is President Yusuf from Somalia. He gestures for us to sit. The proceedings have begun.

I know by heart our lawyers' speeches. We've spent hours with them fine-tuning, condensing, buttressing our arguments. I know the documents that will be displayed won't leave anyone unmoved. The confidential telegram from Harold Wilson on the eve of his secret meeting with Ramgoolam in 1965 about frightening him with hope. Greenhill's cable about his "Tarzans or Men Fridays." The photo of our dilapidated cemetery, in contrast to that of the British dogs.

It's time for the world to hear us.

"The United Kingdom does not wish to be a colony, yet it stands before this Court to defend a status as colonizer of others," the lawyer concludes. "We invite you to help bring to an immediate end"—his voice rises with the force of conviction—"a last vestige of British colonial presence in Africa."

After barely an hour's break, the other side shoots back. No surprise that the agreement legally signed between Mauritius and the Crown in 1965 should be invoked immediately. I watch Judge Yusuf; his face is impassive.

I wait for the refrain on terrorism: "The joint defense facility operated by the United Kingdom and the United States continues to play a critical role in ensuring regional and global security. The facility is instrumental in combating some of the most difficult and urgent problems of the twenty-first century, including terrorism."

There it is. Not admissible information, barely even a form of psychological pressure. The end of the speech has me all the more worried.

"The United Kingdom has to wonder about an essential detail." The lawyer draws out his words. I don't like that. "Why is Mauritius so interested all of a sudden in the fate of the Chagossians? Until 2016, the Republic was perfectly happy when it came to that subject." Exactly what I'd feared. All we've been able to do was lock arms with Mauritius to buck the British; but to choose a side is to accept all its weaknesses. When the British lawyer mentions "Mauritius's expansionist claims" to our archipelago, I suddenly understand the point he's about to drive home. "As the International Court of Justice has no authority to settle bilateral disputes, the United Kingdom asks that the Court declare itself incompetent and to abstain from judgment."

Night will fall over The Hague. The full day of legal proceedings has left me drained. The arguments have come at an unrelenting pace. We find ourselves outside, past the fence. The Peace Palace's brick façade takes on a golden tinge. It's beautiful. In my pocket, I clutch the cowrie shell.

We had to wait. For months, until this Monday, February 25, 2019, when my phone rang over and over. The Court at The Hague had just issued its advisory opinion. My hands were shaking.

> *Present: President YUSUF; Vice-President XUE; Judges TOMKA, ABRAHAM, BENNOUNA, CANÇADO TRINDADE, DONOGHUE, GAJA, SEBUTINDE, BHANDARI, ROBINSON, GEVORGIAN, SALAM, IWASAWA; Registrar COUVREUR.*
> *. . . The Court concludes that, as a result of the Chagos archipelago's unlawful detachment and its incorporation into a new colony, known as the BIOT, the process of decolonization of Mauritius was not lawfully completed when Mauritius acceded to independence in 1968.*

> *. . . The Court having found that the decolonization of Mauritius was not conducted in a manner consistent with the right of peoples to self-determination, it follows that the United Kingdom's continued administration of the Chagos archipelago constitutes a wrongful act entailing the international responsibility of that State.*
>
> *. . . Accordingly, the United Kingdom is under an obligation to bring an end to its administration of the Chagos archipelago as rapidly as possible, thereby enabling Mauritius to complete the decolonization of its territory in a manner consistent with the right of peoples to self-determination.*

I shrieked. It wasn't a cry of joy, or of relief, or of victory, or of sagren, or of pride; it was all of them at once, mixed together, molten into one, a new feeling for which the dictionary had no words. Justice had spoken. The Chagos had to be returned to the Chagossians.

Deep within, a huge wave started to ferry faces. I thought of my father and our name, my wife, Pierrine, Auntielyne, and Ranjit, I thought of my aunt Josette and my cousin Makine, I thought of Marcel, my godfather, and my godmother, Angèle, buried in Grand-Gaube. I thought of Suzanne's laughter, of the children who would be born tomorrow, of my friends, of our supporters and defenders. I thought of my island, of this strip of white sand, of the water's clarity, of all the exiles.

I thought of my mother.

AUTHOR'S AFTERWORD

It's a story my mother told me. Not a fairy tale or a fable, no, but a true story that she scratched at every so often like a nasty wound. An island tragedy. Mothers know lullabies and enchantments. Sometimes, with a flash of their eye, a slight crack in their voice, they betray themselves. The child suspects a secret. Senses anger. The older they get, the clearer the contours become, the sharper the features become until everything is crystal clear: this secret is one of suffering. Of being wrenched away. A daughter doesn't let her mother suffer. So she writes.

I don't remember the first time my mother spoke to me of the Chagos. Was I nine or ten? It doesn't matter. My mother described her childhood in Mauritius, long before—before Europe, before exile, before me—and then a word escaped her lips, Chagos, with its two easy syllables, *sha* and *go*, that could have been tossed just as easily as jacks. Her face darkened. Her gaze was lost momentarily, or rather turned inward, digging deep within herself. The archipelago was tormented. Its poor people had been sold off! Sitting in the kitchen, I could make out the tragedy even though I didn't understand any of it.

My mother is Mauritian. My grandmother, my great-grandmother, my great-great-grandmother are all Mauritian. For me, Mauritius is a pebble in my shoe, a wrench . . . The dictionary is unambiguous: "a wrench in the works" means "a person or thing that prevents the successful implementation of a plan."

At some point there's a black-and-white photo. A square one. Almost a postage stamp. On the far left is my mother, still a teenager, with a floral skirt and a white blouse. Between her and her sister is my grandmother in a geometric-print skirt. In front of the women are two little boys in shorts and white short-sleeve shirts; one day they'll become my uncles. They're staring at the camera and smiling. They're magnificent. Behind them a cargo ship's fo'c'sle and deck are visible. The two boys are holding a life preserver. Above them, the name, *Sir Jules*, is distinct.

My family was among the last free visitors to the Chagos. My grandfather had been named to the Seychelles—a good post that was long-overdue recognition for his years of labor and rectitude in Mauritius—and the Beau-Bassin house was abuzz as a result. The oldest of the brothers, who was dead set on becoming a doctor, would stay in Mauritius. My grandfather would go ahead to lay the groundwork. The others would set sail later on the *Sir Jules*, headed for Mahé. As was customary for ships sailing from Mauritius to the Seychelles, they would stop over in the Chagos.

How many times had my mother told me about that Christmas on Diego Garcia? An extraordinary banquet at the administrator's table! An island right out of a child's dream. Mountains of coconuts everywhere. The villa of Pointe de l'Est, the feasts, the drinks on the verandah, the welter of decorations—another photo I guard jealously shows my grandmother bursting out in laughter, her arms full with ornaments swallowing up her face.

I interrogated my mother about her past. I took notes. The staff who fussed over them. The servants in aprons, the tea brought to their beds in the morning. "The nénènes served and left," she said. I asked her what she thought of the local people, how the Chagossians lived. A moment's silence. "No, we didn't mix with them." The visitors didn't talk to them. A bit farther down, on a page with no other quotes, I scribbled down her words: "I was on the right side of the fence."

And after the deportation? How did the Mauritians welcome the Îlois? My mother wavered. She left Mauritius in 1968, so she wasn't there at the time. But one thing is clear: the people didn't know anything about it. Those spearheading the matter, yes, of course, but not the locals. I compile my readings, my research. It's not enough. I'll have to investigate to get more specific information. I know that a group of especially active Îlois have been fighting from Mauritius for justice: the Chagos Refugees Group, led by a man named Olivier Bancoult. What do I have to lose?

I sent him an email. By some miracle, he responded immediately, suggesting that we meet to talk: in a few days, he'd be coming through London's suburbs. The meeting was wonderful. But as I walked out, one question lingered in my mind. How can his true accounts be united with my mother's memories, with what I've read here and there, with what the photos of that time have shown me? To shift from reality to fiction felt as essential as it was problematic, to write a novel, a pure novel, to put my words wholly at the service of narrative, sometimes at the expense of facts and chronology. I resigned myself to that choice, fully aware that I couldn't forgo a trip to Mauritius.

Down there, in the Pointe-aux-Sables office, a headquarters of sorts for the Chagossian advocates, I meet with Olivier Bancoult again, I open the binders, I delve into the archives, I scan documents.

I record the statements of Îlois still full of wrath. One photo in particular disgusts me. Three nice clean tombs . . .

A major trial is looming. "Caroline," Olivier Bancoult says after a committee meeting, "if you can, I'd like for you to come with us to The Hague. I'd like to have you be part of the Chagossian delegation." His trust is a gift—one that draws me in completely.

We meet in the Netherlands a month later. It's the first time in my life that I've gone into a courthouse, and it's the International Court of Justice. I'm restless. There's hope, tempered by experience. Each trial the Chagossians have won has then been overturned by British courts. How would this one play out? Would the UN be listened to? Like Marie, we'd have to keep faith.

When I was young, my mother told me a story. That of a paradise lost in the farthest edge of the ocean, crushed one day in the jaws of a monster.

In the Bible, David prevails against Goliath. That's my dream. A naïve one, certainly. I know that no book has the power to change the world. But we've already seen opinion change the course of history. Maybe I'll manage, in some way, to use my words to make my wrath yours as well, all while gifting my mother this sliver of childhood binding us.

—Caroline Laurent

ACKNOWLEDGMENTS

I have to acknowledge first and foremost Olivier Bancoult, Rosemond or "Ti Frère," and all the Chagossians I was able to meet and who agreed to share their painful experiences with me. Their courage is immense.

Thanks are due to the invaluable support of the team at Les Escales. And thanks also are due to Véro, Delphine, to the sales reps, booksellers, reviewers, readers, and indeed all those who make space for literature.

My thoughts especially go to my three fairy godmothers: Françoise, Claire, and Charlotte.

And I owe my gratitude to my mother and my Mauritian family, my cradle and my refuge from the very first.

And to Marc, without whom I would be lost.

TRANSLATOR'S ACKNOWLEDGMENTS

To engage with the Chagossians' struggle is to understand how fragile and essential human relationships are. It is thanks to Shenaz Patel and the experience of translating her formidable novel *Silence of the Chagos* that I was prepared to revisit this shameful episode of colonialism. I can hardly express how heartwarming it was to draw anew on the knowledge and insights of Drs. Laura Jeffery, David Vine, and Lindsey C. Latteman, as well as Ariel Saramandi. I'm grateful, too, to have gotten to call on the wisdom of Raza Halim and Philippe Sands, QC, who shrewdly and graciously illuminated the legal front of the Chagossians' fight, and Chagossian Voices (chair: Frankie Bontemps) for their advice on matters of terminology in English.

This book would not exist in English without Gabriella Page-Fort's effervescence; her love for books and the people who make them possible radiates in every aspect of her work. And it would not read half as crisply without Buzz Poole's clear-eyed edits, the expertise of Cheryl Weisman and Lauren Grange as well as that of Lindsey Alexander, and especially Karen Parkin's proofreading acumen and Valerie Paquin's final touches. The map of Diego Garcia, created for this translation, is thanks to the phenomenal Glen Pawelski. My deep thanks go to Rachael Zuckerman, who opened up her home during my toughest stretch. And I'm indebted above all to Caroline Laurent, whose brilliantly woven narrative and warm emails were, in such unsteady times, a wonderfully steady hand.

ABOUT THE AUTHOR

Photo © 2020 Philippe Matsas

Caroline Laurent is the bestselling Franco-Mauritian author of *An Impossible Return*, winner of the Prix Maison de la Presse 2020, the Prix Louis-Guilloux 2020, and the Prix du Salon du Livre du Mans 2020. She also cowrote, with Évelyne Pisier, *Et soudain, la liberté* (And Suddenly, Freedom), which won the Grand Prix des Lycéennes de ELLE.

ABOUT THE TRANSLATOR

Photo © 2018 Carl de Souza

Jeffrey Zuckerman has translated many French works into English, including books by the artists Jean-Michel Basquiat and the Dardenne brothers; the queer writers Jean Genet and Hervé Guibert; and the Mauritian novelists Ananda Devi, Shenaz Patel, and Carl de Souza. A graduate of Yale University, he has been a finalist for the TA First Translation Prize, the French-American Foundation Translation Prize, and the PEN Translation Prize, and has been awarded a PEN/Heim Translation Fund Grant and the French Voices Grand Prize. In 2020 he was named a Chevalier in the Ordre des Arts et des Lettres by the French government.